CHRYSALIS
The Emergence of Emery

Chrysalis
The Emergence of Emery
The Gifted Series Book 1

Maria Macdonald

This book is a work of fiction. Any references to real events, real people, and real places are used fictitiously. Other names, characters, places and incidents are products of the Author's imagination and any resemblance to persons, living or dead, actual events, organisations or places is entirely coincidental.

All rights are reserved. This book is intended for the purchaser of this book ONLY. No part of this book may be reproduced or transmitted in any form or by any means, graphic, electronic, or mechanical, including photocopying, recording, taping, or by any information storage retrieval system, without the express written permission of the Author. All songs, song titles and lyrics contained in this book are the property of the respective songwriters and copyright holders.

ISBN-13: 978-1718046269

Editing by Emily Cargile
Formatting by Swish Design & Editing
Cover design by Dark Wish Designs
Cover image Copyright 2018

Copyright © 2018 Maria Macdonald
Third Edition
All rights reserved.

Dedication

For Paige,
You are perfect, exactly as you are.
You always will be.

GLOSSARY

Light beings are usually good.
Dark beings are usually bad.

Pith – A gifted person's other half. Their core, their essence, the love of their life.
Convergence – A powerful entity who is pure and can live dormant or conscious within someone else's body. Usually using a Gifted being as a vessel before finding a pure human (good or evil) to converge with.

POWERS
Revive – Like electricity, you can 'shock' people and either kill them, or revive them.
Consume – Drains powers – But only works when taking from the persons Pith.
Earthing – Pulling a life force to the ground so that person can't move.
Motion – Teleporting yourself and others from one place to another.
Entrance – The ability to hypnotize someone.

Excelled Vision / Power / Hearing – All standard powers.

Veil – A cloaking ability.

Foresight – Seeing future events. Normally this only appears later in life.

Equalize – The ability to immediately neutralize the powers of any gifted person who poses you a threat.

Command Grip – Taking over another's body, like mentally climbing inside.

Phasing – The ability to manipulate time.

CHRYSALIS
The Emergence of Emery

Prologue

I didn't look back when they called names. I ignored the sharp pain in my back, from the stones and empty soda cans they threw at me when I walked by. I kept my face hidden from them and controlled my tears by biting my tongue, until the familiar metallic taste flooded my mouth. It's what I always did.

I was different, and the children within my small town hated me with a passion that I didn't rightfully understand at my young age.

'Emma the elephant' and 'alien face' were amongst the common names that were used to describe me as a young child. It progressed and evolved to 'salad dodger' and 'wide load.' Though the one I was called the most was 'rat girl,' which was meant to be like *Bat Girl*, but it was more of an insult than anything else. They used the name because my teeth were bigger in the front. Like a lot of children, I had to grow into them. I was alone.

Isolated. Hated and abused. I had no parents, no one to care for me. My whole life had been hollow, empty, and the feeling, it seemed, was to be terminal.

The day my life changed monumentally is one I'll never forget. It was the day I was reborn.

Walking from my job at the local bookstore, the sun had set and I wrapped my arms around myself as a chill started to seep into my skin. That's when I saw them. My abusers.

In school there was a bigger crowd, but tonight I saw only three. Boys… almost men. They were eighteen now, just like me. They hadn't stopped dishing out the insults since they began back in first grade. In fact, after returning this last year, it's become worse.

My looks had changed over the summer. I grew into my gangly body and my teeth, my acne cleared, and my long blond hair is now thick and lush. These boys noticed me, they all did. The taunts never stopped, but I saw it in their eyes—there was an annoyance. Just like it had always been, but now there was also a want… they wanted the new me. They hated craving me. It was new to them and they just didn't know what to do about it. Plus, none of them were brave enough to admit it. Not that it would have changed anything. I hated them all.

When they approached me that night it wasn't with caution. It should have been. Fear would have served them well. I was meek, quiet. I didn't fight

Chrysalis

back. I was an easy target… that's what they thought. *That's what I thought*. Why would they be frightened of little old me?

When they pushed me into the back alley and tried to rip my clothes off, things changed. I listened to their voices, heard the evil inside them, and felt the cruel enjoyment that wept from their pores. I didn't understand it then. But I do now. That fight was monumental and thus began my life.

I was reborn. I was new. I became what I was always meant to be. They started that, but they'll never know, never see. I killed them that day—all three boy-men. They were sons, nephews, boyfriends. Hell, they might have been future presidents for all I knew. Either way, I ripped their lives from their bodies in the blink of an eye.

I still feel that evil, the grime under my fingernails, and it eats away at me. One day it might win and then all could be lost. For now, I hold it back, like a dam impounding water, controlling it and stopping it from overflowing and decimating everything in its path.

That night, as they tried to rape me, pawing at my clothes and laughing among themselves, while I was on the floor assured of my death - or at the very least my violation - my heart rate picked up speed and something sparked inside me. Something that had lain dormant, something that would set me free.

Something that was so unnatural to me, yet felt so very right.

When the light took over it was blinding, I couldn't control it. If I'd have known how, then perhaps they would have survived—maybe. When I touched them with my hands, trying to push them off me, they screamed. The sound was bloodcurdling, and as their flailing arms stilled and their lifeless bodies dropped to the asphalt, I had no time to recover or to make sense of the situation surrounding me. A shrouded figure bounded out of nowhere, grabbed my wrist, and hauled me up.

"Come with me, Emery," he ordered softly, but I couldn't move.

As I tried to blink away the events, dismissing them as my crazy overactive imagination, he must have seen the confusion, or maybe it was fear that was clear in my eyes.

"Emery, you killed them," he told me as gently as possible, pointing to my three attackers on the ground.

I looked down at their bodies but felt nothing. No remorse. No regret. I was just cold from the wind that whipped against my skin through torn clothing and from the ice that I'd allowed to fill me inside, shutting out every truth from that night.

Now that time has passed, I see the vision that I blocked out back then so clearly in my nightmares sometimes. I feel it all now.

Chrysalis

"I need to get you somewhere safe. Then I can explain everything," he told me as he tugged me forward.

I could hear the sirens in the distance. Someone must have seen something, and the cops were closing in. I had no time to think, no time to decide if this person urging me to follow him was good or evil. But knowing what I did, I wasn't entirely sure if *I* could be classified as good anymore. What I knew was that I had no one in my corner. So, I made a choice that night and followed the man who seemed to hold the promise of something else, something better than the lowly existence I loathed.

That was how this started.

Now, the fight that I thought was huge that first night, seems insignificant to what I face ahead of me. What we *all* face. Now I'm in the fight of my life. For everyone and for myself.

But to tell the story, I need to go back to the beginning. Back to my emergence.

Chapter 1

I've never had one of those moments. You know—the ones where you see your life flashing before your eyes? Even now, after those guys just attacked me, or even as

I follow this man—who could be a serial killer—I don't feel fear.

Maybe I should be scared?

"You're safe." The clipped words come from in front of me, and I let my eyes move to the back of his head.

He's tall, he must have at least seven inches on my five foot five frame. He's also lean, but still bulky enough for me to believe he has a six-pack. The blond hair— that I have no doubt usually cascades down his neck—is pulled up into a man bun, and I already know those short whiskers cover the lower half of his face. He's exactly the type of guy I stay away from. Dangerous, cold, and probably hiding a

Chrysalis

sharp tongue – which is something I've been on the receiving end of too many times. He emits an edge that I often find uncomfortable. For the first time tonight a shiver, accompanied by trepidation, runs through me.

Did he feel my worry? Is that why he answered my unspoken question?

"No. I read your thoughts," he says, twisting around to look at me while walking backward.

"You have eyes in the back of your head, too?" I ask flatly, pointing to the road in front of him.

He smirks at me. "That's what you say in reply to my revelation?"

I shrug. "I just killed three of my bullies by touching them with my hands." I watch as he winces at my words, then quickly gathers himself. "Telling me that you listened to my thoughts doesn't seem like the strangest thing that's happened to me tonight."

"Fair enough," he says, spinning back around and continuing in silence. I want to ask him where we're going - how any of this is possible. I want to ask him who he is and why he called me Emery. But I have a feeling I will know soon enough, and while I'm walking, I can pretend it's all a dream or a nightmare. Although strangely, I feel like my real life was more of a nightmare than tonight's adventures. The silence as we walk is comforting. It's something I'm used to, being by myself most of the time. I'm still surprised how well I interact with people when the need arises.

My legs feel heavy, but they don't hurt, and considering we've been walking for nearly an hour—and I've never been good in gym class—I'm amazed I'm still moving at all. Closing my eyes, I breathe in through my nose. Dew hangs in the air and the cold is creeping up my arms.

"Here." The word is muttered, almost subconsciously, by the guy leading me.

"What's your name?" I venture a question. Just the one.

"Elijah. We're nearly back now," he shoots out.

I don't say anything else. Instead, I just follow *Elijah* up the dark lane.

We've walked out of town - so far out of town that I didn't realize anyone lived back here. We crossed the Savernake sisters' fields and traveled through the forest behind. It's somewhere I've never dared go before. I was too afraid to venture here—the woods are dark and creepy, plus there were always whispers, tales about magic and monsters, and I was always alone. I'm not afraid now, though. As we near the solitary house, the lane almost compels me to approach, to enter. There's a warmth about the house, which is confusing since it's a big, imposing, dark place that looks like it's about to fall apart. In fact, it's so decrepit, that it should probably be demolished. There's moss around the windows and

Chrysalis

ivy winding its way up the outside wall, suffocating the chimney. The dark porch surrounding the front of the house looks like a barrier. It's like a scene from an evil fairytale.

"Elijah…" I hear a rumble from the side of the house as a figure steps out of the shadows. My jaw drops at the sight. He's six foot five at least, and *built*, not like a muscle-head gym freak, but like an athlete. His black hair is cut close to his head, but not close enough for it to be a buzz cut, and he has beautiful tanned skin that makes me wonder if he's of Italian descent. His eyes are even more attractive than the rest of him – if that's even possible. They're golden, like actual gold, sparkling and enticing. They're fixed on me, unwavering, and I'm completely mesmerized. I feel myself drawn toward him, but then he blinks and he turns to Elijah.

"You're bringing strays home now?" he spits out with a sneer, before drifting back into the shadows. Elijah sighs, looking down to me.

"Ignore Kade. Come on." He flicks his head in the direction of the door, yet doesn't offer an explanation. I don't ask for one. We walk up the steps onto the porch. I twist my head to the right and focus on the spot where the guy was previously standing. I can't see him, but I can *feel* him, which is weird and makes my stomach clench. Just before I follow Elijah into the front door, I see Kade's golden eyes glimmer in the darkness, before disappearing, like they've been extinguished.

Wow! Weird.

"You might want to stop thinking. Unless, of course, you *want* me, or someone else to hear?" Elijah asks as I shuffle along behind him. I don't answer his question, and he chuckles. "Up here," he tells me, leading the way upstairs.

Quietly moving and taking in my surroundings, I notice the inside and outside of this house are completely at odds with each other. While the façade is dark and almost scary, the inside is a lot brighter and modern. It's as if someone is trying to hide the identity of the house, or maybe trying to warn people away, as crazy as that sounds. We reach the top of the stairs and turn left. I can hear scratching noises, and my fingers start to tingle.

"Ignore the tingling, it will go away," Elijah tells me.

Frowning, I ask. "Did I think that?"

"No, I get the tingles. So, you will, too."

"Well, that's not odd," I reply snarkily.

"Oh, it gets worse," he mutters, and I just know that he's grinning, even though I can't see it. "Your room." Elijah opens a door and moves to the side so I can enter. He follows me in and closes it behind him, while I take in the space. It's nothing special, but it's not too shabby either. A pale blue room—my favorite color—with beautiful white patterns swirled

Chrysalis

all across the wall. There are wooden shutters on the windows and a white four poster bed, with a blue bedspread, matching curtains, and a rug. Two other doors sit on either side of an antique-looking dressing table. Finally, at the end of the bed is a chest with a blue throw over it. Apart from these features, the room is empty.

"That door is your bathroom, the other one your wardrobe," Elijah tells me.

I look around at the pretty, cozy room and smile.

Suddenly realization kicks me up the butt. "I have to go home… get some things," I babble, still staring at everything. My smile is gone.

"You can't go back, this is your home now. Nowhere else is safe for you, not until you know everything."

I look him up and down, then screw my eyes shut, hoping that this is all my kooky imagination, and that maybe I'll wake up in a mental hospital – which seems like the less scary option right now. When I open one eye back up, Elijah is still standing there, now with his arms crossed and the corner of his mouth curling.

"I need clothes," I whisper, looking down at my body, suddenly self-conscious, aware of my tattered state.

A frown flits across his face before he replies. "We'll go shopping. I'll take you to get anything you need tomorrow, but right now you need to rest." His reply is soft, but firm.

"No, I don't need to rest, I need to know what the hell is going on! And *you* need to give me some answers!" I can feel my heart rate ramping up its pace, and I place one hand over my chest, which seems to ease the pressure. Elijah's eyes move to my hand then back to my face, searching for something.

"I'm sorry," he tells me.

"For what?" I ask, rubbing my chest harder.

"For this," he answers, while simultaneously placing his thumb on my forehead. I feel my whole body go numb, and as I start crashing to the ground Elijah catches me.

"What did you do?" I rasp out.

"Shhh… you need rest. I'm just going to help you with that," he says while placing me inside the bed covers. Pulling them up to my shoulders, he stares down at me. "Don't worry, I'll bring in a chair and put it in the corner. Nothing will happen to you, and I'll be here when you wake up."

"Why are you looking after me?" I murmur, my eyes becoming heavy as I realize I'm being dragged into sleep by something other than my own body.

"Because… I'm your brother." His words are the last thing I hear before the blackness takes over. Even then, I'm not sure I've heard him right.

Chrysalis

CHAPTER 2

The fluffy kitty is sleeping in my lap. I rub along his back, from head to tail, just like Jenny taught me. His soft fur is warm, and kitty's tail tickles my knee. I want to laugh, but if I laugh, then Mr. Saunders will hear. Mr. Saunders is mean, he makes Molly cry, and I try to keep him away from her. She's so little. Even though she's nearly eight and I'm only seven, I'm bigger than her. When we make noise Mr. Saunders shouts at us. Last week Molly and me ran into the fields so we could hide until Jenny was home.

Jenny is my big pretend sister. She has the same mommy and daddy as Molly, but not me—I don't know who my mommy and daddy are. We all live here with Mr. and Mrs. Saunders. Jenny makes sure we're all okay when Mrs. Saunders is out. Today Jenny has taken Molly to buy some shoes, and Mrs. Saunders is visiting a poorly lady, 'cause she is a doctor. I came out to the garden so I wasn't under

Maria Macdonald

Mr. Saunders feet, he says we should be seen and not heard.

Farmer Brighton's gun goes off, he's always trying to shoot birds, and his red face is very smiley. He tells me that the birds are annoying, and that Sid the scarecrow is useless, 'cause they sit on his shoulder and head instead of being scared of him.

Today when it makes a loud bang, the kitty must be scared. He cries and digs his nails into me. I try not to wail, Mr. Saunders doesn't like me when I'm loud. But the poor kitty is holding on so tight, I have to pull his claws from my skin. It hurts so badly and I try to be soft, but Farmer Brighton's gun goes off again, and kitty digs back in before running away.

I scream and cry. I must have woken Mr. Saunders 'cause I can hear him shouting. I look at the door and see him. He starts running at me. I can't help it when I whimper, and I can't run 'cause my leg hurts. I need some plasters. Mr. Saunders doesn't say anything as he reaches me, but he pulls his big arm back and has his scary face on, so I close my eyes, like I always do. My punishment for being noisy never comes, though. When I open my eyes, Mr. Saunders is asleep on the floor. I look around, but nobody is here.

My eyes spring open and I gasp, holding my hand around my throat.

"It's okay, you're okay." I hear the soft voice and sit bolt upright. "Breathe… in, out… come on,

Chrysalis

Emery. Get yourself under control." I blink a few times and look into a pair of ice blue eyes. Kind eyes.

"Elijah," I whisper.

He gets up from his chair and moves to sit on the side of my bed, wrapping me in his arms. "It was you, wasn't it?" I ask. He doesn't reply, just rubs slow circles on my back. "It was! That day in the garden of one of my foster homes, with the cat? Tell me it was you?" I beg.

"It was me." His answer is short, but it makes my body sag into his.

"You always watched over me?" I question.

"Not always. I couldn't always be there."

I look up into his face and see sadness pass across his eyes. "Can you tell me what's going on now?" I ask.

"Not yet. You'll find out what you need to know… the stuff that's important. Just a little at a time. Everything else I will tell you when I can. Right now, I need to make sure I don't overwhelm you. I promise you, though, I will tell you everything. Eventually."

I nod in answer. I can see the sincerity in his eyes.

"Okay, but one thing. Why do you call me Emery? My name is Emma."

"No, your name is Emery. You've been called Emma to keep you hidden all these years. That's enough for now. Come, get washed up and meet me downstairs in the kitchen. I'll make you breakfast,"

Elijah tells me, pulling away and standing back up. I raise my eyebrow at him but remain silent. "Go back downstairs, the way you came last night, then head to the back of the house, toward the noise… trust me, you'll hear the noise." He finishes with a wink and walks out of the room.

Twenty minutes later, although I've brushed my teeth with a new toothbrush that I found in the bathroom, pulled my fingers through my hair, *and* splashed water across my face, I still feel dirty. I have no clean clothes yet, so I'm still wearing the jeans and my torn shirt from last night. My jeans have a rip in the knee too, and most of my buttons are missing from my shirt. But I've put them back on because they're all I have. Tying a knot in the hem of the shirt, I stare out of the window, seeing nothing strange outside, just vast fields and sunshine. I shuffle to the door and place my hand on the doorknob. "You can do this. Even if you have no idea what it is you're supposed to be doing," I chant three times before pulling the door open and striding down the hallway, with more purpose than my nerves want to allow.

Feigning a confidence I've relied on almost all my life, I reach the bottom of the stairs. I can already hear the noise Elijah mentioned guiding me to the kitchen. Upon entering, everyone stops what they're doing to look at me. I feel like I'm naked in front of a classroom full of my peers - that same nightmare that most of us can relate to.

Chrysalis

"Hi," I whisper, then wave my hand in a really lame gesture.

Everyone bursts out laughing, and a guy, who must be around twenty, with dark blond hair and a devilish grin, looks over to Elijah and says, "Yeah, E, she's cute."

Elijah smirks and shakes his head, but I hear a growl from the corner, and look that way only to catch eyes with Kade. I'm once again trapped in his stare, but I notice his eyes are hazel brown this morning. I frown, confused at the complete change in color.

"So, you must be Emery?" A female voice distracts me from Kade's intense stare, and I look across the room to a petite brunette standing close to Elijah. Her hair is pulled up into a high ponytail, and it swishes as she talks. She's wearing Daisy Duke shorts and a white tank with cowboy boots. She looks cute.

"Yeah, I guess I am," I reply back with a smile.

"Ahh… yes. I'm guessing E hasn't told you much yet. This must have all come as a big shock. Especially your name. That must be freaking weird, right?" she continues, moving into Elijah and placing her hand on his chest. I can only assume she's his girlfriend.

"Yeah, this is all a bit… um… strange," I mumble, gesturing around the place.

"Okay, enough with the questions, Sicily," Elijah says, looking down to her face softly.

The kitchen door suddenly swings open and a gorgeous redhead saunters in. She looks across at me and sneers. Her disdain toward me is clear enough. "Couldn't get the charity case some decent clothes?" she snaps.

"Katarina, that's enough," Elijah says, stepping away from Sicily and folding his arms across his chest.

She raises one eyebrow and smirks, looking at Elijah then back at me.

"Maybe you should've let those guys have her. She might have learned something."

I feel my chest compress at her words, and once again there's a growl in the room, but this time it's from behind me. Katarina looks at me with disgust. As her lip curls, she moves her eyes above my head, staring at whoever's behind me for a moment, before spinning around and stomping back out of the room without another word.

I look around at everyone. Their eyes are mostly on me, and they're all filled with something akin to pity.

"What did I do to her?" The question pops out of my mouth before I can consider it, but I'm confused as to why someone can so obviously hate me with no apparent reason.

Chrysalis

I've been bullied my whole life, and I have always dealt with people hating me, but not at first sight. "Nothing. She's just a bitch," Sicily says, looking toward the door with anger. Her eyes move back to me, and they soften. "Come on, I'm going to take you shopping today," she says clapping her hands together with excitement. "Before we go, though, I'll introduce you to everyone."

Next to her, Elijah rolls his eyes but smiles.

"So you met Miss Stroppy Panties, Katarina. Ignore her, we all do. Obviously, you know E, and I'm Sicily. This is Tristan," she tells me pointing to the blond guy from before who apparently thinks I'm cute, "Tess, who's Tristan's twin sister, and Miles, are out today." Her eyes glance quickly around the group. It suddenly feels awkward, and I'm guessing she can't tell me where they are. She coughs and then continues, "The growly guy behind you is Kade." I glance over my shoulder, catching Kade's scowl and wonder when he maneuvered behind me.

"Hi," I whisper to him with a small smile. He doesn't say anything. Instead, he just stares at me, like I'm a puzzle. One he wants to unravel.

I turn back to the rest of the group. "It's nice to meet you all, and I hope I'm not sounding ungrateful, because I'm totally grateful... especially... you know..." I look over to Elijah and then down at my clothes, "...that you saved me last night from those guys." I hear Kade growl once again, but ignore him and continue, "I just… I want to know what's going on. I mean… what I did last night, those guys…" I look to Elijah again, not saying the words. I have a feeling that everyone here knows what I did, but I don't want to say it out loud. A bang makes me jump, and I turn to see Kade marching out of the room.

Swinging back around to face Elijah, he's staring at the door through which Kade just left, a muscle twitching in his cheek.

Sicily claps and brings my attention back to her.

"Come on, let's go shopping. I have some clothes if you want to change?" she offers.

"That's lovely of you to say, but you're kind of tiny. I'm pretty sure if I wore any of your clothes, I would look like the *Incredible Hulk*, you know, without all the green." I bite my lip and crinkle my nose, hoping I haven't offended her. I know that's not the case when she giggles.

"See, told you E, she's cute," Tristan says winking at me.

I look between Tristan and Sicily, then my focus is back on Elijah. "You need to explain some things to me," I state crossing my arms defiantly.

"I will, I promise. Go shopping. Have fun. Sicily will look after you. We'll talk when you come back."

I sigh, but quickly realize I'm not going to win this argument anytime soon.

"Yay, shopping!" Sicily says excitedly while bouncing up and down on her toes.

Chrysalis

My feelings are mixed. I want to know what the hell is going on, but it's also nice knowing that I might be making my first real friend since I was eight years old. Rolling my shoulders back and smiling, I look around at this new bunch of people. When my eyes land on Sicily, I nod my head.

"Come on then, show me how to shop." I hope she doesn't see the nervousness that I can feel zipping around every inch of my body as she grabs my hand and drags me outside. I have a feeling today will be a whole new experience for me.

Chapter 3

I can't pull my eyes from Sicily as she bounces along. Her movements are excitable, like a bunny on speed. She somehow manages to 'people watch' while walking through the shops. I see her eyes roaming and scanning everyone as I struggle to keep up. We're in the mall, and it's a task trying not to lose her while negotiating my way around crazy-ass shoppers.

"Here!" Sicily chirps, looking back at me, as she enters yet another shop. I roll my eyes at her back in jest. I can officially say I'm over having a girly shopping day. We've already bought more than enough clothes and shoes, hair products I've never heard of, and makeup I don't need. It's all been added to the growing collection of belongings I apparently can't live without. "This has to be the last shop, Sicily," I complain in an overly whiny tone, and she grins at me.

Chrysalis

"Don't tell me you're tired. I won't believe you."

I frown at her reply. "Okaaay… " Drawing the word out, I turn away, ready to creep outside. I want to find somewhere to sit while she carries on her shopping extravaganza. The idea of letting her go it alone, while I sit and wait, is as close to bliss as my imagination will stretch right now. We're at the point where she's shopping for herself more than anything. She doesn't need me, and I really don't want to be here.

Sicily is great, in small doses. That's not me being mean, she's just… a lot. I'm used to being alone. I've gone from having no one, to being thrust upon a bunch of people that I don't even know. On top of that, Sicily is probably the most overwhelming person I've ever met. She's lovely, just a bit much over an extended period of time, when truthfully, I don't really know her at all.

This group of people, specifically my brother—I still can't get my head around that—they all seem so *cool.* I've never been part of the *in-crowd*. Actually, I've never been part of *any* crowd. I usually avoid people at all costs. Being the butt of cruel jokes so many times over the years has cemented my place in society. There's also the fact that I've never had any friends. Any time a new person started at our school, it was explained to them that being friends with me would be social suicide. I'm so used to it that somewhere around sixth grade it just became the *norm*. I don't know any other way. I don't think I've said so many words to one person, or had someone speak to me so much in one day since... *Molly and Jenny.*

Their names pop into my head involuntarily, and I glance over at Sicily. She either doesn't read minds or she's giving me my privacy because there's no response from her.

"Emery, where are you going?" I turn around and look straight into Sicily's narrowed eyes.

"I was just going to go outside and sit down. I'm tired and sooo over shopping." I whisper the last part, but watch as hands move to her hips, and she starts tapping her foot.

I'm thinking she heard me.

"Emery! This is supposed to be a fun girly day!" She stamps her foot and I know my eyes widen. Biting my lip to stop myself from smiling at her childish behavior, the realization hits me, Sicily *is* like a child. That's why she can be quite draining. She constantly asks questions or chatters away. She likes to get her own way and throws a fit when she doesn't get it. The term 'spoilt brat' springs to mind, but I also realize that the childlike sweetness in her manner allows her to obtain things others wouldn't be able to. And although I have only spent today with her, I can already see she uses it to her advantage, often.

Chrysalis

"Sorry, Sicily. I'm done. I've not had a girly day before." I watch as her eyes soften and she pulls her hands from her hips. "I've loved it, but I'm tired… and, well, to be honest, I want to speak to Elijah. He owes me some answers," I explain, noticing her eyes light up at the mention of Elijah.

"You're right. I'm sorry, I get carried away sometimes. Let's go back," she replies quickly. I watch her. My gut is telling me she really wants to get back to Elijah, but I have no proof that's really how she feels - not that it matters. Getting back is my ultimate goal, so it's a win.

The house isn't home, but I don't miss where I've been living. Having been bumped from one place to another, a mixture of foster places and children's homes, I'm at the stage where I'm about to leave school and need to stand on my own two feet. The last six months haven't been easy. Living at the only children's home in the county meant more ridicule from my peers at school. I have no family, well, I thought I had none until Elijah. I only know that my parents died when I was a baby. I've been alone ever since. I had Molly and Jenny for a couple of years when I was younger, but they were blood sisters. A family member eventually came and rescued them. Ultimately, my life has been lonely since then.

Sicily grabs my hand and drags me forward, down the side of a shop into what looks like a cut through.

I feel an emotion pass through me. Nerves? It's nervousness I feel, but it's not me I'm feeling it from.

"Are you nervous?" I splutter to Sicily before I can engage my brain.

She stops suddenly and turns to face me. "I hate that Elijah can do that. It figures you would also be able to read people, too." She's talking to me, but her eyes keep flitting over my shoulder.

"What? Read people? And what do you keep looking at?" I ask, spinning around.

The moment I do, I'm trapped. I'm unable to move anything, not even my lungs, so I can't breathe. I feel my insides seizing, and my chest actually hurts, like I'm in a vise grip. I hear hollow laughter, and as my breath is released, I cough out a harsh breath just as a figure walks toward me. The rest of my body remains frozen. As a dark blur moves into my line of sight, I can see that it's a guy, about twenty, with auburn hair and silver eyes.

He's tall and broad, but because my eyes are frozen, they can't roam over his outline or his face at great length. I can only pick up bits as he moves in and out of the area where my eyes are fixated.

"So… you're the famous Emery. After all these years, here you are in the flesh. Finally."

I can't see the smirk, but I can hear it in his voice. I can also feel arrogance and evil radiating off him. I try to reply, even though I have no idea what I'm going to say, but all that comes up from my throat is a strangled noise.

He laughs again. "You really are clueless aren't you? Hmm… that will make my job easier. More boring. But still… easy is good. And I'll be rewarded massively for you. A daughter of the Laird."

There's noise behind me, and before my brain can take in his last comment, I remember that Sicily is back there.

"Now, Sicily, you know it's rude to interrupt." He tuts at her, then clicks his fingers. I hear a thud but can't look to see if she's okay. "Now, what shall I do with you?" he asks, moving into my personal space. "So pretty. It's a shame." He leans forward and runs his fingers down my cheek. My stomach starts cramping, but not because of what this guy's doing. "I should introduce myself. I'm Zeit," he tells me as his fingers travel down my throat. They stop when he reaches the collar of my new top.

The first outfit Sicily made me buy today I changed into immediately so I could throw away the clothes from last night. He tucks his fingers into my collar and yanks it down, tearing it open. *Great, that's another top I can't use again.*

"That's better." He smirks, and he's so close that I can see his face in detail now. Before I have the chance to study him, three things happen at once.

My stomach twists and turns and I feel like jumping beans are inside my body.

I hear a loud growl.

Then I see a flash of light.

"Zeit, you'd better run while you can." Elijah's voice is loud, and as Zeit moves out of my space, I'm released from the stranglehold I was in.

Before I can drop to the floor, I'm caught in strong arms, and I look up to see Kade. He's not looking at me. Instead, he's glowering up at Zeit.

"Stay down. Don't move," Kade snaps angrily, never tearing his eyes away from Zeit as he places me on the ground. Just like that, in a few words, I feel like a naughty school girl. Like somehow, all this is my fault. Elijah quickly moves to my side as I sit up looking back over my shoulder at Sicily.

"Is she...?" I say no more.

"She's fine. He just put her to sleep," Elijah answers.

Another one who can put people to sleep. How many are there?

"Not as many as you would think."

"Get out of my head," I grumble, but he just smirks at me. I look past him to Kade. He's fighting with Zeit. Well, it's kind of a fight. Kade has Zeit pinned against the wall. He punches him, then moves to slide his hand around Zeit's throat, dragging his body up the wall. Zeit puts his palms up and shoots a dazzling red light out of his hands, straight into Kade's chest. Kade just laughs at him. Suddenly, I hear a scream and see a woman standing at the

Chrysalis

entrance of the alley. Kade drops Zeit, who wastes no time in running away from us, his laughter ringing through the air.

"Quick, come on," Elijah says looking between Sicily and me.

Kade jogs over. "Grab Sicily," he orders Elijah, while holding his hand out to me. I reach for him and feel a zap shoot between our fingers. I glance up to his face and see him narrowing his eyes at our joined hands as he drags me up. "Try to keep up," he snaps. Then before I know what's happening, he's running, and I'm desperately trying not to fall.

In what can be no more than three minutes we're back outside the house. I look around, but can't see Elijah and Sicily.

"It will take them longer to get here. Especially with Elijah having to carry her. She was still out cold," Kade answers my unasked question.

"We… that was… I mean…" I can't seem to pull my thoughts together. Confusion addles my brain as I stare at Kade in bewilderment.

"When you work out what it is you need to say, then come find me," Kade snaps, walking inside. Leaving me with more questions than answers.

Once again I'm alone, and even though I've only been in the company of others for less than twenty-four hours, I already know I don't want to go back to feeling alone again. Not anymore.

Chapter 4

I'm still standing outside when I hear a whirring sound. Feeling a gust of wind on my left side, I turn toward it, and suddenly Elijah is there with Sicily in his arms.

"Emery? I thought you'd be inside?" he says the words like he hasn't just run over ten miles while carrying someone.

"Yeah, well, I've only just arrived," I answer, shrugging and looking down at Sicily, still sleeping in his arms.

"You couldn't have. Kade is way faster than me." His eyebrows pull together and he shakes his head.

"Well, maybe he had to slow down for me?" I offer.

He shakes his head again and looks at the ground, mumbling to himself. "No, you wouldn't ever slow him down—" He's cut off mid-flow as the door opens.

Chrysalis

"Get inside. *Now.*" Kade's words are like a lash across my back. He turns away, stalking inside and I look to Elijah, who sighs.

"Come on, he's right. We should go inside." He turns to leave, but I can't move my feet. "Elijah," I whisper.

The moment he looks at me, his eyes widen. "Kade!" he shouts, but before the name has left his lips Kade is already out here. A gold flash lights the sky. Then he's in front of me.

"Inside *now!*" he shouts back to Elijah, who looks torn, but nods his head and moves inside still holding Sicily.

Kade turns to me. "Wrap your arms around me."

"What?" A million emotions are running through me, and I know they're not just mine. Although, I don't understand how I instinctively know that. It's too much to think about right now.

"Your arms, wrap them around me. *Now,*" he demands, stepping closer.

I do as I'm told and hold onto him. I haven't held anyone for, well... forever. Not like this. The second I'm latched onto him, his hands slip around me.

Immediately, I relax, and I know without any doubt that I'm protected. Warmth starts prickling my skin and seeping into my bones.

"Close your eyes. *Feel,*" his hot breath whispers into my ear. I succumb to his order easily and without question, and as soon as I do, my feet free themselves.

I'm pulled up and carried, much like Sicily, but I know the arms holding me belong to Kade.

The moment we're inside I hear the door click shut and Kade says, "You can open your eyes now." He lowers me to the floor and I look up to him. His eyes capture me as they move over my face. Then he slips his hands from my body, takes a step back, turns, and walks away.

"Emery…" Sicily's voice is soft and cautious. I turn around to face her. "I'm so sorry we got into that situation. I should've known. I wasn't careful enough." Watching as she fiddles with her fingers, I notice the childlike gestures shine through again.

"Sicily, I appreciate you saying sorry about the situation, but you have to understand, I don't *know* what *that* situation even was. I know nothing. Nobody is telling me anything, and I've had enough." As I step away from her she grabs my arm, but I wrench it free and continue walking. I can't leave this place, at least not tonight. I understand that I'm in danger, and whatever quirks I do have, they don't include being suicidal. Making my way back upstairs while ignoring the tingles, I slam the door behind me, attempting to cocoon myself in the bedroom I've been given. Within minutes there's a tap at the door and before I can say anything it opens. Elijah appears in the doorframe.

Chrysalis

"I could have been changing," I tell him flatly.

"No, I would have sensed it." His reply doesn't even surprise me, which is scary. "Can I come in?" he asks.

"If I say no are you going to come in anyway?" I counter.

"Probably." He grins at me as I roll my eyes, so I close them and lay down on the bed. The door clicks shut and the bed depresses as he sits next to me. "I'm sorry. I know I haven't been very forthcoming." I open my eyes and stare at him while raising an eyebrow. "Okay…" he holds his hands up, "…not forthcoming at all." I close my eyes once again. I want to know everything, but I'm already so confused. I know my life before was lonely, but at least it was structured, there were no expectations. Every day was the same, even down to the words that would inevitably be spat at me from the jocks and cheerleaders at school.

No.

Feeling sorry for myself is *not* going to help me. I sit up and push myself backward until I'm leaning against the headboard.

"Tell me," I demand, pulling my legs up to my chest, wrapping my arms around myself, and resting my chin on my knees.

"We'll do a bit at a time," Elijah says. I can see that he's waiting for my reaction. But I'm too tired to care much anymore. Something is better than nothing. So my face stays blank.

His shoulders sag and he turns, looking over to the window. "You're nearly nineteen. I'm twenty. As you know, we're siblings, there was only ever you and me. We lost our parents, but they had powers, as do we. However, back then, only I displayed any abilities. It seemed like you were never going to come into your gifts."

He rises from the bed and walks over to the window. Lifting his arm above his head, he places it against the wall and leans down looking out of the glass panes, a far-off gaze blanketing his features as if he's reminiscing. "Because it was deemed you didn't have any gifts, it was decided that the best course of action was to allow you a normal life, away from all this…" he moves his hand, gesturing outside, then continues. "I've watched you my whole life. Even when I was young. I started displaying my abilities when I was only two. I've developed them well. I'm strong, one of the strongest, and as such I've been asked to move away from here on more than one occasion." He straightens and turns to me. "But I couldn't leave you. You've never known me, but I've always known you. I'm a stranger to you, but you're my sister… completely, and I love you."

My chest compresses at his words and I feel my heart rate pick up speed.

Chrysalis

"Stop," he says as he moves back to the bed, sitting down and grabbing my hand. "You need to calm down. I don't want to have to put you to sleep again." My eyes widen and my heart rate doubles its speed in response to his words. "I'm serious Emery, you can't control your powers right now, and you need to calm your heart rate down before you do something accidentally. Like last night with those boys. Breathe deep... come on... in and out."

I let his words wash over me and close my eyes, taking in deep breaths through my nose and letting the air pass out of my mouth slowly. I can feel my heart calm.

"Wow that was quick. When I first came into that power it took me ages to calm myself," he tells me, pride tinging his words.

"What power?" I gasp out, noticing that he said the heart rate was attached to a specific power.

Elijah chuckles. "You caught that, huh?"

I nod in response. I'm trying not to go back to the part where Elijah said he loves me. I need some time to process that.

"You know that we have powers, that *you* have powers. There are many different gifts, probably more than any of us know—"

"Who's *us*?" I interrupt him.

He folds his arms across his chest and grins. "What answer do you want first?" he replies.

"Urm… the power." He smirks at me. "*Then…* the other one." I grin and he laughs. It's a deep, genuine laugh. The realization seeps into me, I could have had this my whole life. I could have had him, which means it's been kept from me. Suddenly my body goes cold.

"Don't," he snaps, his laughter stopping abruptly.

"Don't what?" I mimic him.

"Whatever it is that you're thinking, whatever made you go cold and stiff, stop thinking it. You can ask me anything. I will attempt to answer you and try to calm your fears, but you need to ask me."

"I thought you could read my mind?" I taunt.

"Only when you're thinking something consciously in your head. It only works when you're basically having some inner dialogue with yourself. It's hard to explain." His answer doesn't make sense to me, but I don't question him. I need his continuing explanation of everything, and I'm not going to get it if I keep interrupting him.

"Are you ready for more now?" Elijah tips his head to the side, awaiting my reply. I nod, which makes him grin. "Okay. The power you used the other night. You saw a light before you touched those guys, right?"

I nod and swallow. I remember their bodies dropping to the floor.

I killed them.

"Stop it. They weren't good people," he replies.

"They might have been. They may have grown up, got better." My voice is raspy as I force the words from my mouth.

"No. The guy that attacked you today? They were like him," he tells me, his eyes narrowed, anger swimming in his pupils.

"How do you know?" I reply.

"Emery, you're making this explaining gig real hard. Can you be quiet, just for a minute? Let me get some stuff out, yeah?"

I smile at his complaint. Now he looks like a big brother.

He closes his eyes and shakes his head. "The power is called *Revive*. It can bring someone back to life, or jolt their hearts to kill them. This power runs throughout your whole body. When you get worked up, it can appear without you wanting it to. In time you'll be able to summon it at will. It was running through your body the night those pieces of scum attacked you. When you touched them, they were effectively zapped with a high voltage. Even if you hadn't touched them yourself, the same thing would've happened the second they made contact with your body. And it can be any part... they could have touched the tips of your hair, and it would have still ended the same way.

"You were *live*, Emery, like a live wire, and they were out of time. Had they realized that you'd come into your powers, they would've been more careful.

The power you felt today when you were attacked and then again outside the house, it's called *Earthing*. They Earthed you. They pulled your life force into the ground, basically freezing you to the earth."

Elijah stops and rubs his hand down his face. "I should never have let you go with Sicily alone. I didn't think it through, I just assumed they wouldn't attack you in public. Sicily feels bad. She pulled you into that alleyway, she knows better than that. Still it's done now." He sighs long and hard.

"How did you know that we were in trouble?" I question.

Elijah rubs the back of his neck. "That's harder to explain. We could feel you."

"We?" My stomach starts clenching, then a knock at the door causes me to jump.

"Elijah. You need to come downstairs. Debrief. Bring your sister." Kade's voice growls through the door.

"Is he ever happy?" I ask, quickly biting my lip when I realize, yet again, my mouth has gotten away from me.

Elijah smiles at me. "Rarely. Although one day I hope that might change," he answers, staring into my eyes. "Come on. Let's get downstairs." Elijah stands, holding out his hand.

"But… I still have loads of questions," I complain, pouting.

Chrysalis

"That won't wash with me, Emery. We already have a pouter in the house, we don't need another." Winking, he grabs my hand, hauls me up, and pulls me down the stairs.

Great. This place is driving me nuts. I'm surrounded by crazy people.

"I heard that," Elijah mumbles with humor as I find myself, yet again, following him blindly, understanding still eluding me.

Chapter 5

Waking up to Elijah sitting in the room is a surprise. We argued last night. The meeting we were summoned to was filled with a lot of information that made no sense to me. They discussed developments regarding people

I'd never heard of. Aside from meeting Tess and Miles, I was completely lost. Nobody made a point of explaining anything to me. Maybe they assumed Elijah had already filled in the blanks. So, I sat in the corner of the large living room, staring at a video on my phone for most of the night until they noticed.

"What are you doing?" Elijah said to me, and everyone stopped talking to look my way.

I glanced up at him. "I was just watching a video," I answered slowly, feeling like it was the wrong thing to say.

Chrysalis

"A video about what?" Miles had jumped into our conversation, and I briefly saw Elijah look at Miles, a frown passing across his face.

"Err, it's anime." When nobody spoke I carried on.

"It's something I like to watch. I watch it quite a lot." I started babbling and suddenly felt really uncomfortable.

"She's supposed to be here to help, and yet, she's ignoring everything and watching cartoons!" Katarina complained, crossing her arms. Miles sat next to her nodding.

"They're not cartoons," I disputed. "And anyway, if any of you were willing to explain what the hell was going on here, maybe I'd be more interested." Standing up I walked out, going to the only place where I had my own space.

"You need to get her under control." I heard Miles say—I assume to Elijah—as I left. The words were quickly followed by a snarl, after which nobody spoke. Once I went upstairs I heard nothing for about an hour, then Elijah appeared following a knock at the door.

"I wanted to see if you were okay?" he asked me.

"Really? You want to know now? How about standing up for me back there? Or even better, actually telling me something substantial, rather than giving me snippets which always leave me even

more confused than before!" I shouted, turning away and going to sit on the bed.

"I'm sorry, I truly am. I want to tell you everything, but to be honest, there's a lot to tell. It's going to take time." He stopped talking and I looked back at him, feeling bad that I shouted. Then he continued on, and my regret quickly dispersed, "Of course, it would help if you actually listened ct the meetings, and didn't just sit playing your silly cartoons." He hammered his hand down on the dressing table.

"Just leave me alone," I whispered, feeling rejected and once again lonely. I got what he was trying to say. I understood that I probably should have listened. But nothing made sense and nobody was forthcoming with explanations. So, I ended up doing what I always did. I sat in the corner trying to go unnoticed. Now he was shouting at me, and I'd had enough. I laid down curling onto my side, staying still until I heard him leave. Only once I heard the door click behind him did I allow myself to close my eyes and forget about my day. I pretended that I was someone else, someone strong, as I drifted into sleep.

Chrysalis

It's morning now. The sun is almost blinding and he's here again, just like yesterday, sitting in the corner of my room, looking disheveled and worn.

"What are you doing in here?" I question, sleepiness making my throat tight.

"I wanted to watch over you, make sure you were okay," he responds, his eyes fixed on me.

"Why wouldn't I be? I mean I'm safe in this house, right? That's why I'm here." I watch as his jaw ticks.

"You *are* safe here, but I like to make sure, and I thought…" he glances away and swallows before turning back to me, "…maybe you were here to get to know me. After all these years, it's nice to be able to talk to you. My sister." Elijah rubs the back of his neck, looking a little uncomfortable with his admission

"I know. I'm sorry, I didn't mean… well, it's… of course I want to spend time getting to know you. I just wish it wasn't under these circumstances. I have magical powers I know nothing about, and I'm being chased by God knows who. Katarina seems to hate me as much as the jerks from school always have. And Kade doesn't seem too impressed either. So excuse me for wondering what the hell is going on!" I jump out of bed, stomping like a child to the bathroom, not giving Elijah time to answer. Turning on the shower I decide that I need to refresh, wake up properly and then face the world. Sighing, I sit on the floor, resting against the bathroom door and closing my eyes.

"I feel you in there, I know you're not in the shower. I can also sense that you need me to leave you alone for now. When you're finished come downstairs, I'll make you breakfast."

I release a breath when I hear him leave, then I haul myself up, stepping under the shower and trying to let all my fears and confusion wash away.

"I'm sorry about Miles and Katarina last night." I hear the voice as I walk into the kitchen and spin around, seeing Tess behind me. "Katarina is just having a hard time with it all. Miles though… he can be a dick anyway. And ever since Elijah and Sicily… well, let's just say he's gotten worse." I feel myself frown. Tess is pretty, with short dark blond hair and almond shaped brown eyes that match her brother's. She's every bit as good looking as the rest of them. She smiles at me and I notice that she has exactly the same smile as Tristan—not surprising since they're twins.

"What do you mean? Elijah and Sicily are dating, right?" I ask her the questions, but realize I'm still frowning, so I quickly soften my face, hoping she doesn't think I'm crazy.

Chrysalis

Tess nods, sitting down at the kitchen table. "Mmm hmm, yep, but she used to be with Miles."

My eyes widen at her words, and I sit next to her at the table. "Really? Oh, I bet that didn't go down well." I forget everything and concentrate on the gossip. It's actually nice to do this with someone. These people are starting to give me things I've been missing for years. They all have their own ways, but each one offers me something I never really noticed I was missing until now.

"No, Miles is still pissed, and regularly takes it out on everyone. He saves the best for Elijah, but he can't really do much to him because… well… you know." She gets up and moves over to make coffee, gesturing to me. I nod, accepting her offer of a coffee.

"I don't know. What?" I exclaim, totally drawn into the conversation.

"Elijah is one of the strongest, he's a level eight. Very few people are at that level, and there's only one I know who's higher. Miles is only a level five, there's no contest," she mutters while making coffee for the both of us. I'm completely confused by every word she has just uttered.

"What's a level eight? I mean… what are the levels?" Slowly she turns around to face me. Her eyes widen as she holds a cup of coffee in each hand.

"You haven't been told? I thought Elijah would have…" She stops talking and I feel a wall building inside her, even though I have no idea how I know it.

"Stop…" I say to her, holding out my hand, palm up. She nods to me and I look at my hand, wondering where that command came from. "Come and sit down. Tell me what the levels are, please?" I ask softer this time. She nods once again and moves to sit next to me. It's like she's hypnotized. Her mouth opens as though she's a robot. It's weird and freaks me out a little bit, but I have no idea what's going on, or why she's acting like this. It's obviously something I've done, I just don't know what exactly that is, or how to reverse it.

"Every one of us has a level. They start at one and move through to ten. Ten being the highest you can ever be. These levels are based on our gifts… the specific powers we have, and how strong they are. You can't earn these powers or win them, they're what you're born with. When we get to about sixteen our levels are usually pretty set. Most people have all the abilities they're ever going to get by then… except you. I've never met someone who only came into their powers at the age of eighteen. That's unheard of." She stops talking and sits drinking her coffee.

"So, Elijah is a level eight. You said one person is higher?" Her reply is to smile at me and nod, still in a trance-like state. "Well, who is that?"

Chrysalis

"Kade, he's a level ten. I've never met anyone stronger." Her words surprise me, although I'm not sure why, since somewhere in my gut I feel like I knew that already.

"Tess, enough!" I hear the words shot through the air like bullets from Elijah's mouth.

Tess blinks a couple of times before looking between Elijah and me and frowning. "You *Entranced* me!" Tess shouts angrily. I look up at her not really knowing what to say.

"She didn't know, Tess. I haven't told her anything yet," Elijah explains to her. Tess shakes her head and walks out while Elijah comes to sit next to me, taking Tess's empty seat.

"So I can entrance people now? Whatever exactly that is?" I mumble, looking down at my hands.

"Maybe," Elijah replies, rubbing his chin.

My head whips up, and I look at him. "Maybe?"

"Well, I'm not sure if this is a power you possess or…" he trails off, looking out of the window.

"What, Elijah? Please, tell me something," I beg.

"It might be a power you're drawing from someone else."

"Who? How?" I rush out my one-word questions, excited and scared at the answers I might receive.

"You can sometimes borrow abilities from someone else. It doesn't remove their power. It can cause it to weaken while you're using it, but other than that there's no long-term damage, not that we've seen so far. However, you can only borrow powers from your other half," he answers, closing his eyes.

"What do you mean by other half? Like, someone you're married to?" I question.

He shakes his head. "No. Not even close. Your other half, well, for us, is the other half of your soul. There is only one person we're meant for. But when you pair up it can make you vulnerable, because the other person can ultimately steal every ability you possess, meaning you're open to being attacked and killed. A lot of us pair up, but not with the other half of us, because it means we have to trust them one hundred percent or risk our own lives. If we come across our other halves at any point during our existence, we will recognize them. That is if we're lucky enough to find them before they're killed. But we have to make a choice whether to be with them or not." He scratches the back of his head and sighs.

"A lot choose to live without them because it's easier. However, the other side to that is if you meet your other half, or even see them from afar and then you let them go…" Elijah breaks off and grinds his jaw, before continuing. "Suddenly you know what you're missing. Supposedly it feels like half your soul is ripped away from you. It can cause some to break completely. I've witnessed it. I've seen people take their own lives or live hollow, lost, and lonely existences because they've given up on their other half." He bites down on his lower lip. "It's usually

Chrysalis

worse if their other half has been killed. It's haunting. There are few who have turned their backs on that love and been fine. But not many can endure the loss, and some move over to live in the dark, hurting others, hoping it will give them some kind of sick release." He scrubs his hand down his face.

"So, I might have this power, or I might be drawing it from my other half?" I rush out. "There are so many questions I want to ask Elijah. Firstly, how would I be able to draw it? Doesn't the other half of my soul have to like, I don't know, agree to be mine or something before I can take their powers?" I question him, happy that he's finally opening up and explaining some things.

"No, well… actually, yes. It's different for you, though. I mean we come from a certain family, one I haven't explained yet. You should get some abilities that make you more unique, but for now we have to wait and see. The other option is that your other half recognizes you, and is already falling in love… or trying not to."

"Falling in… *Are you serious?*"

"Completely." Elijah nods and grabs my hand.

"Who?" I ask.

"I can't know for sure." His voice is laced with worry.

"But you have an idea." It's a statement. Elijah knows who. I'm sure he does.

He nods in reply.

Suddenly, as if a mask has been unveiled from my face, I see everything. Emotion washes over me as all the puzzle pieces slot into their rightful place. I open my mouth and one word drops from my lips.

"Kade."

Then, slowly, Elijah's head moves up and down, giving my brain the confirmation that my soul never needed.

Chapter 6

Kade…

I can't stop repeating the name in my head. Elijah gave me a boatload of information this morning, and I'm struggling to wrap my head around everything. Even so, the one thing I can't see past is the idea that Kade might be the other half of my soul. It's ridiculous.

"You need to stop thinking about it," Elijah murmurs from next to me.

I glance across at him. "I wasn't talking in my head."

He smirks. "No, but I can feel that you're all knotted up inside. I can think of a few reasons, but only one thing really stands out." He shakes his head but doesn't look at me. We're currently on the way to school. I wasn't overly keen when Elijah suggested I attend today, but he said it was the right thing to do, that we needed to keep things as they were. Personally, I think there's more to it, but if there is, then as per usual I'm out of the loop.

"I don't see how he can be the other half of my soul. Wouldn't I know?" I question.

"Emery, you have to remember, I didn't say he was, just that it might be a possibility. The other possibility is that you've developed the power yourself." He frowns.

"What?"

His arm flexes as his grip on the steering wheel tightens. "Usually, in families, the line is pretty straight.

What I mean by that is the *bloodline* is pretty straight. So, siblings look similar. Traditionally, we all have names that start with the same letter. That would be the same for the whole house, and the same house colors—"

"House?" I cut him off mid-flow.

"I wish you'd stop doing that," he complains.

"But if I did then I'd forget what I wanted to ask," I whine. Elijah looks my way and chuckles.

"You're everything I imagined you'd be up close." He smiles and once again it rocks me inside. I swallow and look away, not accustomed to the affection I hear among his words. "It's okay," he tells me softly, reaching over to hold my hand.

"What's okay?" I croak.

"Being scared." I start to shake my head, opening my mouth to tell him he's wrong, but I don't get the

Chrysalis

chance. "You are. Before you try to explain how you're not scared, how you've been doing fine being alone all these years etcetera, save it. I can feel you, remember? You're scared. I get it, you still don't know me, but you will. Then you'll love me like everyone else does," he says winking, and I giggle at him. His attempt at placating me a little is working.

"So, the house?" I prompt after a few moments of silence.

"Well, we're from the House of Laird."

"That sounds like we belong in an old fancy English movie," I reply, thinking how cool it would be to have a big ol' house in the English countryside.

"You really do have an overactive imagination," Elijah says, biting his lip.

"Really? You're gonna go there, after the freaky crap you've shown me in the last few days?" I respond, grinning.

"Okay, I have no answer to that."

I laugh. "So... we're the House of Laird. What exactly does that mean?"

"There's a lot to it, so don't expect me to tell you it all now." I frown at him, and he catches it when his eyes flit to mine. "Before you go all postal on me, I'm not trying to keep anything from you. It's just... I will forget stuff. There's so much you don't know. I've learned this over the course of my whole life, and you expect me to tell you all twenty years, and then some, of information in a couple of days? It just doesn't work that way, Em," he says sighing.

"Okay, I'm sorry. I'm going to shut up now." He glances at me quickly. "I will, I swear… okay? I'll promise to try and keep my mouth shut." I roll my eyes.

"Not every bloodline is special, that's the first thing you need to know. But there are some families who are a part of what is known as a House. That usually means they're very wealthy or important. If that's the case, then they're called the House of whatever their surname is. So for us it's the House of Laird. Usually within these Houses, all members have the same initial for their name. We also have house colors that you are to wear to represent your House. However, the color tradition was lost long ago, when all the houses were torn apart."

I really want to ask Elijah a million different questions, and I bite my lip to stop myself from saying anything.

"Bloodlines usually have the same powers. Not necessarily exactly the same, but if you have the power to entrance, and it's not from Kade, then that's a new power to our House."

"I know I said I'd be quiet, but I still want to know about something I asked earlier that you haven't answered yet."

"What?"

Chrysalis

"Well, if I'm the other half of Kade's soul, wouldn't I know? I mean you said that we all know the moment we lay our eyes on that person." I ask him, rubbing my temples.

"Usually, that's an easy *yes*, but you're the first person we know of, who's come into their powers so late in life. I guess there is a chance that because your gifts appeared so late, you wouldn't realize meeting your other half. Your abilities aren't even all showing yet, so being able to control them and being aware of little signs will take time. If Kade is your other half, then you probably don't yet know it."

I nod at his response. "So why do you suspect he is?" I question, biting my lip.

"Little things," he shrugs. "He knew you were in trouble. He never explained why, but I could sense something from him, I'm just not sure what. Kade doesn't have the ability to feel, but he has many other abilities, and I know Tess told you how strong he is. Kade's better than the rest of us at almost everything. He never allows me to read him, I can never feel him. The fact that I could the other day threw me. There's also no other real explanation for him knowing you were in trouble. I didn't know." He pulls the car over and I'm vaguely aware that we've reached my school.

"When I asked you how you knew I was in trouble you said, '*We* could feel you.'" I narrow my eyes on him, and he turns in his seat to look at me.

"I could feel you, but only as I drew nearer while I was running to you. Kade burst into my room that day, shouted that you were in trouble, and bolted. I struggled to keep up with him, he's so fast. But I had to. If I lost him, I wouldn't have known where you were. He guided us to you, to your exact location. We arrived just at the moment Zeit ripped your top. Kade froze. Honestly Em… I've never seen him react like that. The more I think about it, the more I realize it's the truth. You're his other half."

I sit opening and closing my mouth. For once, I have not a single thought or question in my head. I turn and watch the other kids arriving at school. A couple of popular girls in my year notice me sitting with Elijah, and I watch as they tap the boys, bringing their attention to us. The boys' eyes light up as they notice Elijah's car. I turn back to my brother. "What happens now?" I ask flatly.

"You go to school." He smirks.

"But I thought you said the only place I was safe was with you?" I rush out, worry powering up through my chest.

A look of agony slips over Elijah's face. "I'm sorry… I need you to continue as normal, just for a couple of days. I want to get all the paperwork for you cleared. Legally removing you from both your school and from your living arrangements. I can't have anyone sniffing around because you go missing."

Chrysalis

"But I'm eighteen!" I complain.

"I know, but the less mystery, the better. I don't want anyone missing you."

I snort at his statement. "No one will miss me."

He puts his hand on the back of my head and pulls me into him. "You *would* be missed, Emery. Don't worry, I promise someone will be watching you all the time. You're safe," he says, letting me go.

Off to school. Great.

"Now Emery, go play nice with the other children. And if they upset you… don't zap them." He winks and I cross my arms. I don't know whether I'm more worried about hurting someone, or about being their scratching post whenever they have an itch.

"Fine. Will you be picking me up?" I ask, pulling myself from the car.

"You know it, baby sister." He laughs and salutes me, pulling away from the sidewalk with a screech of his tires.

The rest of the day I ignore the stares and whispers directed at me. Though this time it's not because people are saying nasty things, this time the chatter is because they all want to know about Elijah.

Things come to a head after the fourth period. Jennica corners me as I leave the library. "So, you have a boyfriend. I'm surprised. He seemed hot, kinda cool too with that car. I'm not sure what you could offer him?" She holds her hand up like she's looking at her nails. "I bet you're still a virgin. He's gonna realize what a mistake he's making soon." She stops, then claps her hands together excitedly "I know Emma… introduce me to him, that way when he dumps your fat butt he can hook up with me. At least then you'll still see him." She looks at her friends, then back to me. "From afar, while he's kissing me." They all laugh, amused with themselves.

I roll my eyes and walk away, I'm so used to their harassment that it bounces off me, for the most part, these days. How different their attitudes would be if they knew who he truly was.

Walking outside the building toward the parking lot, I desperately need some air. Passing under some trees, I'm suddenly yanked back and thrown against the library wall.

"Emma, or Emery." The words are whispered, and as I look up, I see a face I know only too well. My body jolts as fear flits through me. In front of me is Michael. One of the boys I killed the other night. "I… you…" I stutter.

"You killed me. Yes, that's right, you did. But I was stronger than the other two, and with some help from Zeit, I reconnected with my life-force. Although, I guess technically, I'm still dead." He laughs and it's a creepy sound. He doesn't sound like

Chrysalis

the Michael I knew from before. He was always horrible - one of the meaner boys.

Now, though... now he's truly scary.

He smirks, and I feel pure evil flutter in the air. "It's amazing to think," his eyes roll, "...all these years you've been under my feet. Emery fucking Laird. In *my* school. I had you here at my fingertips, and I just played with you from afar, when I could have been playing with you up close and personal." He leans forward and sniffs my hair.

Suddenly, everything seems to happen in slow motion. I watch as he moves back from me, his hand closing in on my face. It's like he's about to stroke my cheek, but it's so slow, and it confuses me. As I look around I realize that *he's* not making everything slow, something else is. Before I can question my sanity, his hand is ripped away from my sight and I turn to see Kade holding him against the wall.

"Stay away from her or I will end you," Kade says in a low, menacing voice that sends a shiver down my spine.

Michael—stupidly I think—laughs. I feel my stomach dip and swirl as Kade leans into Michael. "Believe what I say. I don't lie."

Michael's eyes widen slightly, and he grabs at Kade's hand, which is locked around his throat.

"I'll kill you..." Kade leans closer, and I can just hear him as he whispers, "even if you're already dead." I can feel Michael's fear. It's saturating the air surrounding us all.

Kade drops him. "Come on," he commands, grabbing my hand. I feel like my arm is going to come out of its socket as he pulls me from the school grounds. We stop at a shiny motorbike.

"Here." Kade snaps, passing me a helmet. I look at it then back at him. "Put it on. I'm taking you home."

I've never been on a bike before, and although I don't know Kade well, I'm sensing this is one of those times when I shouldn't argue. So even though I'm not entirely sure I want to, I grab the helmet he's offering me and slip it on. He nods and gets on the bike, indicating for me to climb on behind him. The moment I do, he grabs my hands and pulls them around his waist.

The ride we take to the house is probably one of the top five moments in my life so far. I'm not sure if that makes me really sad, but I don't care, not at this moment on the back of Kade's bike, feeling the wind hitting my body, my cheek laid against his back. And when we get on the freeway, for those five minutes, Kade places his hand over mine, allowing his thumb to drift back and forth. I don't think he even knows he's doing it. I've been pinned in a corner for so many years, shunned and humiliated, feeling confused and alone. But this moment right now, I feel free. I feel like I've broken out of a shell,

Chrysalis

a prison I've been trapped in. I pull my visor up when we pull off the freeway and close my eyes, allowing the wind to blow in my face.

Happy. It's an emotion which has often evaded me.

We arrive back at the house and Kade helps me off his bike. "Are you okay?" he asks, a soft look on his face.

One that I haven't had the pleasure of seeing yet. It's breathtaking.

"Yeah, thank you for saving me... again," I tell him, staring into his hazel eyes. "How did you know?" I ask, and bite my lip waiting for the answer. Kade says nothing his gaze moving over my face, I can sense he's trying to work something out. "Did you feel me? Because Elijah says you might be my other half, and honestly, I'm still trying to understand it all. But I thought, maybe you could tell me if it's true?" I play with my fingers, hating that I've exposed myself, but I have so many questions, and this would have been one more answered.

Kade's face changes. His eyes narrow on me as his jaw ticks. "It wouldn't matter whether I am or not. I will never be with you. *Never,*" he barks and walks inside.

In that moment, right at that second, I know the answer to my question.

He *is* my other half.

I realize it the instant his words jolt me backward, and my body goes stiff because I feel like the bottom has just fallen out of my world.

Chrysalis

CHAPTER 7

"What happened?" Before I've had a chance to pull myself together following Kade's departure, Elijah appears in front of me.

"Nothing. I want to leave." My voice sounds hollow even to my own ears.

"Sure, where do you want to go?" Elijah looks around while moving into my space. "We can go somewhere away from here, maybe have a night out?"

"No Elijah, you don't understand. I want to leave *here*," I demand, pointing at the house. "I can't be in there anymore, with them… with him." My words trail off and I look down at my feet, fresh humiliation coursing through my body as I remember Kade's cutting words.

"What happened, Em?" he asks, slipping his arm around me and bringing me into his chest. I sigh ruefully, determined not to cry.

"I just want to go," I repeat, swallowing hard. My throat feels like it's coated in chalk, all dry and dusty.

Elijah looks at the house then down to me.

"Sure, come on." Grabbing my hand he leads me to his car, settling me inside and moving around the hood to slide in. The car comes to life with a roar, and I don't look back as we peel away. Sitting in silence for the whole journey, both of us are obviously inside our own thoughts. I only start taking notice as we pull into a hotel downtown.

"Where are we?" My voice is tired, and suddenly I'm drained.

Elijah remains facing forward, staring out the windshield of his car. "We're at the Vallarta Hotel. I figured we need to talk, and you need to be away from the house." He sighs, turning to face me. "You need to understand that you're not leaving me, Em. Never again." His tone is sharp like he's annoyed. But right now I don't care, even if it's me that's upsetting him. I nod my reply and follow his lead as he walks up to reception, asking for a two bedroom suite. Remaining silent as he guides me to our room, Elijah unlocks the door, checking the whole place before he relaxes.

"Tell me what happened," he demands firmly but gently before I've even sat down.

"Tomorrow," I whisper.

"No, Em, not tomorrow. I want to know what happened back there. Why you're suddenly all quiet

Chrysalis

and withdrawn. You look pale, and I'm worried about you." He slumps down on one of the brown leather sofas in the living room area as if exhausted. Then, leaning forward, he lays his head in his hands. "I need to know you're okay." It's a plea, and I feel it deep inside tugging at my heart.

Padding over to the sofas, I gently lower myself into the seat next to him. "I'm okay, at least I will be. This is better, I know where I stand."

"What do you mean this is better? What's better?" Elijah raises his head from his hands and turns to look at me.

I bite my lip and contemplate how much to tell him. My eyes slide to the left and I take a moment.

"Emery, I need to know everything. I need to take care of you, until you're in a position to look after yourself, to control your powers. You need to be completely honest with me, it's the only way I can protect you," Elijah explains clasping my upper arms and making me look at him.

I blow air out from between my lips and nod. "Kade. He said it doesn't matter what we are, or what we're meant to be." I pull my gaze away from his, looking over his shoulder, staring at the skyline. "He said he would never be with me." I shake my head, shrugging from his hold, standing up and taking the few steps over to the window. "It's not like I asked him to be with me… I only wanted to know if we were joined. There's so much I don't understand, so much I want to understand. I really only asked for clarification. I've never had a boyfriend, I wasn't asking him that. But he was so…" I break off and turn back to Elijah. He's grinding his teeth and I can feel a coiling in my stomach, which surprisingly, isn't from me. "Elijah," I whisper.

"He was so what, Em?" he asks, his tone controlled.

"Cold. He was cold," I answer, feeling my insides deflate, and this time I know it's all me.

"Stay here," he orders.

Before I can answer, I feel a gentle breeze and he's gone, the door slamming behind him.

I walk around the suite. There are two bedrooms, both exactly the same. I make my way to the bathroom and decide to take a shower. When my legs are struggling to keep me up, I step out from under the water and wrap the fluffy turquoise towel around me. Kicking my clothes to the side, I'm annoyed that I have nothing to change into *yet again*. Shuffling into one of the bedrooms, I find a white robe and throw it on.

I slide between the sheets of my bed, snuggling under the covers and burrowing my way under the pillow. I try to ignore the constant jabbing, both in my head and heart.

It's a feeling that's been there since the moment I realized Kade was my other half—then just as quickly found out he'd never want me. It's all so

Chrysalis

confusing. I've never had a boyfriend, I've never really had the opportunity. Although, there's never been a boy I've been interested in. Let's face it, they were all horrible to me. Kade hasn't exactly been welcoming, but he has saved my life. More than once. That has to count for something, right? He's probably been acting on instinct. I mean, he does know when I'm in danger. He's a good guy, his hero personality wouldn't let him leave me to die. Even if he wants to stay away from me.

God, he must hate being connected to me.

I need to help him. I've got to do the right thing and get as far away as possible. He can't leave that house and those people. They are his family.

He can't leave, but I can.

I know that Elijah said not all of the *other halves* get together. In fact, it sounds like most of them choose not to. Through fear maybe? Whatever the reason, I need to let Kade have some peace, and being able to always feel when I'm in trouble is not going to help him. I need to get out of his life.

It's amazing, I've come alive. I have all these feelings that have somehow ignited inside me.

Right now, though, I need sleep and can feel it pulling me under.

"Emery." Elijah's muffled voice pulls me from my dreamless sleep. "Emery… Em…" I twist my head and force my eyes open. He's sitting on the side of my bed, and the room is almost entirely dark.

"What…" I smack my lips together and reach over to the bedside table that somehow holds a bottle of water now. Flicking the lamp on and grabbing the water, I take a big gulp. As I put it down and turn back to Elijah, a screech escapes me. "What happened to you?" I ask reaching up tentatively and touching the cut above his eye, then moving my hand down to the bruise forming on his cheek and lastly the tear on his lip.

"Just a little… disagreement. Listen, I'm sorry I woke you. I wanted to tell you that you have clothes now." He turns his head, nodding, and I follow his gaze to the chair in the corner, which has a blue duffle placed on it. "I got some things for you. For us. We'll be here as long as we need to be. I've sorted it with the hotel. I booked us this room for the next few days, then after that… well, we can see what happens."

I say nothing but grab his hand for comfort. I can feel his emotions, but not clearly, and I'm not sure if that's because I'm half asleep, or because he's holding back from me.

I wonder if I can mask my own feelings.

"You can," Elijah tells me with a smirk, and I fake punch his chest. Which makes him hiss through his

Chrysalis

teeth. "What happened, Elijah? Tell me!" I practically shout at him.

Sighing, he rubs his chest where I punched him. "Kade and me... we got into it."

"Oh God, Elijah. Why did you do that? I didn't need you to defend me. Kade didn't do anything wrong!" I feel my heart rate pick up speed and start using the breathing techniques that Elijah explained to try and calm myself.

"I know," he replies, and it throws me.

"What?" I ask.

"I know that Kade wasn't doing anything wrong. I mean I was pissed with the way he spoke to you, but that's kind of Kade's way. He always seems grumpy. When I left here I wanted to hurt him. In the short time it took me to run back to the house, I realized that he can make the choice not to be with you. We can't control people - that's what the others want to do." *Others?*

"That's for another time, Em," he tells me in reply to my unspoken question. "When I got back to the house I was annoyed, but I knew there was nothing I could do. Kade is within his rights to decide not to be with you. It's not like you've even dated. Hell, you didn't even know him a few days ago." Elijah rubs the back of his neck, and I can see another bruise on the underside of his forearm.

"Then why did you fight?" I mutter.

"Because I wouldn't bring you back. And I wouldn't tell him where you were."

My chest seizes at his words. "What?" I huff out.

"He can feel you, but only when you're in danger or when you're near to him. It's so complicated, Em, and not really a discussion for two in the morning. Just trust me when I say he's pissed that you're out here, and this…" he stops and points to his face, "…was him getting his point across. It shows just how deeply he truly feels for you because believe it or not, he actually likes and respects me. I may be a level eight, but I'm not stupid. I know what Kade is capable of, but I also know he wouldn't seriously hurt me. These bruises will be healed by morning. Still, I could see the control on his face when we went at it. He might be telling you that he'll never be with you, but his actions are saying something entirely different."

I pull my hand away from his and rub my eye. "This is a lot to digest. We need to have a longer chat tomorrow, Elijah."

"Yes, but after you've been to school," he replies. I open my mouth to protest, but he continues talking before I can get a word out. "I know what happened today. That's one of the reasons I'm so late. After Kade calmed down, he explained about school. That guy, Michael, he won't come near you again. If he doesn't heed Kade's warning… well, simply put… Kade will end him. One thing we have on our side is

Chrysalis

that Kade can feel when you're scared or in danger. He will always come for you," Elijah tells me rubbing my shoulder. "It will be okay."

"What if he's too late?" I ask, biting the inside of my mouth.

Elijah chuckles and I arch my eyebrow at him. "Sorry, Emery, it's just, there's nobody faster than Kade. You've seen what he can do. He ran back to the house with you in tow after that attack in the alleyway, right?" he asks.

"Well, yeah. But even though I knew we were running fast, it felt weird, kind of like we weren't running at all." I lay back down in bed, snuggling under the duvet and wait for Elijah to explain. He must know what I want because he smiles at me. I can sense his love for me, it's pouring out of him in waves. It makes me feel warm, knowing I finally have a family.

"Kade can manipulate time, it's called *Phasing*, and before you say it, he can't time travel or anything like that. He has the ability to slow things down, or maybe it's just that he's so fast everything else seems slow. I'm not sure. But no matter how fast one of us… or one of them are, Kade is faster - always"

"When he saved me from Michael, I felt like everything was in slow motion," I say, trying to stop my eyes from drifting shut. "Michael had just sniffed my hair," I mutter sleepily, and immediately I feel Elijah tense. "He pulled back but was about to stroke my cheek… I think. He never got that far because Kade must have slowed everything down, and then he pulled Michael's arm away before he touched me."

Elijah works his jaw, and I can feel his emotions warring with each other. "Michael is lucky Kade didn't rip his arm from his body." He shakes his head out and relaxes slightly. "Yeah, he probably didn't slow time down as such, he's just so fast. The reason you felt like everything was slow too is because you're his other half. Like I said before, you can take on his power."

"But I thought I had to ask for his power, or he had to share it freely or at least agree to be my other half before we could exchange powers… or something. Damn this stuff is confusing. Now my head hurts."

Elijah grins and ruffles my hair. "Okay Em, before you fall to sleep, the short version is that you do need to freely share yourself with your other half. Well, usually. Whatever is happening with you and Kade, there's more to it. When he saw Zeit rip your top the other day he stopped, frozen. It confused me at first, but I think I've worked out that it was because he felt like he was a few seconds too late. Kade is never too late. I'm assuming that's why Michael never got to touch your cheek. I have my theories, and hopefully, in time I'll get all the answers, meaning you will too. For now, though, my main

Chrysalis

concern is making sure you're okay, training you to use your powers and generally getting to be the big brother that I've always wanted to be. Now sleep. Tomorrow is a new day, Emery."

As his words drift down to me, I close my eyes, knowing that when I wake Elijah will be right there to make sure I'm okay. To watch over me. I'm not alone anymore, and that makes every other confusing and scary thing that's happening right now seem perfectly okay.

Chapter 8

Waking up this morning I feel different, stronger. My eyes scan the room almost expertly, noticing little things like the fingerprints on the door frame, or a smudge mark on the wall next to the light switch. It's like I've been doing it for years. Elijah is asleep in the corner chair. I slide from the bed grabbing the blue duffle and make my way to the other bathroom, giving him peace. He needs the rest. I move through my daily routine quickly. Digging around in the bag after my shower, I pick out black jeans and a red hoodie. When I'm finished I make a coffee and move to the balcony, opening the doors and stepping outside. I breathe in the aroma coming from my cup as I take in the dawn rising. It's around five, and the sun is appearing behind a few scattered white clouds, making me think it's going to be a beautiful day.

I slept well last night, apart from Elijah's interruption. I actually fell asleep pretty early, it was

Chrysalis

about seven in the evening, so I've had nearly ten hours of sleep. That has to be why I feel more alive. But there's something else too, something stirring inside like I have a power that's just waiting to be used. One of the strangest things about all of this is that I never would have recognized that feeling before, but now I can. I know something's about to happen, I just wish I was more prepared for it.

The hotel phone rings, causing me to jolt from my thoughts. I run across the room with such speed that I manage to knock a small table over on the way. Stopping abruptly, I stare down at my feet.

Did I move that fast?

I look back to the table now laying on the floor. It would appear the answer is yes. I shake my head and grab the phone.

"Hello," I answer, sipping my coffee with a smile. I place my cup on the kitchen counter and fan my lips when I realize how hot it still is.

"Emery..." The voice is cold and dark. It makes me stop what I'm doing and immediately pay attention. Even through the phone line I can sense powerful evil, hate, and viciousness.

"Who is this?" My voice is firm, and although he sounds scary, I don't actually feel fearful. Maybe it's because Elijah is in the next room and I'm only talking on the phone, or maybe it's because of whatever has happened to me.

He chuckles darkly, "that's right, you really should start asking questions, little girl. You need to find out who your friends… and your foes are. One day, if you don't die first, you'll be expected to make a decision. You need to catch up quick."

I take a breath in, then hiss out, "You still haven't told me who *you* are."

I hear his chuckle down the line again and feel goosebumps slither across my skin. "I'm the other side to you. I'm the one they'll say you shouldn't want to be like, but I'm the one who's free. I don't have to contain my powers and I have no limitations. There's a reason that you came into your powers late, Emery. When your brother starts digging, you will find out. All the ones who knew are either on my side now, or dead. One day we will meet, Emery. One day."

A click followed by the dial tone tells me he's hung up. Slowly I place the phone back in its holder. Now I'm even more confused. Picking up my coffee and clutching the warm cup in my hands, my goosebumps recede and I walk out to the balcony.

"Emery." I hear my name whispered, and my eyes move instantly without my brain directing them. They travel straight to a man on the ground. We're seven floors up, but I can see his smirk as he stares at me. Then suddenly, he disappears.

Chrysalis

"He found you," I hear Elijah's voice behind me, and although he must have just woken up, he's completely alert and sounds concerned.

"Who's found me?" I ask, turning toward him. His eyes move over my face searching for something.

"You're different, Em."

I nod. "Yeah, I know."

Elijah's eyebrows pull together, his unease is clear.

"You know? What do you know?"

This is a different Elijah than I've seen before. He seems grumpy, annoyed… unsettled.

"I'm not sure what I know," I tell him, and he raises an eyebrow. "All right, that sounds stupid. What I'm saying is, when I woke this morning I felt different. Stronger. Like I have more power, but I don't know why… or how. What I can tell you is that I saw that man's face from up here. I've never needed glasses, but even so, it's a stretch to see someone's face from seven floors up."

Elijah taps his fingers on the doorframe. "You must have started building your basic powers, strength, speed, vision, that sort of thing. Either that or Kade is near. Have you seen him?" His head darts around.

"No, and it's not Kade." I blush looking away. "I feel him when he's near."

His eyes widen in surprise. "You do? You haven't mentioned that before. I didn't know you could feel him, too."

Biting my lip, I sigh. "Yeah, I wasn't sure what it was at first, but I've figured it out. I guess with everything going on I haven't told you, but in my defense there are always more questions to ask, more things to find out. Every time something gets answered it brings another five questions, Elijah. At this rate, I'm going to be in a never-ending state of confusion and will have to always rely on someone else to keep me safe. I want to be able to keep myself safe." I complain. Draining the last of my coffee, I move back to the kitchen to pour myself another.

"You want?" I ask him, lifting my cup.

"Ugh no, I don't drink that crap." He leans down and pulls a bottle of water from the small fridge.

"Okay. Back to the original question. Who was he?"

Elijah takes a few gulps, wipes his mouth with the back of his hand and shakes his head. "Sorry, Em. You do need to know, but there are two things I want to do first." I cross my arms but say nothing. Elijah smiles then continues, "Training. First, you need to train. Secondly, to get to him, I need to give you a history lesson. Change of plans. Are you up for some home-schooling today?"

I feel a grin spread across my face. "That works for me," I reply.

Chrysalis

"Focus Em. Close your eyes and listen to my voice. Feel the power, the life-force. It flows through us. For me, it's like a zinging under my skin… Find your own feelings, then let them bleed into you and simmer on the surface of your body. When you feel it, take some deep breaths to make sure you're calm. You need to control it. It will be the same for every power you have. In time, as your abilities grow, you'll be able to choose the one you require on command." He stops talking and I keep my eyes closed, enjoying the silence.

I listen to my heart beating, it's a slow steady pace and the constant noise is like a buzzing, starting in my chest, but spreading slowly through my body. As the buzzing expands with every heartbeat it quietens, turning into a continual hum. All of a sudden it stops, and I feel a cool balm wash over me. Then—nothing.

"It's no use, Elijah, I can't do it." I sigh.

"Open your eyes, Emery," Elijah whispers.

I do as he says and am shocked that the once dark room we're training in, is now lit up like Christmas. A bright blue light bathes the entire room. As I look down, I notice it's coming from me. Pouring out of me.

"I'm the light," I whisper, gazing down at my body in absolute awe.

"You are," Elijah replies softly. "This is what you do. Every time you use a power it will feel like this. As you train more you'll be able to focus the light into one area, like just your palms, or eyes, or whatever body part you want it to come from. You will control it, guide it, and channel it. It's not yours to own, it's just *you,* an extension of you. If you always remember that, then it will get easier. The power you need will flow from an instant decision in your mind. For example, if I want to use *Revive,* I don't command it, my body just knows what it needs to do. This will help if you're in a fight at any point because your reactions will be automatic. However, what we did today you need to practice, at least once a day, preferably more. When you're better at controlling it, you won't need to train in a dark room, but this is a necessity right now. We don't want someone seeing your light."

I smile at him. "Okay, so how do I turn it off?"

"Well, here's the fun part. Say 'stop' out loud." He winks.

"Stop!" I command. Instantly all the light is lost, and the room is dark. I hear Elijah shuffle over to the wall and then the room glows from the lamp. "How does that even work?" I ask, throwing my hands out.

"Remember when I said our abilities are a part of us?" I nod and he continues, "Well, that's why. You won't have to say the word out loud in the future.

Chrysalis

Much like the way you use your powers, you just have to think what you need, and it will happen."

I bring my hands out in front of me and turn them over and over. "I can't believe I have powers... Wait. What powers *do* I have exactly?" I question, tilting my head toward Elijah.

"I don't know. I mean you have *Revive*, that's pretty obvious from the other night. Any other powers you get could come to you at any point. I think what I need to do is explain my powers to you. You should get some, if not all, of the same abilities as me. I need to explain some of Kade's too, seeing as you can use them. However, I don't know every gift he has. I'm not sure if he knows every gift he has," Elijah tells me scratching his head.

"Before all that, though, I need to go back to the beginning and explain the basics. Let's go sit in the living room area. I'm gonna use the bathroom. Will you grab me a bottle of water?" he asks walking away.

I make my way to the kitchen, collecting two waters and take them to the sofa. I wanted so badly to get away from here last night, as far away from Kade as I could. But his reaction to Elijah has me all twisted up inside. Now I know what we are, what we're meant to be. I'm not sure if I can be away from him myself.

Realistically, I need to talk to him, but he doesn't seem up for that. So, at the moment I'm stuck. I'll have to speak to Elijah, get his advice, or maybe Sicily or Tess if they're still talking to me. For now, though, I need to sit with my brother and listen to as much information as he is willing to impart.

"Thanks," Elijah says as he returns, taking the bottle from me and sucking down half of it while lowering himself into the seat opposite. "Now, Em. You know and I know, that you like to interrupt. It would be great, fantastic in fact, if you could keep your lips sewn together for just a little while," he tells me, placing his thumb and forefinger on the top and bottom of my lips and smooshing them together. He smiles before letting my lips go and continuing, "And let me get through the information as much as I can. When I've finished you can ask me anything. Do you think you'll be able to sit still and keep quiet?" He raises an eyebrow at me and smirks. I narrow my eyes back at him.

"Yes," I grind out, pushing my nose into the air. He pulls in his lips and I see his shoulders gently shaking. I feel the laughter he's trying to suppress, and it causes me to start giggling. When my laughter has died down I pretend to zip up my mouth, Elijah rolls his eyes at me.

"I promise," I tell him without opening my mouth, so it doesn't really sound like much more than a grunt.

"We basically have superpowers, over and above the normal human—"

Chrysalis

"Like *Superman*?" I interrupt. "Sorry," I quickly say, remembering my promise.

"No, to your question. *Superman* was an alien, Em. We're human." He pulls his hand down his face then continues, "Since humans have existed, so have we. Maybe we're over-evolved, or maybe something happened to our ancestors. I'm not sure. It's like when people talk about Jesus. Nobody alive today knows the truth, so everything comes from historical documentation. It's the same with us. We don't live forever. We're not immortal, but we do have a slower body clock. So we often live until we're around one hundred and twenty… well, if we aren't killed before. See, I'm not good at explaining this stuff." He shakes his head and closes his eyes.

I say nothing and wait for him to carry on.

"Okay, so years ago there were houses, we're the House of Laird. There was a structure to our society, which meant we had six head houses, and Laird house was the leader of the six. Everyone had a place in our society, and largely, it was peaceful. Our ancestors tended to live in their own communities, often away from regular humans for fear that one of the children would display something they couldn't explain. Country villages were always good, so that's where you would mostly find them. However, the dark and light communities were split and lived apart." I frown with confusion and he grins. "Dark and light represent good and bad. We're the light Emery, the good."

"Is it always the case?" I can't help but interrupt.

Elijah shrugs. "That's what we've been taught." I smile my thanks and he continues. "Back then a lot of people did join with their *other half.* The fear of vulnerability wasn't really a concern back then, it was just the natural way. If you loved this person, the other half of your soul, you knew there would never be another being that you could love more than the person you belonged to… so why not be together, as it was intended? A few years before I was born things started falling apart. Some houses turned dark, maybe they always had been." He ponders. "They started by striking out within their own families. Then, when one person beat the others back, they took over and used their new-found placement as ruler to try and battle other houses, ultimately wanting to take over that house, too. Obviously the more they ruled, the more power they had at their disposal, even though traditionally they couldn't rule a house unless they were a blood member. More houses fell. When there were only the six head families left, they thought it best to disband and separate members, to try and keep everyone alive. The intention was to bring this new monster down… but that never happened."

I can feel my heartbeat picking up speed as Elijah explains our story. I take a few deep breaths, and he notices, pausing the history lesson so I can gain control. Once I calm he carries on.

"Our mother, Zarina, was from Alposco House. She was paired with our father Edrin way before the family wars started. Her house, like Laird, was one of the major six. All six houses were similar to royal bloodlines. Those houses always made the decisions, decided our laws. And they had many followers, people who chose of their own free will, to believe in their values. They were respected, revered, and loved. I don't know anything about the other four houses." He says, rubbing the back of his neck. "The information is captured in documents that the dark have stolen from us over the years. I believe you and I are the only people from one of the major six houses within our circle." A small smile plays fondly on his lips for just a second "Laird was the Head House. The blue of our family, the blue light that shines from your power, it is the royal blue, the Laird blue…" Elijah pauses, and I watch his eyes move above my head. They become unfocused, staring into the distance.

"Our mother died not long after you were born. I don't know how. Our father disappeared after she went. Many think he committed suicide, unable to live without her." His eyes move back to mine and are now sharp. "The man you saw this morning, the same one who you spoke with on the phone, he is Zed. When you were attacked the other day while out with Sicily, can you remember the name of that man?" I shake my head no. Everything was so rushed, and then I was dragged back by Kade. "His name was Zeit. He's Zed's son and our cousin."

I gasp at his revelation.

"Zed is our uncle, our mother's brother, and he's from the House of Alposco. Emery, he wants us… we're the heirs to the Laird House. Stay away from that man. He will try and win you over. But if you refuse to bend to his will, make no mistakes, he *will* hurt you, maybe even kill you. Although that's a stretch, you'd be much more useful producing another heir." I feel my eyes widen, and he nods his head in agreement. "Yeah, scary, huh? Zed is a level eight like me. You need to learn your powers, and quick. It would also help if you learned Kade's. You may need every advantage in the months to come. Now, do you have questions?" he asks, and I watch his lips twitch.

"I have loads." I sigh. "I think I'm going to have to go over everything you've said and maybe ask you tomorrow. Like, why would I use Kade's powers? I mean, that would be an invasion of privacy, it would be a violation, seeing as he hasn't allowed me to use them, surely? I wouldn't feel right." I stop, wondering how Kade might feel if I was to use his powers.

"Anyway, at the moment, I'm still trying to decide whether being nearer or further away from Kade is best. Let's face it, he doesn't seem to like me. He can't leave that house. They're his friends not mine. I need to be the one to move away from him so he can have some peace." Elijah opens his mouth, but I hold my palm up to him.

"You've done enough talking for one day, and anyway, I'm going to bed," I say, getting up and walking away. As I do, the thought hits me… *I'm not alone…* it's something I forget easily, since in the past I'd never wanted to think about the fact that I'd had no one. I take the few steps back to Elijah, lean down and wrap my arms around him. "Thank you for sharing… my brother," I whisper, then walk back to my room.

Twenty minutes later I'm annoyed at having to get out of bed for a drink. When I get to the door I can hear Elijah talking. I pull the door ajar and listen, realizing my hearing must also be more enhanced than it was before.

"We're at the Vallarta. No, Zed called her today, he was down in the street. Okay, shit, don't growl at me. She's coming into her powers. I wasn't going to tell you, I mean if you can't be nice then why should you know anything? Yes, I know, but Katarina isn't always right. I'm telling you now because she thinks it would be better if she moves as far away from you as possible. Shit! Apparently, she doesn't think it's right that she takes on your powers without your agreement, something about violating you. She feels it's best to get as much distance from you as possible, give you peace or some crap. It's not my fault, this is entirely on you. Hello. Hello. Shit."

Then there's silence, and I'm just about to creep back into bed when I hear. "Hello, Tristan. Yeah, what happened? Smashed it? Another phone, damn. Okay, well, I'll check in tomorrow, but now he knows where she is. If he feels any fear, he'll be able to get to her a damn sight quicker. Okay, later."

I tiptoe back to the bed and throw myself under the covers. As I lay there struggling to find sleep, I'm not sure if my brother just did something wonderful, or broke the newly growing trust I'd found in him forever.

Chrysalis

CHAPTER 9

I can feel Elijah's surprise when he enters my room.

"Practicing already, Em? I'm impressed," he tells me, but I ignore him, keeping my eyes closed and concentrating on the power buzzing across my skin. I feel it cascade down my arm as I stretch. Opening my eyes, I shoot a white flash from my fingertips. The spark flows across the room, shattering a vase before it even touches it.

"Damn, Em." I look over to Elijah to see his eyes are fixed to the now vaporized vase.

"What?" I snap. The annoyance of what I overheard last night is still clinging to me.

His head spins toward me, and a frown crosses his brow. "Em, what's wrong? I can feel the conflict in you."

I stand up and pull the sneakers that I found in the duffle this morning onto my feet. "You know, I would probably understand more of what's going on if you explained, but you don't. And when I wanted to leave your house, *on my own*, you chose to come with me. I didn't ask you to come." I stand and grab my jacket.

"Em, what the hell are you talking about?" I can hear the confusion in his voice, and I can feel the uncertainty tinged with worry inside him.

"I left that house to get away from Kade. I need to sort out my own head, make my own decisions. You had no right to tell him where I was. Now I'm leaving. Alone this time."

"I don't think so, Em." Elijah steps in front of me, crossing his arms and working his jaw.

"You don't get this, Elijah. I'm leaving. You don't control me, or command me, and you can't bend me to your will." When he doesn't move, I sigh. "Listen, I'm pissed. What you did, telling Kade? You betrayed my trust. Now I just need some space. I know you want to protect me, but that doesn't mean you can leave me out of the decision-making process, especially when it's my life we're talking about. With that said, I *am* coming back. I want to have a family… I want to have you. It's all just a little bit too much, and I need a couple of hours to myself."

Elijah stares at me. His jaw still working, but it's tense. Then he pins me with his eyes. "I'm sorry, again, Emery," he tells me before leaning forward and pressing his thumb to my forehead. I expect to fall and for Elijah to catch me. I expect that I'll sleep, waking even more pissed. But I don't. Before I realize what's happening Elijah is falling. I catch him at the last moment, and surprise blasts through me when I can lift him—although it is a struggle—onto the sofa. I watch for a few minutes as his chest moves up and down, his breathing even and calm. Then I grab my bag and haul ass out of the hotel.

As I sit sipping my diet coke and watch people as they walk by, I second guess my decision to leave the hotel.

I'm not in danger since I'm in public, and it's a highly built-up area. Still, I feel guilty for leaving Elijah like that. But at the same time, I'm also aggravated that he thinks he can control my life. I know he's trying to keep me safe, but he can't do that forever. Withholding information isn't the way to help me, either. If he didn't hold back so much, then maybe my understanding would be greater.

I know that he's right, that he can't tell me everything in one go, but it took him so long to even start to explain.

On top of that, I'm now getting powers I can't grasp, having feelings I don't understand, and I'm trying to decide how best to navigate my life. Included in this mess is the decision whether to leave the other half of my soul behind, which, from what I understand, means I'll live some kind of half-life for the rest of my days.

I let out a heavy sigh, my chest sagging and decide it's time to leave. Leaning down to grab my bag, I jump slightly when I see Zeit has taken a seat in the chair opposite me.

"Emery..." he drawls the word out while leering at me.

"Zeit," I return, keeping my tone even.

"Ahh, you remember me then? Glad to see I made an impression on my cousin." He clicks his fingers in the air, and a waiter appears beside him.

"Yes, s-sir." The waiter stutters, even he can feel the darkness that rolls off my *cousin*. I watch as Zeit's silver eyes sparkle, amused with the fear he's summoned in the clueless waiter. Strangely, I don't feel scared. If anything I'm perturbed. I wanted to have a quiet afternoon and hash some things out in my own head. The last person I needed to see was him.

"Get me a latte. My cousin here will have a diet coke," he snaps.

"No, I won't. Thank you anyway," I say to the waiter who scurries away.

Zeit brings his hands to the table and arches his fingers together. "So how much has Elijah told you so far?"

"Enough," I reply, trying to think of a way I can get him away from the people around us.

Chrysalis

"Hmm… I don't think he has. Father told me you had no clue who he was. I think your big brother has been keeping you in the dark, Emery. You do realize the dark is the best place for you to be, right? You could come and join us, you know." The corner of his mouth curls up. "Unlikely," I answer, looking over his shoulder.

"Emery. You can sit there and pretend like you're not listening, but you should pay attention. I'm going to enlighten you… and that's not something I do very often."

I look back to him, torn between wanting to get away and anxious to find out what he wants to say.

"Better," he murmurs running his fingers jaggedly through his auburn hair. I can feel his simmering anger. "Elijah thinks he knows everything. He doesn't. He's the highest level in all the elder houses. That, however, does not make him invincible. There are factors that he hasn't considered. Has he told you about your parents?" His question catches me by surprise, and I find myself nodding. "Well, if that's true, then he's fed you a pack of lies. Although it's doubtful even *he* knows the truth."

"And that would be?" I question, almost kicking myself for asking him anything.

"Your mother, my aunt, was from Alposco House… my house." I nod at him but say nothing. "I don't think Elijah knows much about our history. All the details, the books, the documents, they are with us. We collected them as we collected the houses." He sneers as the waiter places his latte in front of him with shaking hands. "My house, it's dark. It always has been. We had a house in a light community, for those pathetic members who wanted to live in the light. *To be good*." He sneers. "The *real* members of Alposco have always stayed away from the light. The two sides should never have mixed." Zeit picks invisible lint off his arm and a curls his lip. "I wouldn't say we ever lived in peace, but we kept a distance and seldom crossed paths, choosing to run our houses in different ways. The two sides rarely saw things in the same way. You brought an end to that Emery… *you*," he emphasizes, pointing at me.

"I don't understand." My words are soft as my brain tries to make sense of his tale.

"Okay, so you know your mother was an Alposco." I nod. "She was dark, Emery. Dark and light don't combine. Ever." I feel my frown as confusion washes through me. "Oh for God's sake Emery, how stupid are you?" Zeit snaps. "Your father was light, and your mother was dark. Their union was the first time those sides mixed together to make an heir."

"But… but… Elijah?" I blurt, knowing he's older than me.

"Zarina, your mother… she wasn't *his* mother. He's light, you're dark. One day the dark will call to you, and unless you come to us you'll destroy

Chrysalis

everything you hold dear. Elijah, Kade... all of them." The smirk turns into a full-blown grin and for the first time I feel a frisson of fear zip through me. *He's obviously delighted to be enlightening me.*

"You're stronger than Elijah. You have dark and light power, it's only appearing late because the dark side develops slower. Kade will have to fight you one day, to save them, because he's the strongest of us all. Except... maybe you." He says tapping his finger against his lips and smirking. "You'll drain his power and kill him, too. One day you'll have to leave them or obliterate them all." His eyes sparkle. "It's amazing, you're like our own little bomb, waiting to detonate, and they're welcoming you into their fold with open arms. We just have to sit back and watch the fireworks. But make no mistake *Emery,* until that happens, as long as you choose their side, we will keep trying to kill them. To capture you or kill you if need be." He shrugs at the last comment as if it's no big deal, and he hasn't just threatened my life.

I make a move to leave, but I can feel myself pushed down into the chair. "Stop it," I whisper and watch as Zeit chuckles. It annoys me, and I can feel the zing of my power. Slowly, I pull myself up and from the pull of his *Earthing*. His eyes widen a fraction.

"You're already stronger than I thought. This will be interesting to watch." Suddenly, the smug look drops from his face.

"That's if you live long enough to see," Kade bites out from behind me, and I can feel his heat warming my back.

"Now, now, Kade, we're in company," Zeit says, gesturing around at the pedestrians.

Kade places his hands on my shoulders. "There will be a time, Zeit," he says, then runs his hand down my side. He slips his fingers through mine and pulls me away. I glance over my shoulder and catch Zeit's wink as I leave. The minute I turn back, I realize we're running. Kade looks back at me. His eyes scan my face, then he continues forward. I feel power coursing through me as my body keeps time with his. We slow, then come to a stop. Kade pulls me in front of him and he searches my whole body.

"I'm fine," I tell him, but he ignores my words until he's done his own assessment. "Kade…" I say softly and his eyes meet mine.

"I felt your fear," he growls, and I nod.

"Yes, but I knew he wasn't going to hurt me. My fear came from the things he told me."

"What? What did he say?" Kade asks, grabbing both my hands in his, and I wonder if he even realizes he's holding them.

"He said I'm dark."

Kade shakes his head. "Not possible."

I nod my own reply. "Yeah. Apparently, Elijah and I have different mothers, Elijah just doesn't realize that. The mother he thinks is his, is actually

Chrysalis

only mine. Zeit said that historically, light and dark families don't mix... like ever. And I'm the first mixed child to be born, which makes me super powerful and also capable of destroying everyone." I sigh and look around realizing we're now in a secluded area of a park.

Pulling my hands from Kade's, I sink down onto the grass as Kade paces back and forth. His muscles are all bunched and he scratches the scruff of his chin in thought, he obviously hasn't shaved for a couple of days. As I watch his movements I know that I could love this man so easily. I already feel it there, just waiting for me to accept it, so it can cover me. I can feel him, too. I know Elijah said that he can't read Kade, something about him being able to block it, but I do get glimpses sometimes, like now. It's strange, usually in those sparse moments that I can *feel* him, it's power, strength, and ferocity that I feel. Today it's fear. "Are you scared?" The words are out before I have a chance to stop them, and he halts looking down at me.

"Fuck, yeah." His answer is startling. "I don't know what exactly you are, except that you're my other half. We need to stay away from each other, but every time I try to keep away from you, it kills me. The first time I saw you, Emery... you were eleven, I was thirteen. I accompanied Elijah on one of his many visits to check on you. The second I saw you my whole world slotted into place. I knew who you were, instantly. For years I've hoped you weren't going to come into your power, that you'd never come into our world. You would remain safe, and I could watch you from a distance. My mistake was thinking *that* would ever be enough. I can't ever be with you. I can't allow myself to have a weakness, and Emery, you *would* be a weakness."

I feel my chest compress as pain crushes me inside. He kneels down next to me, lifting his hand up he cups my cheek and whispers, "Emery, no matter what, wherever you are, I promise I'll always keep you safe." I close my eyes and feel the pain inside me disappear… replaced by emptiness.

Chapter 10

"Emery." Elijah's tone is cold as I enter the hotel suite. He stares at me, his legs slightly apart and his arms across his chest. I can feel the tension in the room. It's everywhere and emanating solely from him.

"What?" I ask, slinging my bag onto the sofa.

"Don't *'what'* me like this is some game," he spits.

"You tried to put me to sleep. It's not my fault it backfired!" I shout as I catch Kade's questioning gaze skim over me.

"I shouldn't have needed to even try. You should trust me enough to know whatever I do is for your own good," he growls.

I shake my head, laughing hysterically, then throw it back for dramatic effect. When I snap it forward and cease laughing, Elijah's eyes momentarily widen. "I've known you for four days, Elijah. Four days!" I shout. "Don't tell me I should trust you, I don't even know you!" A flash of pain hits me in my stomach, and I know it's his pain from my words. "I'm trying here, trying to trust you, all of you. It's not easy, the stuff you've told me so far… the things I'm seeing. Hell, the things I'm *doing*... It's all unbelievable. I feel like at any moment I'm going to wake up from some crazy dream." A cold laugh slips from between my lips. "You want to know what the hardest part is? The feelings. I try to ignore them, but they're smothering me, they flow from all of you. Most people I guess I can't tap into yet, but you lot…" I gesture toward Elijah and Kade. "I can feel you. Maybe not all the time, but enough that it's driving me crazy. I needed a few hours away today. I was coming back. I knew I was safe—"

"Em—" Elijah tries to interrupt me, but I hold out my hand.

"No. I get that people are after me, but I intended to stay in public places. And since you said Kade could feel me when I was scared, and that he's the fastest one of us, I figured, unless he doesn't care if I die…" I move my eyes to meet Kade's and take note of the frown marring his face before looking back to Elijah, "…then I was safe."

Sighing, I sit down, all the annoyance and frustration drains out of me. "Look, I'm sorry, I didn't know when you tried to put me to sleep it would backfire, and yes I took advantage of that moment, but I needed space. I've been alone my whole life." I ignore the looks from both of them, close my eyes, and lay my head back on the sofa.

"You know she's your other half."

I can hear the voices, but my mind can't quite reach them.

"Yes. Of course. I knew the moment I laid eyes on her when I was a boy. That doesn't change anything."

"How can you say that? It changes everything."

"No. You know what happened with Kale and Tessa."

"Yes, I'm very aware, as are we all, but you can't believe that will happen to everyone. Emery is different."

"You're right. She is different."

"Then why, Kade?"

"Because if I let her in… she'll consume me."

I wake with a start and instantly notice the room is quiet and dark. Rubbing my eyes, I move to search for the light switch.

"Here, I got it." Kade's deep voice rumbles somewhere in the black of the room, making me jump. Then a dim light glows, outlining everything.

"You scared me," I whisper.

"I doubt much can scare you these days. Far as I can tell, you were a survivor long before we entered your life." His words floor me, but if Kade notices he doesn't show any reaction. He only raises what looks like a beer bottle to his lips and takes a swig.

"Was that supposed to be a dig at me? I know that I'm not what you want in your life right now, and I'm sorry, I didn't ask for any of this... not that it makes any difference." I mumble the last few words, realizing that no matter what's happened, there's no one to blame. And what's worse is that I could be creating more danger for Elijah and for Kade. The thought of Kade being hurt slams into my chest, and I finally understand the power he has over me. This other half business is starting to become annoying, especially when I have to be around him and my feelings grow daily. Soon it won't be him struggling, it *will* be me.

"You scared him," he offers, and I try to find his eyes.

It bothers me that I can't see his face.

Suddenly, with that thought, his eyes blaze into the gold color I saw that first night.

"What is that?" I ask, standing and moving over to him.

Chrysalis

"What?" he asks, frowning.

As I make it into his personal space my hand reaches up, almost of its own free will until I'm touching his face. "Your golden eyes," I whisper.

Kade grabs my hand tenderly but doesn't move it. "When I can't control my feelings, my eyes glow. It also happens when I'm fighting. Not scuffles with dicks like that guy at your school, but real fights, ones where I'm using my powers and my strength, or when someone I care about is in danger," he tells me without even blinking.

"So right now… you have feelings you can't control?" I ask softly.

The muscle in his cheek jumps. I bring my other hand up, laying it on his chest, much like I've seen the popular girls at my school do with the guys. I've never behaved in this way. I've never flirted, and I have no idea why I am now. It's like there's a puppet master pulling my strings. Kade is resting on a stool, so he isn't too much taller than me. Without thinking, I take a step forward and raise up onto my tiptoes, leaning into him until my lips are nearly touching his.

"What feelings do you have?" I whisper the question, willing him to kiss me.

Kade opens his mouth to speak, and I can feel his breath against my lips, hot and minty. "The way you feel right now… that's not you, it's all me." His words are like cold water running down my back. I take a step away, pulling myself from him and hiding my face behind my palms. His big hands gently pry my fingers away from my eyes. "It's okay. I can control myself… just." His eyes have morphed back to hazel and he shakes his head slowly, standing up and moving off his stool. "I have feelings for you, Emery. You're my other half, it's only natural. I've always had my powers, so I'm strong, but I'm also experienced, and I can control those feelings. I hide my emotions since I know others, like Elijah, can feel them if I don't. It appears, however, that I can't hide from you. I guess that's because of our connection. So, when we're around each other, you need to learn to control yourself."

"God! You make me sound like a silly schoolgirl who has a crush on you."

Kade chuckles. "I know how this feels, remember? I do understand. But I've learned to command my body. You have to learn to channel your powers. Elijah says you've been practicing." I nod, pleased that I'm doing at least one thing right. "It's not just *my* feelings projecting onto you anyway. You left here before, went off because you needed space. All that amounts to is not being able to control the emotions that filter into your body. You need to shut them off, so you're not swallowed up by everyone else's emotions. It will take time. I still struggle you know." He rubs the back of his neck.

"You feel?" I ask.

Chrysalis

"No, I mean not like you and Elijah. I can't feel people, I just feel you." He sits back on the stool.

"Just me." I contemplate his words. "But you have it under control?" He doesn't answer. "I have feelings for you," I tell him, and a blush creeps up my neck.

"Of course you do." His reply is clinical and a wave of unease washes over me.

Deciding to change the subject before we travel into unchartered waters I ask, "Where's Elijah?"

"He went back to the house. He wants you to go back there, and he needed to speak to the rest of them. I told him I'd stay with you until he's back."

"I just fell asleep, in the middle of our argument… he must hate me." I stand and walk to the balcony, worry climbing up my stomach.

"No, he's fine. Elijah is strong, and I've never known him to be scared of anything. Until you. He's so scared that something is going to happen to you, Emery. It's making him all kinds of crazy and overprotective. You've only known him for a few days, you were right when you said that earlier and you can't help the truth. But you need to understand that he's been watching you for a long time. Cut him some slack."

I lower my head feeling awful. "I need to tell him about our parents, about me. He needs to know I'm dangerous."

"You're not a danger to us," Kade declares.

I spin around. "I am! Don't try to downplay this. I may have known you all for only a few days, and I *know* I said some harsh things to Elijah earlier, but the truth is I *feel* for you, especially you two, and these aren't feelings that have been projected onto me, these are from me. They're mine to own." I declare, jerking my thumb into my chest. I move inside to sit back down on the sofa, pulling my knees up and wrapping my arms around them. I rest my chin on top and stare at Kade. His eyes search mine and I release a breath whispering, "I can't bear the idea that I might cause either of you pain."

Kade comes to sit next to me. "Listen, I know I've probably seemed cold over the last few days, but I had to make sure you knew where we stood. I will always care for you, but I'll never want to take it further. I just can't, Emery."

"I know that. You don't have to keep telling me," I say, feeling humiliated again.

"Hey, that doesn't mean we can't be friends. If boundaries have been firmly established, then we can both move forward. I'm not going to lie, it will be hard. But seeing as we can use each other's powers it might be good to work together, so you can learn mine."

"And you can learn mine," I chip in.

Kade grins. "Let's take one step at a time… *you* have to learn your powers first," he says, and I grin right back at him.

Chrysalis

"Why can I use your powers without your permission? At least I think I was using your powers..." I ask, realizing Elijah never answered that question for me.

"You're a Laird. The six head houses have some kind of ability passed through the ages. The head female, if she ever meets her other half, can use his powers at will without his permission. You're kind of like a princess."

"Princess..." I mumble.

"You like that huh? I'll make sure to remember that," Kade tells me still grinning.

"This is the most time you've ever spent near me," I say, tilting my head and taking him in.

His grin drops. "Yeah. You can be addictive. I need to get a handle on that," he mutters quietly.

"Why can the head female take the power without consent?" The question dissipates the sudden awkwardness that started to saturate the room.

"Legend says that as the female would carry on the line, they needed to be protected, and historically the head houses always had females who were the other halves to very strong men. We don't know if this was somehow created many centuries ago, or if it has something to do with magic, which I've never seen by the way, so have no idea if it actually exists." He sighs.

"We just don't know enough to have definite answers, but as the head female of the Laird House, you can take my powers at will. But I can't take yours, not unless you freely give them. The only problem with that is, unlike the rest, if you freely gave me your powers for as long as I use them, you would have nothing to protect you. The other couples find their powers slightly weakened, and unless they're stolen by a dark partner, they will never lose them completely. But with us… we're different. There is a lot about us that's different, Emery, that's why I think it would be good for us to spend some time together." He drops his head on the back of the sofa and stares at the ceiling. "Elijah hated school in every capacity, so he never really took too much notice when we were being taught about our history. I used to be like that. Then the day I realized you were my other half, everything changed." Kade's voice is gentle as he explains, and as he raises his head and gazes at me, I can see the same gentleness mirrored in his eyes. "I knew I would need to protect you in the future. I knew how special you were and that if you ever came into your powers, you could be hurt. From then on, I never missed a class. I learned everything I could and asked to take extra classes on our kind. Even so, because of the lack of historical documentation, our understanding only goes so far."

I sit stunned that he's told me so much. "I'd like to learn more. I'd like to spend time with you… as a friend," I tell him quietly.

Chrysalis

"Okay." He nods then glances at the door. "Elijah should be back soon, then I'll be going, but I *will* call tomorrow and we can start our arrangement."

He stands up and walks over to the kitchen area to grab another drink. I glance at the time and am stunned to see it's nearly three a.m.

Elijah must love his middle of the night jaunts!

"Kade, I'm going to bed, if that's okay?" I ask, and he raises his bottle and nods. I stop and turn back. "Oh, Kade… I meant to ask you… does anyone other than you, me, and Elijah know that we're each other's partners?"

A frown crosses his face. "Only Katarina."

I'm surprised at his answer. "Katarina?"

"Yeah, my sister."

Oh, joy.

Chapter 11

Staring at myself in the mirror, I take a long hard look. My blue eyes are bloodshot, and my bright blond hair looks like straw, poking out in different directions. "Em, come on, we need to practice," Elijah shouts through the door. I sigh, grab some tissues, and wipe my face. He's been on my case since I woke up this morning.

I apologized, he did too. We decided to drop the issue, and he asked me not to run away again. He said if I needed space he would give it to me, but until I was capable of looking after myself, he wanted to know I was safe. I agreed. After everything that's happened, and realizing how much Elijah has been there for me over the years—protecting me without me knowing—the least I can do is let him continue now that I do know about him. He just wants to be a brother, so I need to start acting like a sister.

Chrysalis

I walk out of the bathroom and find Elijah standing looking out over the city. "Elijah, are you okay?" I ask, coming to a stop. He looks like he's in his own world and fear whips and zings in my stomach when I realize he's not moving. I run over and knock him completely off his feet, forgetting the speed and strength I now possess. We both land on the floor. "Elijah!" I screech and turn to him. He shakes his head as the door to the hotel room swings open, and Kade stands there, snapping his head around, taking in the room.

"It's okay," Elijah rasps, and I get up pulling him to his feet. He looks toward Kade. "It was Zed. He trapped me for a moment, I wasn't on my guard and he managed to pull me in." Elijah turns back to me. "You broke it, Em."

"What exactly did I break?" I ask, taking a seat and watching Kade stalk fully into the room, shutting the door behind him and moving over to the window.

He's perfect. I jolt as the thought pops into my head and I hear Elijah chuckle.

"Elijah," I hiss and he smirks at me. I sneak a glance at Kade and see his eyebrows are pulled together. He catches my eyes, and I can *feel* the heat in them before he breaks the stare.

"It's a gift Zed has, that our mother had." I feel my stomach pitch and know that these feelings are all me. The guilt is festering, I haven't told Elijah about the conversation with Zeit yesterday, and I feel awful. "You okay?" Elijah asks softly.

"Yeah, I'm fine. You were saying…" I control my emotions, pulling my stomach in and mentally telling my brain to stop. I have no idea how this stuff works, I just know that the feeling in my stomach quells and breathing comes easier again.

Watching as Elijah shakes his head, obviously trying to work out what's going on, I know he felt me, for that one moment before I could muster up my control. Sighing, he continues to explain. "The gift is called *Entrance*. You used it on Tess the other day, remember?" I nod my head, remembering Tess was not happy and will probably still be annoyed when I face her again. "We don't always get all the gifts our parents had. I don't have that power, and I assume you don't either. I figured you'd pulled that from Kade, right?" He asks, and I shrug, still having no real idea of what I'm capable of.

"No," Kade says, and I can feel his warmth as he sits on the arm of the sofa behind my back. "I don't have that power," he continues, and Elijah looks from him to me.

"So you do have *Entrance*." He rubs his chin. "Usually, we'd get the same powers from our parents. Strange, although not entirely unheard of."

"Elijah, I have to tell you something." The words are out before I have a chance to really think, and Kade places his hand on my shoulder, squeezing it to

Chrysalis

give me comfort. "When I went out yesterday, Zeit came to see me." I feel Elijah tense. "It's okay, he didn't hurt me." Looking up at Kade, he meets my eyes and I see a swirl of emotion filter through them. Turning back to Elijah I continue, "He told me... please don't be cross." I swallow, not wanting to let the next words out.

"Emery, what is it?" he whispers.

"Zeit, he told me that my mother Zarina, she's not... I mean she wasn't... Elijah, she's not your mom." I drop my eyes and feel Elijah. He lets everything hang out in that moment.

It's a mixture of shock, denial, pain, sadness, and anger.

Disbelief.

Suddenly, I feel like my stomach is shrinking, and my lungs seize as I struggle to breathe.

"Elijah. Control yourself," Kade snaps from behind me, and instantly the pain stops.

"Sorry," Elijah says grabbing my hand and pulling it to him. "I'm just... I don't know what to say. Although what Zeit says can't be trusted, Em."

"He was telling the truth," I state. "My head says he wasn't lying. There's no explanation, it's just something that I know."

Elijah nods. "Yeah, being able to read feelings, it gives us a lot of extra abilities. I'm not sure that I've worked them all out myself yet. We know things we can't explain, like when people are being honest. But don't mistake that for something else, Emery. When we know, we just *know*. Don't let your brain get jumbled into thinking something is true or false when your gut doesn't feel one hundred percent certain. Never try and work out what something is when you feel conflicted because you'll probably get the wrong answer." I stare at him, confusion seems to be a constant lately.

Understanding my new life is going to take time. Elijah smiles. "Don't worry, Em, just trust your instincts. I think that your powers are stronger than you realize, and somehow, they're protecting you."

"What does *that* mean?" I quiz. If it's possible, I'm now even more confused.

"Emery..." Kade says my name low from behind and I turn to face him, causing his hand to drop from my shoulder. I feel cold all over at the loss and a burning sensation where his hand was. As always, his eyes capture mine, and I have to internally remind myself— while not thinking it aloud so Elijah doesn't hear—that he isn't mine. He doesn't want to be mine.

A frown crosses Kade's face, then it clears and he explains, "We've been trained from when we were young. Every gifted person we know has come into their powers earlier than you, so we can't be certain, but there are theories. We believe that to a certain degree, your powers take care of you. Like an automatic defense that naturally occurs even if we

Chrysalis

don't command it. Now as adults, because we've grown with our powers, we know how to use them. But because you're inexperienced, it's possible that your powers may work without your command, like a natural sixth sense that keeps you safe." He stops talking and I widen my eyes.

"Wow." I breathe out, amazed that my powers might be looking after me when I'm unable to. I stare at Kade and he stares right back, neither of us wanting to blink first. I love his eyes. I want to submerge myself into their depths.

Elijah breaks the moment. "Em, I hate to say it, but with Zed and Zeit continuing to find us, we could really do with being back at the house. I know you don't—"

I cut him off. "Elijah, it's fine. We can go back. I need to make some apologies anyway."

"Apologize to who?" Kade interrupts.

"Well I need to say sorry to Tess for using *Entrance* on her, and I need to apologize to Sicily for not telling her it was okay when we were caught by Zeit. She felt so bad about his attack, and I just walked away from her," I explain.

Kade's eyes narrow on me. "Tess will deal. We all know you're just learning, you can't be held responsible. Sicily was stupid. She knows it. You don't need to apologize to anyone."

"Kade, Sicily didn't mean any of it." Elijah injects his thoughts, but his feelings spasm in my stomach, and I realize he's torn. He wants to be angry at Sicily because he worries about my safety, but he cares about her too much.

"You love her," I whisper and watch as Elijah grinds his teeth.

"I hate that you know what I'm feeling," he states, cutting his eyes to me.

"Sorry," I mumble.

"No." He sighs. "It's not your fault, Em. It's just, I'm usually the one who feels others… I'm not used to someone seeing inside me. You knowing what's going on inside my head. It's unnerving."

Laughing, I cock my eyebrow. "You don't say." My sarcastic tone makes him smile, and he reaches over, catching me around the neck and scraping his knuckles back and forth over my scalp. "Ugh! Elijah!" I complain in mock annoyance.

He chuckles, releasing me. "Just doing my big brother duty."

Right then, something clicks inside me, it's like a blindfold has been lifted and I can see outside for the first time. I stare at Elijah as thoughts and feelings ripple throughout me.

He's my brother. He loves me. I finally have family.

Now, I'm realizing that this is something I have needed, something I've craved, and by opening up and dropping my guard, I can allow my heart—that's filled with love for my brother—to expand, showing

Chrysalis

him what he means to me. Reaching forward with my hand and placing my palm on his chest, I open my mouth. I stop as he smiles, wide and dazzling.

"I know," he whispers, and I feel the emotion gather in my throat. Wrapping his arms around me, I'm pulled forward as he holds me, protects me, loves me. Just like he has always done.

We sit there just clinging to each other for so long.

When we pull apart, I look behind me, but Kade's gone.

"We'll go home. To my home… it will feel like your home soon, I promise. If nothing else, Em… he'll be there."

I nod and smile, but I have to wonder whether I'm just setting myself up to be hurt over and over again by being so close to Kade and agreeing to be his friend. I know what tradition says I *should* feel for him. I know what my body automatically tells me whenever he's around. What I'm finding hard to get past is the feelings that are growing in my head and heart—the ones that have nothing to do with our natural connection.

Chapter 12

"I need a minute." As soon as the words are out, Elijah looks at me with worry. "It's okay, I'm not going to change my mind or run, I promise. I just… need a minute."

His shoulders drop, and he looks beyond me into the darkness frowning, but he nods. Then he turns and walks to the door. Stopping before he enters the house, with his back still facing me, he says, "Just, keep your senses open if you're staying out here, and don't be long, Em.

Please." Then he disappears inside.

Taking a few deep breaths, I keep my emotions on lockdown. I don't want anyone knowing what I'm feeling, at least not before I'm able to work it out myself.

I'm not sure how long I stand in the darkness, but when I hear the clicking of the door, signaling that someone is joining me, I realize it might be time to move inside.

"Emery, I'm sorry to interrupt your... contemplation. I just wanted to talk to you." The whispered words come from Sicily. I close my eyes. Hearing her pain is hard. I feel so much conflict inside of her, and I wonder if Elijah feels it too. The overwhelming emotions make my insides feel tight, and I take a couple more breaths before turning to face her.

"Sicily, hi," I reply, smiling. Immediately something lightens within her and she reflects my appearance with her own smile.

"I wanted to speak to you before you went inside. I needed to apologize... for before, with Zeit. I was stupid, and you could have been hurt because of it." Her stilted chatter is just one indication of how worried she is. Even if I didn't feel it inside me then I would still know how hard this is for her. It's very obvious that she's nervous and worrying that I blame her. Whether it's because she wants my friendship and likes me, or because she thinks she'll lose Elijah, I have yet to determine.

"Hey Sicily, it's okay. You weren't acting maliciously. It was just carelessness. I don't blame you, and you shouldn't feel bad. As far as I can tell, this world, the new one I'm still learning about... it's hard and confusing, complicated and scary. Worst of all is that to me, it seems no matter how long you've lived in it, there are still lots of unanswered questions." I sigh and turn back around, looking into the darkness. "There's a whole world of unknown."

"I just wanted you to know I was sorry. I want us to be friends."

"We are," I reply.

She says nothing else. Without looking at her, I know when she leaves because the emotions inside recede.

Letting my head drop backward, I look up at the dark sky and mutter to myself, "No stars tonight. Even in the heavens the outlook is bleak. How am I ever going to survive this?" I ask nobody and everybody all at once. Solid arms slide around me. The warmth engulfs me, and my muscles relax into him. I wonder what he really wants when he's telling me one thing but his body is telling me another.

"I told you. I'll keep you safe. As long as I'm breathing. That's my vow," Kade rumbles in my ear. "Come, let's get you inside, you're freezing."

As with everything Kade related, my body just follows him, blindly.

It's been nearly a week and all I've done is stay in this house and continue to train with Elijah - understanding how my new powers work takes up a ton of time - or go to school. The fact that Elijah has

Chrysalis

been taking me to school and picking me up every day has made the popular girls want to hang. They don't like that I'm not interested. I guess they thought I'd be clutching at any little crumb they sent my way. It shows that in all the years they've picked on me, not once have they paid any real attention to me. If they had, then they would have realized long ago that with or without Elijah and the others, I will never be their friend. I will never suck up to them. In fact, the further away from them I get, the happier I am. Now though, I don't need to worry. I'll never see them again. As from today, I'm officially home-schooled and will graduate by going back and sitting my exams. Although at eighteen, I can now make my own choice whether I do or not, but Elijah kept saying it was good to tie things off in the right way, so nobody got suspicious, and starting sniffing around as he put it.

Rubbing my hands together, I hop from one foot to the other trying to get warm. Giving up, I sit on the bench in the back garden. Kade hasn't spent any time with me since the night I came back here. After holding me and saying he'd always protect me, he dragged me inside, clasping my hand tight. When we got through the door Miles was standing there, arms crossed, his eyebrow arched. Kade dropped my hand like a hot potato, and since then it's like he's vanished.

I feel so lonely despite having people around me and

I wonder if it's just because of the distance between Kade and me. I've spent time with Sicily and have spoken to Tess, although I think she's wary of me, and I haven't found time to apologize to her yet. She's warming up… slowly. Tristan, I've come to realize, is your typical arrogant guy. He'd fit in well with the jocks at school. But to me, he shows a softer side. He rarely shows it in front of others, opting instead to make jokes or flirt. I think he flirts to upset Kade, who did drag Tristan off one night after some particularly explicit comments. Usually, though, Kade just growls or leaves when the comments start. Kade has also been hiding his emotions from me, it seems he's gotten better at it. I feel stupid because knowing what he was feeling was something that only I had, not even Elijah could get a read on Kade, so I felt special. Without it… I'm more disconnected from Kade than ever.

Katarina I haven't seen. After passing Miles that night, I went back to my room to get settled. Elijah has since told me that Katarina and Miles have gone somewhere for five days. They're due back tonight, and I have no idea where they've been.

"Hey, you okay?" Twisting my head and shoulders around, I find Tristan looking at me with concern. Everyone in the house knows I can feel them, just like Elijah can, and for the most part

Chrysalis

they're pretty good at keeping themselves hidden. It helps that I don't want to get a read on them. If I tried, I probably still could - that's what Elijah tells me anyway. But since I don't want to, my days are much more blissful. It's only Kade that I've actually tried reading, but when I do, I can feel his walls shoot up, and that's as much as he lets me feel.

"Yeah, I'm kind of bored actually." I grin, but it's fake, and he can see it.

"Did you go to school today?" he asks, and I nod.

"Why don't any of you go to school or college? I mean you're around my age, so you could still be studying."

"Well, my little Emmy…" He calls me the nickname he's blessed me with and comes to sit down. I've taken to sitting in the back garden specifically at night, so I can watch the stars. I find it calming, and it lets me have the space I need. "We all studied, but it was in the home-school sense. Kids with powers can't study with regular kids… you know… in case we fry them or something," he explains, and I giggle. "Well I didn't say it was pretty, Emmy, but there you have it. Plus, I'm so smart that they would have noticed I was different. You know… the whole 'mastermind kid' dynamic. I would have been on television and everything, zapping people left and right." He winks at me and I shake my head, grinning like a crazy person.

"You always manage to cheer me up, Tristan, even when I feel really down or vulnerable. It's like you have the power of feeling and can read me."

"Naa, I'm just super smart… didn't we just go over that, Emmy?" he asks, tapping my temple and smiling. I shiver and realize it's getting too cold to be out here, but as always, I'm reluctant to go inside. "Here, come closer," he says, pulling me into him and wrapping half his jacket around me until we're tucked up together on the bench. I lay my head on his shoulder.

"What's really bothering you, Emmy?" he asks quietly.

"I'm falling in love with him," I blurt, and my body goes solid.

"It's okay. I know." His reply startles me.

"You know? How?"

"Well, it's kind of obvious. The way you look at each other. Plus, for those of us who know Kade… he's never been like this with anyone. *Ever.* I can't explain what's different, except to say *he is different*, only with you. He's tender. Even with Katarina, who he loves dearly, he isn't tender. I can't see him changing so suddenly unless it meant something, and there's no way you don't feel the same. I just don't understand why he pulls away from you. I've seen it. He's so strange, it's like he's fighting an internal battle. I guess we'll just have to see what part wins," Tristan says, giving me a squeeze.

Chrysalis

"The only problem is he doesn't want to feel that way about me. It's only our natural connection that's making him feel like this. My feelings, though… they're more. I know it. I can't explain it, but I know it's real. If I spend much more time with him, Tristan, I won't be falling for him, I'll be *there*. Everything is so new, I'm still learning all this stuff." I sigh. "I'm scared and not of the people trying to kill me." Letting my words hang in the air, Tristan pulls me tighter and we both gaze at the stars, caught within our own minds.

"When you've both finished whatever the hell you're doing out here, Katarina and Miles have come back, so you're needed for de-brief. Don't want to stop this moment, though, so take your time." The growl of words are like knives stabbing into my body. For that single moment, Kade drops his walls, and the pain hits me everywhere. Then just like that, it's gone, and so is he. "He doesn't have good thoughts about us," I whisper to Tristan, who chuckles.

"Maybe he'll get his head out of his ass then. Come on, Emmy, let's get inside."

With quite a bit of reluctance, I follow him into the house, through to the kitchen and take a seat. Tristan moves to stand at my back, and I watch as people filter in. Kade must have been collecting everyone up when he came outside because he's the last person to come in, and he leans his long taut body against the kitchen counter opposite where I'm sitting. I look over, willing him to meet my eyes. But he doesn't. He looks everywhere but at me.

"So, Miles and I went to Ruston. We'd heard through the grapevine that the Alonso's were hiding there. Every place we hit up was a bust though. Iric and Isobel must have moved before we got there. We'll have to be quicker next time," Katarina states, looking at us all one by one.

"Erm, can I ask who these people are?" Although my voice is strong, I'm aware that they may ignore me. But I'm sick of not knowing things, so I've decided that I'm going to ask anyway. They brought me here, so they'll have to suck it up and answer my questions at some point, even if they're stupid questions.

Katarina's eyes cut to me. "Iric and Isobel are siblings. They're some of the oldest people we know that have powers. We need answers and they could help. But for years they've been hiding, one of their special powers is the gift of *Veil*. They make it as hard as possible to contact them. The last time we did was just under two years ago now," she explains, and although her tone is cold, I don't get the feeling that she hates me.

"Okay, and why are you looking for them now?" I throw out another question.

"Because of you!" Miles spits out. "We're out there risking our lives because of you. Kade won't

Chrysalis

come with us like he usually does, offering his protection. He chooses you over his own sister now!" Miles gets louder, and at his words my eyes cut across to Katarina. I watch her wincing. "You have been nothing but trouble since you came here, and I for one, wish that you'd stayed where you were. If it weren't for Elijah..." he stops, letting those words hang in the air.

"Don't speak another word. You've said enough," Elijah hisses, glaring at Miles.

"I'm sorry, Elijah," Miles replies casually, like he's anything but sorry for his words.

I look around the room and note that most of the people are looking at the floor or out the window. They obviously feel the same way as Miles, they just don't want to say it. Looking back to Kade, his eyes are now on the back of his sister's head. His brows are pulled in, making little lines appear across his forehead. I drop my head down, staring at my lap, and my shoulders sag.

"It's okay," I hear the whisper from Tristan, and he starts rubbing my shoulders, trying to ease the tension.

My head whips up when a loud smash echoes around the room, and I manage to catch Kade's back retreating out of the door. I see remnants of a glass laying shattered in the wash basin.

"You have to push him, Tristan. Really?" Katarina shouts, throwing her hands up and marching out after her brother. Miles filters out, then Tess gets up, glaring at Tristan and follows the others through the swing door.

"I want to go out," I say, looking at Elijah.

He raises his eyebrows at me. "Really?"

"Yeah, you said I needed to tell you when I wanted space. Now is that time. I want to go to a club or a bar or something and have a drink. Let my hair down."

He chuckles at me. "Okay, Em, we can go out to a club. You can dance, but no drinking. You're not twenty-one yet."

"Whatever." I shrug.

Twenty minutes later, Elijah, Sicily, Tristan, and I arrive at Quarz, a place I've heard about but have never been to. The queue outside is huge and snakes around the building.

"Ahh, this is going to take ages!" Sicily moans.

"Not if Emmy *Entrances* the bouncer." Tristan winks, and I'm starting to see that nothing remains a secret with this bunch of people.

"I have no idea how to do it… I think it was a fluke before, I mean I didn't purposely *Entrance* Tess." I quickly explain with a bite to my tone. The sudden realization that Tess is Tristan's twin dawns on me.

Tristan chuckles. "I know, babe. Don't worry. Just walk up to him and stare into his eyes, then will him to let us in. I promise your powers will do the rest."

Chrysalis

Nodding, I make my way to the bouncer. He looks neither impressed nor surprised. No doubt he has hundreds of girls trying to get into the club every night. I stop in front of him and wait until he looks at me. Craning his neck downward, I catch his eyes. Before he even gets a word out I can feel the sizzling of my power firing up.

"My friends and I want in," I whisper.

He nods, opening the rope and ushering us through. People complain behind us, but we ignore them. When I get inside I feel energized.

"Wow that was incredible!" My excitement is evident for them all to see, and they catch each other's eyes, smiling.

"I need a drink," Tristan states immediately.

"I want to dance," Sicily says next.

"Oh… me too. Come on let's go." I turn, but before we go anywhere, Elijah grabs me, spinning me back to him.

"Tristan and I will be over there," he says, turning to point to a section of the bar. "You two just stay here." He spins back around and gestures to a small dance floor space from which he he'll be able to see us. I nod even though I'd rather go up to the top floor and dance. I'm just happy to be here, feeling free, and now that I'm able to shut out people's emotions easily, I feel like any other nearly nineteen-year-old.

Sicily slots her fingers through mine and we rush onto the dance floor.

Glancing over to the bar, I can see Elijah and Tristan. My eyes wander back to them every few minutes. We've been dancing for ages. The sweat across my brow and dotted down my spine reinforces it, even if I have no idea what the time is or how long we've actually been here.

"I'm gonna go grab a drink, you want to come? Or do you want me to grab you some water?" Sicily pants.

"Grab me a water, please." She nods and turns toward the guys. It feels like mere seconds later when someone pulls me back into them.

"What the hell?" I complain, assuming it's a guy wanting to dance.

"Be quiet and listen to me. I'm Iric. I have no idea if you've heard of me yet, but I need to speak with you. *Now*. Before Kade turns up. He'll be here any second, he can feel your fear. You're a danger to them all. If you don't want to hurt them, come with me."

I look across at the bar and notice Elijah is talking to Sicily while Tristan orders another beer. With no time to spare I make a decision based on my gut and slink back into the shadows, allowing him to take me.

"We must hurry!" a lady says, appearing behind him. "Kade is near." With that, I hear a snap and pop and then I see Kade across the room. Suddenly, all I can see is white light everywhere, but it's just for a millisecond before the regular light is restored, and

Chrysalis

I'm standing with Iric - and who I assume is Isobel - in a living room.

"What the hell?" I manage to choke out before everything goes black.

Chapter 13

My head hurts.

"She's coming around."

Ugh. That man's voice is hurting my head.

"That's quick. I've never known anyone to wake this soon."

The woman's isn't much better.

"Yes. It's certainly concerning. Be prepared, she may already be stronger than we can comprehend. If she's aligned with her mother's family, all may already be lost. Stay vigilant, Isobel."

Shoot, I'm with Iric and Isobel. I'd better stop thinking, they might be able to hear my thoughts too.

"We can, but it's okay. There's only certain words we can pick out," Isobel tells me.

Groaning, I open my eyes and take note of the room.

It's dark red almost everywhere. Both Iric and Isobel blend into the space behind them, only

Chrysalis

distinguishable by the slight color variations in their clothing.

"You told me I was a danger. How?" I ask immediately. My question is direct as I stare at Iric. My voice doesn't waiver. I've had enough of this situation, I want answers and I'm not willing to wait any longer.

Iric raises his eyebrow at Isobel, then looks back at me.

"You see us?" Isobel asks, and it throws me slightly.

Confused at her question and still reeling from everything, I stand. When I move, they both step back.

"Of course I see you, I'm not blind. Now why did you just step back? You two brought *me* here."

They glance at each other, then Isobel speaks. "Child, you should sit down." She pulls a chair out from under a mahogany table.

As I sit she mimics me, seating herself opposite.

"Child?" I question, tilting my head.

"You're nearly nineteen now, yes?" I nod. "Iric and I are a year apart. We remember the birth of your father, my dear. We're in our seventies now."

I feel my eyes widen but can't do anything to stop it. I'm shocked at the revelation, they look no older than late forties at most. Both have copper colored hair and dark brown eyes and wear matching frowns as they try to blend in unseen.

"In your seventies?" I sit stunned, my mouth agape.

"It seems she needs more information than we have time for, Iric. Maybe this was a fruitless task," Isobel says, looking across the room to where Iric stands.

"No. She has already proven that she's strong. We need her to know. The rest will be up to her."

"Know what?" I snap and feel flickers of power in my palms. Looking down, I'm startled to see that the ends of my fingers have a white glow.

"You don't understand quite how powerful you already are. How much more powerful you'll become. You may get sucked into the power once you grasp it fully, and then, my dear, you may turn dark. This would be unfortunate. Iric and I have the *Foresight*, we can see things in the future—"

"Some things," Iric cuts her off.

Isobel glances over to him. "Yes, quite… Some things. What we see isn't the future confirmed, more like a possible future. Most of our kind gain the *Foresight* ability with age. We did when we were in our fifties. Unfortunately, that was the same time as the Houses started crumbling and the dark became too powerful. We knew our gifts would be sought after. We've been in hiding ever since. Your coming was foretold, my dear, many moons ago. You have both dark and light. It is new, unknown, and many are fearful. We have known about you since your

Chrysalis

birth, and as such, have taken a greater interest after your parents were lost and you and Elijah were split. Occasionally, we've watched you. It seemed as though you were never going to come into your powers, and this made sense, as not one of us had experienced a child of both dark and light before. It was concluded, therefore, that because of the two sides mixing, you may not ever have powers. We thought that maybe it was a natural occurrence to stop the dark from growing a formidable army." Sighing, she searches my eyes. "You don't seem worried my dear."

"Nothing surprises me anymore. If what you say is true, if I'm so powerful because of being both dark and light, then why haven't people on either side tried to create a child like me before?"

They both stare silently before Iric moves forward, settling himself next to me. "You are the only one as far as we know. There have been stories told for centuries, of one like you who came before, one who almost destroyed both sides. These stories kept our sides apart. I think even the dark was fearful of creating a being with such scope to control all things."

Everyone is completely silent for a moment as we all sit in our own heads.

"So essentially, you're trying to tell me that I'm like a bomb waiting to explode, and I'll take everything and everyone with me when I do?"

Page | 135

Iric places his warm fingers over my upper arm, and it reminds me that I was brought here from a club, that I still have a dress on… that I'm still trying to be a normal girl, when the reality is I'm anything but normal.

"My dear, there's much we don't know. Isobel and I are the oldest that we're aware of who live in the light. There may be elders on the other side, this we cannot know. A lot of our documentation and books were taken or destroyed by Alposco House. They have become what everyone always feared. Unbeatable. We have lived in the shadows for eighteen years now, and we're tired."

"Listen," I say, pulling away from his grasp, which is beginning to feel like something more than just a gentle gesture to make me feel better. "What is it you pulled me here for? Tell me. Be specific. I need to get back to my brother and friends, they'll be worried."

Glancing once again at each other, Iric nods and speaks. "From what we have seen, along with what we already understand from the books we've read and the tales we grew up listening to, you *will* be very powerful. Your gifts are unknown, as you must be aware of by now. Each of us has a unique set of gifts. Nobody can predict what powers they will possess. What we do know is that you *will* have many of them. What you do with your powers will be your choice. The concern is that you may turn to your mother's

Chrysalis

house. You may join them and then… honestly…" Iric pauses and closes his eyes, screwing them tight, before opening them. I see something almost ghost-like swimming in their depths, "…if you join them, Emery, all hope will be lost. With you and Kade, the light, the good, against them… we stand a chance. Without you… there will only be dark, and it will be that way until time is forever extinguished. Dark bleeds into the rest of the world, it seeps into normal human life, in a way that's hard to clean up. Kade is the only person who's stronger than you. That's the way it is, that's why he's your Pith."

"My Pith?"

"Yes, your Pith… your core… your essence. Names like *other halves* have more recently been used, but the ancient name for your other half is your Pith. God! You're completely clueless to this world." Iric stops talking and instead glares at Isobel before having some kind of internal freakout. "She's going to get everyone killed. She has no basic understanding of anything. How can we help her?" I can't help but inwardly agree with his statements.

"Shh Iric, calm yourself. She's still learning, but that does not mean dark will win. Only Emery can decide her fate." She turns to me. "Listen, child, for I now need to be quick. Kade will find us soon. He can pick you up anywhere, even when you're cloaked. It's lucky that you haven't shared your powers with him yet, for he would have been here within minutes of us arriving. We brought you here to explain that people will tell you things about yourself, but what you need to remember is that nobody alive today knows what the past brought. We only have the knowledge of books. The future is not set in stone, it's ours to determine. Yes, you have both dark and light within you, but from the tales we've been told, the ones we mentioned before. The person like you who came before, he was deliberately created to be dark, to destroy. You must understand, wherever your mother came from, she was not meant for the dark."

I feel a tug in my chest at her words. Since Zeit revealed the truth about my mom, I have felt a heavy weight on me. Like maybe I was somehow damaged or stained by being the child of a dark mother.

"Zarina was always meant for the light, my dear. She and your father came together after the passing of his first wife Jemima, who died when she was giving birth to Elijah. It can be a struggle for us. If there are no doctors nearby with powers, we don't always make it. Going to a normal hospital isn't an option. It's not about showing our gifts, it's because when we're in pain, or if someone tries to treat us, our powers can go into a sort of self-defense mode, and then we run the risk of killing people. Many of us don't bear children. Each of the big houses always had a doctor on call, so it wasn't as dangerous. For Edrin, when he lost Jemima, he was very sad. But

Chrysalis

although many were shocked, he knew, as did your mother, the moment they set eyes upon each other, that they were Piths. You were born of love, Emery. You weren't made to serve a purpose. *You can choose.* You have the blood of both a good father...*and* a good mother. The worry is that when people are very powerful it can taint their minds, they can fall prey to the dark. And with you already having some dark blood in your veins, we worry that you may become something that you don't really want to be. Then, by taking Kade's powers too, you'll be unstoppable. On the other hand, it is a hardship for Kade no doubt, because if you start turning to their side, he's the only one who'll be able to stop you. And that will forever damage him in a way that will not be repairable if he has to kill you... his Pith."

My heart picks up speed, and I take a few seconds to just breathe and calm myself.

"Why were you surprised I could see you?" I ask, trying not to focus on the last statement, the one that makes me feel like my insides are being ripped in two.

"You're very sharp. Not much will pass you by if you don't want it to," Iric tells me with a smirk. "You weren't supposed to see us. We're gifted with *Veil*. It is as described, the ability to veil, or cloak ourselves. You shouldn't be able to feel us, either."

At his words, I concentrate on trying to feel them and get a sense of apprehension, but not much else. I shrug, and Isobel smiles.

"You could feel something?" she asks.

"Only some apprehension."

"Hmm…" Iric mumbles, raising his eyebrow to Isobel. "Soon she'll be able to see through cloaks, anyone who's a *Veil* will not be hidden from her," he says with concern in his tone.

And I know right then, as all the feelings come rushing into my body—that even though these people initially brought me here as a warning—they're also frightened of what I may become. They feel they have to do something to stop me in case I destroy everything.

"You brought me here under the guise of helping me, but you're not going to let me go are you?" I shriek, stepping back from them.

"You're going to get too powerful, you will hurt and kill people and ultimately destroy the world as we know it," Iric snaps, and I can feel the power crackling under my skin as his eyes widen.

"You aren't even giving me a chance?"

"Please Iric, let her be. She deserves a chance to grow into all she can be… for good, for light," Isobel pleads, but Iric shakes his head, stepping toward me.

"I'm sorry it has to be this way, Emery, but I cannot take any chances. Our world is on the edge

Chrysalis

right now. It's so fragile, and any slip toward the wrong side could change... *everything*."

As he reaches out, I instinctively raise my hand, but the crackle fizzing across my palm dies suddenly, and I have nothing—no power, no speed, no strength, nothing.

"I have the *Equalize* gift. It's the ability to neutralize powers that pose a threat to me, Emery. Only two males living at any one time get this power, and I am one. He pushes me back, and I fall to my butt.

"Iric, stop this!" shouts Isobel.

He immediately throws his other arm out, pointing at her and zaps her with a white light that has a red tinge.

"You will not stop me! I have had enough of being in the shadows. I want to stop hiding. If this world gets any darker, that will *never* happen. You would have never agreed had you known my plan was to eliminate her before she was unstoppable, and I needed your power of
Motion so we could teleport her here."

"But Iric, it goes against everything we believe in," Isobel gasps from her place on the floor.

"There's nothing I believe in now. I haven't since they took Sandrine from me." He flips his hand the other way, still aimed at Isobel, and zaps her with the light again. She then flails for a second before becoming still. If I could still use my powers, I'd be able to feel if she was still breathing.

Turning to me he grins coldly. "Now it's your turn." I close my eyes and try to keep my breathing calm.

Not able to feel anything, I'm surprised when a warmth flows through my chest, a soft heat that can only mean one thing.

He's here.

My eyes struggle to take in the sight before me without my powers, because everything is happening so quickly. But then, with a rush, I realize that Iric has been captured by Kade. His gold light is twisting in the air, making a whirlpool, and all my power rushes back into me now that Iric doesn't have me in his hold. Kade's eyes glow gold, and I'm momentarily mesmerized, wondering how he can still use his power on Iric. Watching him, I miss his shouts.

"Emery!" he bellows, and I snap from my trance. "Leave. *Now.* Take Isobel with you. Go out through that door and follow the corridor. When you get to the window… jump. Don't look down. Then call to Elijah, he *will* come."

I sit there just staring, once again feeling my heart pick up speed as my chest pulses with feelings for this man.

"Emery… please go," he implores. I can hear and feel his panic building up, he's worried about me,

Chrysalis

and it snaps me into action. Grabbing Isobel while Iric shouts garbled, muffled words that I can't make out, I run at speed out of the door, down the corridor, and I only stop upon reaching the window. Looking out, my stomach drops at the sight. I've never been good with heights and this looks like at least a sixty-foot drop. Isobel moves and murmurs on my shoulder and that thankfully pulls my thoughts into a good place, now I know she's still alive.

Kade will only ever protect me.

Remembering that, I yank the window open, close my eyes, and take a leap. Instantly, I land and spin around to see the window right behind me. It was an illusion. The window was actually on the ground floor. Dropping Isobel at my feet, my stomach pulls me toward Kade. I know he's fighting, but I can't feel much, which is a good thing… I think. Shouting for Elijah, it takes no more than ten seconds for him to appear.

"Emery. Thank God." He sags forward, and his fear infuses into me, showing just how worried he truly was.

"Let's get you both away from here."

"But Kade," I say, looking back through the window.

"He'll be fine," Elijah says, frowning.

"No. Take her, I'm waiting for him." I insist.

Don't try and stop me. I mean it. I purposely push the thought to him.

He needs to know that I'm deadly serious. Elijah grinds his teeth but nods, grabbing Isobel. He then turns, and with a gust of wind, he's gone.

I pace back and forth not knowing whether to go back in or not. A minute passes and I've had enough. I hoist myself into the window and with one leg on either side, I see Kade appear in the hallway. "What the hell are you doing?" he snaps.

"Don't you snap at me! I was worried," I shout. "How come he couldn't neutralize your powers?" I question. He only shakes his head and frowns.

His frown drops and he chuckles. "You were worried about me?"

His turnaround surprises me, and I open and close my mouth, not knowing what else to say. He walks up to me, then stops. He looks down but says nothing.

"What?" I ask.

"Well, could you maybe move out of the window so I can get out?" He grins.

"Oh. Yeah, okay," I mumble, climbing back out the window. I walk off, and within seconds Kade is next to me. I feel his warmth deep in my stomach and it causes butterflies.

"I was worried about you, too," he says seriously.

"I'm sorry. I went with them out of choice. I trusted my gut, thought they were good. I'm seeing my gut can't be trusted."

Chrysalis

"That's not true. Iric and Isobel *are* good. Iric lost his other half—"

"Pith," I correct him.

"What?"

"They told me the correct term for your *other half* is 'Pith.' It means your core or essence," I explain.

"That makes sense," he mumbles. "Either way, Iric lost her. Sandrine. She was killed only six months ago.

He's suffering, I have no doubt that when his head clears he'll feel awful."

"*What?*" I shriek, causing Kade to stop and pull me to face him.

"What's wrong, Emery?" His eyebrows cave inward, as concern washes over his face and swirls in my stomach.

"He wanted to end me, and you're saying he'll feel better when his head clears?"

Kade scowls and works his jaw. "He was never going to end you. If I'd had to, I would have killed him first. But I know him, he's a good man. When people lose their other... Piths... it can make them crazy, and some do join the darkness, unable to see clearly anymore. It's why a lot of us choose not to be with our Piths," he tells me. Then he stares at his feet and wraps his hands around the back of his neck. I feel his pain coursing through me.

Either he isn't masking it anymore, or I'm getting stronger because I feel everything, all his hurt, all his anguish. It's all wrapped up in me.

"I-I... " My babbling stops as I collect my thoughts. "I'm hurting you by being here. You can't help your feelings. Maybe it's worse... me being near you?" His head snaps up to me, but I place my palm up, asking him non-verbally to wait until I've finished. "I feel it, remember? I hate that I'm doing it to you. Your pain is my pain, you know? Because you're my Pith," I say smiling, trying to break the ice.

"If you feel the pain, do you also feel how much I care, Emery?" he grits out, and it's confusing because he looks angry, but I can feel his heartbeat picking up as he steps to me. "No," I answer.

"You block it out. That's why you only feel the pain," he says pushing his hand into my hair at the back of my head.

Whatever he thinks and whatever he says, I know his feelings for me are all a fabrication of an ancient tradition or spell... or maybe it's a curse. Either way, they aren't genuine.

"You feel the way you do because you've been built to or cursed to... or something. Don't you see, Kade? Whatever it is, I know one thing... it's not real."

He steps back and lets his hand drop. "You just don't get it, do you?"

Chrysalis

I shake my head, my own confusion filling my chest now.

"I first saw you when I was thirteen. I've had nearly eight years to shut myself off from you, from the feelings we're *supposed* to feel. I could have moved away, I could have turned away from you, I still could. When we meet our Piths, we don't love them because we're *told* to, or because our body *makes* us. Yes, we have a natural reaction to them. They are after all, our perfect fit. But if we couldn't live without them, then nobody would ever choose not to be with them, and I can tell you, Emery, there are more people these days who decide *not* to travel that road. It's because it makes us vulnerable. The truth is, we *can* live without the other person. We can. I can. *You* can. But, the more time I've spent with you after all these years of just watching has made me realize that I don't *want* to be away from you. I've been trying to push you away from the beginning." He sighs and starts walking. I quickly catch up to him, but he remains silent, leading us to a bench and sitting down. I sit too, then turn slightly to face him.

"There are reasons I tried to push you away. It's every reason I've ever said, but it's also more. I'm the strongest, I fight a lot." He grabs my chin and pulls my eyes to him. "A lot, Emery."

Nodding, I feel the weight of his words.

"This whole time I've been thinking about what I would feel like if I lost you, but it's just as likely you'd lose me. I'm always on the front line when it's needed, I could easily be killed. I don't want you suffering that pain." He drops his hand and closes his eyes, and I wrap my fingers around his hand, making him open them back up.

I stare into his eyes, the deep hazel pools are filled with emotion. I decide then that it's time to open up.

"What I feel, what's growing every day inside me… it's real. Completely real. I've been trying to deny it, knowing you don't want me." Saying it out loud makes me catch my breath. This has been one of the hardest things I've had to deal with since learning about this new world.

He surprises me by interrupting. "Emery, this is me being totally honest. I can't stop it anymore. It's bigger than me, than us. It's not an ancient prophecy telling me I should feel like this, it's simply my heart screaming that you're the one for me. I'm in love with you, Emery, and there's no alternative. I'm not fighting it, not anymore. I'm taking you, and I'm keeping you forever."

I jolt, standing up suddenly. His words have shocked me. Kade stands too. Prowling forward, he clutches my upper arms and pushes me backward until I'm against a tree.

"Thought about this so much more than is healthy," he says, slipping his hand around my neck

Chrysalis

before leaning in and kissing my mouth softly. The kiss builds like a slow burn until I thread my fingers into his hair, and then it turns frenzied. My whole body is warm and soft, and it feels like bubbles are rushing through me as I enjoy my first real kiss. I notice with every second, every breath, every moan, that I can feel both of our emotions, entwined, mixed, fused with each other. Love being the strongest feeling of all.

Pulling away from me, Kade smiles and I try to bring my senses back into focus. "You feel it too, don't you?" he asks, and I just nod, knowing exactly what he means.

"There's a lot of crap swirling around us. But you have to know, Emery, it's you and me against the world. I have to know you're right here with me," he states.

"Kade... I-I..." I look across the field we're in, back to the house where Iric was and notice the flash of light. In a split second, I see Kade's eyes widen, and he spreads himself wide to cover me. Then instantly, I'm immobilized. I try to scream but my voice is tied tight. Moving my eyes slightly, until they fall upon Kade, I see that he's on the floor, unmoving. He took the whole hit, straight to his back.

I look back up into the face of a man I've never seen before. Cold, dark, heartless eyes stare at me, and a feeling of death washes over my body.

"Block her vision and hearing. She's *Earthed*, she isn't strong enough to pull free yet, and Kade's not a concern. Collect them both. We leave now." There's a click, followed by a loud clash, and suddenly everything is dark and silent.

I'm in my head, somewhere I've been so many times before, but never like this, never forced. Now it's scary and empty, and yet all I can think about is how I didn't get the chance to tell Kade that I'm in love with him, too. That I *am* his to keep. *Forever*.

Chrysalis

CHAPTER 14

Motherfu—

Kade?... Wait... what?

Emery. The word is a whisper from him, but none of the words coming from either of us are spoken.

Kade, am I hearing your voice? Is this a dream?

My body throbs. I've been in my own head and I'm not sure for how long, but it's been killing me. Finally, I know he's okay, unless it's not real.

It's me. I'm able to reach you with my mind.

What? How?

There isn't time to explain right now. Just answer me one question.

Okay.

Do you trust me?

Yes. My response is instant because everything in me knows instinctively that I trust him one hundred percent.

Maria Macdonald

Good. I want you to feel inside of yourself. Feel deep down. Search for your power, it's there. What they've done to you has placed your body into a kind of sleep-like state. You need to look past the darkness inside your mind. The black that you can see right now is only a cover. Locate the light that's hidden, and imagine it getting bigger.

I search inside myself and feel like if anyone knew what I was doing, what I was searching for, they would undoubtedly question my sanity.

It's not working. I whine.

Emery, concentrate. You can hear me... can you feel me?

I imagine Kade in my mind. Extremely tall, with a beautiful body, one I've felt up close but never seen. I imagine his dark, almost black hair and his deep hazel eyes. Then I see his eyes in their golden state. Suddenly, I can feel emotion beyond my own, fear, worry, anxiousness, but it's his and it's all for me, for my safety. Anger bubbles on top of it, so much anger that he's ready to kill someone. Again, it's all because they have me. He doesn't want them to hurt me. His fear pulses again, but there's more. There's an overwhelming river of love, flowing from him.

It's all for me. I stupidly think out loud.

What?

Nothing. I can feel you. You're scared, angry, and worried about me.

Chrysalis

Yes. I am. Now, take those feelings in again. Concentrate on them. Let the light come out.

Wanting to sigh at his bossiness, but instead doing as he says, I feel him. Allowing his emotions to penetrate starts a whirlwind inside of me. Then I focus on his golden eyes. They get bigger—no, *closer*, much closer to my face, and they're burning with love. It makes my heart skip, then skip again. I hear his words from when we were at the tree, him admitting how he feels. As my emotions grow with his, my heart skips more beats. Then my mind moves to Kade being shot with power in the back—*skip skip*—him protecting me—*skip skip*—his body motionless on the floor—*skip skip skip*—not being able to tell him I love him too. My heart stops as a wall of darkness shatters, and light emerges through. I can't breathe. Spasms start in my chest and I feel like I'm falling. Noises filter into my consciousness.

"Look! She's slipping out of it."

"This can't be possible!" "Re-*earth* her! *Now!*"

"I can't, she's too strong."

"Re-*earth* her!" The words are bellowed as my heart stops skipping. It stops pulsing, the beats cease altogether, and I feel like I'm about to die.

Emery, listen to my voice, let me guide you.

Hearing Kade, I try to pull myself back, but there's something tugging me, something stronger, making my body shut down.

Maria Macdonald

Emery, it's you and me, don't give up now. Fight, baby, come back to me. I was scared of destroying you. Prove to me that you're stronger than anyone knows. Take me, I'm yours.

Screaming silently, I force the darkness out from the inside and draw up the light. My eyes spring open, and I only have a second to take in the three men in front of me before they push different colored flashes of power out of their hands. Their fear fills the room, draining it of oxygen. I look down at myself and see that I'm lit up. Blue and white light covers every inch of my body, and I'm hovering in the air like an electrified angel. When the bolts hit me, they're immediately absorbed by the light, and that's when they run. I raise my hand, and a blue flash blazes from my palm, splits into three, and hits all the men at the same time. They shatter into pieces like glass, then they disappear. My power stops. The light extinguishes and I gently lower until my feet hit the ground. I'm shaking hard from the exertion and fear.

"Kade…" I whisper but get no response.

Closing my eyes, I try again. *Kade.* I think his name aloud repeatedly, still there's no answer.

I start walking, trying to find my way out of wherever I am. The room I'm in is practically empty, except the bed I was laying on, a table, three chairs, and a couple of doors. Trying handle one, I turn my nose up as the smell of a bathroom shared by three

Chrysalis

men hits me square in the face. I move to door two, turn the handle, and peek outside tentatively.

Kade. I think again while walking along the dark corridor.

There are no windows, and if I were to place a wager,

I would say I'm underground. Passing a door, I jump in fright as I see a woman. Freaking for a second, I raise my hands, and blue flickers appear. It's then I notice the woman has done the same. Moving my left hand gently, my mind catches up with my eyes, and I see that it's a mirror. I can almost hear my blood pumping in my ears as I move toward myself.

Cupping my chin, I'm confused. It's not me, I look different. I've got auburn hair, not my normal bright blond. My face is similar but not entirely the same, and the eyes are not mine. The clothes I'm wearing cause me to take a step back and look down at myself. Only then do I realize these weren't the clothes I had on before. They must have changed me. Barely covering my body is a sheer nightgown. Underneath is lingerie.

What were they going to do with me?

Backing up, I twist and start running through the corridors. Every turn seems to lead me somewhere else, and before I know it I'm back where I started. *Kade!* I scream in my head.

When I get no reply I move back to the start, taking a deep breath and trying again. Making a different turn brings me somewhere I feel is new. However, the walls, the floors, the ceilings, and everything else looks the same. Then I see a sliver of light at the bottom of the wall opposite where I stand. My memory jumps back to the window and the illusion. Walking over and laying my hand on the wall, I close my eyes and push my hand. It melts into the brick. I try with my whole body, and suddenly I'm through. The sun hits my face, but so does the fist that I didn't see coming. Stumbling backward, I jerk to the right and luckily miss the next fist swinging at my face.

"You should be dead. Why are you here?" a man with scary crazy eyes shouts.

I back up slightly, then ask, "Who are you?"

"If you were alive, then why come back? Nobody will accept you now. You ruined us all. You should have let them in, let them take over, then we'd still have our House," he shouts. His hair is blond, his eyes blue. Though right now they're tinged with red, like someone on the edge. He's making no sense and I have no idea what to do. "You can't even feel me anymore, can you? What have you been doing, and who with? It doesn't matter... don't tell me... I'm sorry, but you need to die now."

He reaches toward me, and I take a step back. "I have no idea who you are," I tell him. His eyes

Chrysalis

narrow, and he shoots a blue and red light out toward me. I don't quite manage to move in time, and it hits my neck. The pain forces me to my knees, then he steps forward and punches me in the jaw.

"I hate you," he hisses and raises his hand. The light flickers across his fingers again, and instinctively I put up my palm. My power zaps him, running up his arm.

"What trickery is this?" he shouts, holding his hand in the air. Just as he's about to bring it down again, he's tackled sideways and falls to the ground. Elijah is on top of him, punching and hurling abuse.

"Stop, son!" The man shouts, and my insides freeze.

"Don't call me 'son!'" Elijah hisses, but it's obvious he knows this man. He knows this is our father, and what's more... he hates him. I can feel it.

"But Elijah—"

"No," Elijah states, pulling himself off the disheveled man who's still on the ground.

"But—"

"I said... no. Come on, Emery," he says, turning to me. I can't pull my eyes away from the man in front of me, a man whose own eyes have widened, a man with a shocked expression that matches the pain and confusion racing through his body.

"She can't be," he whispers.

Elijah looks down to him. "She is. Look..." He clicks his fingers, and I feel a coating being pulled off my body. I look down and see my hair is now back to its natural blond. I want to ask Elijah what that was, but he continues speaking. "No matter, though, you lost your chance with either of us when you never came back. Now you're nothing, we don't need you. Go clean up their mess, be no more than a lowly scout, or messenger, or whatever else they have you doing. You sold out, father, and when you did, you hung our asses out there. We were kids, but you still didn't hesitate. Now you have what you want." He turns back to me, holding his hand out.

"But you looked just like your mother," the man whispers to me.

I touch my face and feel pain piercing Elijah. "Come, I'll explain, later," he says, dragging me away. He quickly pulls me around a corner, and I try to pull back, wanting to know what's happening. Elijah faces me. "We have no time for explanations right now. Kade needs you."

His words slam into my body, and I close my eyes.

The minute I do, Kade's face appears. He whispers my name, and suddenly my insides throb, making me double over.

"Emery." Elijah snaps. I drop to my butt and bring my knees up, breathing deeply. "Emery, push through this. Kade needs you."

I glance up at his face. Elijah's concern is evident as his worry washes through my every pore. "What do you mean? You keep saying that."

Chrysalis

He sits next to me. "Emery, we don't really have time for me to explain, so I'm going with the quick version." Nodding, I remain quiet, allowing him to continue, "I found Kade. He's not good. When he took that shot for you, he was momentarily knocked out. That shot was a kill shot. Kade's tough, though, so it's gonna take more than that to take him out. When he was down they hit him with some other shit… fucking cowards." Elijah works his jaw as my head starts hurting. I will myself to keep my emotions in check. "They tried to drain him, Emery, tried to take all his powers." I suck in air, as an ache courses through me. "They didn't succeed, he's too strong for them all. So they all sat around taking pot shots while he was out—"

"How do you know this?" I ask.

"Because they knocked him out momentarily, but he woke up, he just couldn't move. When I found him, he was able to tell us—"

"Us?" I interrupt him again.

"Yeah, me, Sicily, Tristan, Tess, Miles, and Katarina. We all came. We needed everyone to help rescue Kade. When we disposed of the people in that room and he was able to speak, we could see that he was gradually gaining his strength back. It wouldn't have been long until he would have taken all those guys out anyway, even without our help." A flash of pain passes across his face.

"What happened?" I whisper, as dread fills me.

"He asked after you, Em. He wanted to make sure you were okay. When I told him we hadn't found you, that your emotions were untraceable for me, he lost his shit.

Honestly, I've never seen him so on edge. He reached out to you. Em, you have to understand, Kade speaking to you in your head normally is not a problem, but they had put some kind of old-time power on you, something even I don't know about. It cloaked you, switched everything inside you off. To find you, to connect, he had to push through all the power that had been used to hide you. It took everything in him, all his power, all the strength he had, everything. He reached you, Em, he told us where you were, and managed to pull you out." Elijah drops his head and grabs my hand.

"What, Elijah? What aren't you telling me?" Every hair on my skin is on end. There's something coming, something I don't want to hear.

"He's not got long, Em, he used whatever he had left to save you. He's… nearly gone." Elijah's voice breaks, and there's an ear-splitting scream circling us. It's so loud, it makes me feel like my body is about to shatter. "Shhh…" Elijah says wrapping his arms around me, and I realize the sound is coming from me.

"Take me to him," I demand, sitting up straight.

"Em—"

Chrysalis

"*Now* Elijah," I bark out. The time for talking is done. He nods, getting up and pulling me with him. We run. It's only a short sprint, and when we arrive he guides me through a doorway. All the others are crouched down, crowded around a body lying sprawled out on the floor. I move forward and ignore them as I push in-between like they don't exist. Because they don't. If he doesn't, then nobody does.

As I clear them, I see Kade. He's lying still on the floor, looking perfect, like he's asleep. At that moment he opens his eyes, and it's then I see the pain, the power he still holds, even if it's seeping out of him. And more than that, I can still see the love. Feel the love. "Princess," he says, reminding me of our earlier conversation. A tear escapes my eye, dropping onto him.

"I'm sorry," I whisper.

"Why?" he whispers back.

"Because I got you in this mess... Because you did this to save me."

"Emery, I will always choose to save you. That must be something you understand by now? What did I say?" he asks quietly, and I frown, trying to think of what he's remembering. "I told you, I'd keep you safe, always, as long as there is breath in my body." He smiles and then looks over my head. "Can I have a minute with Emery, please?"

I hear everyone shuffle out. I'm not sure they're happy about it, not if the muttering is anything to go by, but I ignore them. Nothing but Kade can penetrate my consciousness anymore. I'm living and breathing for him.

"I'll gladly give my life for you. I know what I bought by saving you. I know, Emery. And still, I'd do it again in a heartbeat."

"Kade…"

"No, don't take it away. I'm aware that I'm dying, nobody can do what I've done and survive. I'm lucky to still be talking now…" At that moment Kade starts coughing, and I can see and feel the pain he's in.

"Maybe you should stop talking, Kade?" I offer, stroking his forehead.

Smiling, he reaches across and holds my hand. "It's always been you, Emery. I knew when I first saw you, and I know with my last moments on this earth, it's always been you. I only fear for your safety now. What might become of you? Promise me something?"

I nod as tears freefall, dropping onto his chest. "Promise you will practice your powers. You're stronger than them. You need to listen to Elijah. He *will* look after you. I need to know I'm leaving you safe, princess." The nickname is like a hot knife plunging into my heart.

"I promise," I whisper. He nods, and I can see how much his pain has amped up. He's struggling to talk, and so I glide my finger across his lips, quieting him. "Kade, when we were at the tree, I didn't get a chance

Chrysalis

to tell you something. I love you, too." I watch as his eyes flame gold with the last bit of love he holds, and then like his flame is doused, the spirt is gone, and his eyes are empty.

"Kade!" I shout and hear thundering steps as everyone tramples back into the room. Everyone is shouting and screaming. My heart slams against my chest.

Thump… thump… thump.

I struggle to catch a breath. My insides are hollow. Empty. Cold.

Thump… thump… thump.

The pace quickens, and my limbs start shaking.

Thump… thump… thump.

The white and blue colors start glitching across my body as though it's electrifying itself.

Thump… thump… thump.

All of a sudden, everything gets blocked out, all the noise, all the feelings, all the thoughts. There is nothing but my heart.

Thump… thump… thump.

Then I'm floating, about four feet off the ground. I look down, and my whole body is covered in a cocoon of white and blue, just like earlier, but this time I have a red tinge around me, like a current around my body.

Thump… thump… thump.

All I can feel is the remnants of Kade, his smell, his touch, his voice … the look in his eyes.

Thump… thump… thump.

Then suddenly his words '*I'm in love with you*' float around my head on repeat, and all his love crashes into me. It breaks something, and before I know what's happening, my body rises up and starts shaking in mid-air. I can see the others shouting, but I can't hear anything from them, they're on mute. Light propels out of my body, shooting and pinging. It whizzes around in three separate color strands, then it comes together, pauses for a second, then shoots into Kade's body. He raises off the ground, mirroring me, while my power continues flowing into him. I have no idea what's happening, but somehow, I know it's healing him. All I keep thinking is that… I want him alive.

I *need* him alive.

Now my body is automatically carrying out my orders.

The smile spreads across my face as I watch Kade's eyes opening. They widen as he takes me in.

"I love you," I whisper, then I fall to the ground. I'm suddenly completely spent. "Emery!" I hear him roar before I lose my grip on consciousness once again.

Chapter 15

"Kade, you need to go get some sleep."

"No, Kat. I need to stay here in case Emery wakes up."

"She's fine. They've said that she is. It's up to her now. She'll wake up when she's ready. What are you going to do… wait here forever? She could be like this for years."

"She won't. She's a fighter. *My fighter*. She'll be back with me soon."

"You're going to get yourself hurt if you don't pull away from her now, Kade. You need to leave her behind.

We can go somewhere and start anew. She's strong. You've seen that nothing will happen to her. Plus, she has Elijah and the rest of them."

"I think you should leave, Kat."

"You don't mean that."

"Absolutely, I do. I've denied the feelings I have for Emery for years. You of all people know that. When I finally admitted them to myself it was still with chains holding me down, chains I gave myself, not willing to trust in her, in us. I was so focused on the past that I tried to block out the possibility of this future. I can't do it anymore. I love her, whether she's lying here silently, or fighting at my side. Loving me back or running away from me… she's the one. *The only one.* I want to breathe the same air as her for all eternity. She's my Pith, my soul, my essence, she is the core of me. More than that, Emery is essential. Without her I can't be me."

"There's nothing I can say to change your mind, is there?"

"No."

"Okay, then I'll go, but when she's better, I promise to make an effort to get to know her, for you. Kade, you know the only reason I've been completely standoffish is because I'm afraid she's going to be the end of you, my brother. But if you're destined, more than that, if you're *determined* to be with her, then I will stop showing her this side of me and try to let her in."

"That would be appreciated, Kat."

Chrysalis

I can hear the beeping of machines, although they're drowned out slightly by what seems to be wind chimes. *Odd.*

A sharp sound jolts my body, and I try to pry my eyelids open but fail. The heaviness is too much.

"Kade, let me sit with her a while. You've been here for four days. Dude… you smell."

"Shut up, Elijah. I'm not gonna leave and risk her waking without me here."

"Okay, I'll just park my butt in this chair a while." The room goes back to just beeping and wind chimes. I remember everything that happened, although I'm not quite sure why I passed out. I can only imagine it's because I revived Kade, and it's depleted my energy. The one thing that is clear inside me is the longing for him. The love I feel for him, and the happiness, knowing he feels the same. It's all-consuming. I hear him sigh and feel his fingers fold around my hand.

"I just wish she'd wake up." His voice is raw and raspy.

"I know, man. I know," Elijah replies.

Trying again to move my eyes, I fail once more.

Kade. I speak in my mind, but he doesn't reply. My heart rate accelerates slightly as fear starts ramping up. The inability to do anything is strangling me.

"I can feel her fear," Kade states to Elijah, the concern evident in his voice.

"What? I can't feel anything."

"Well, we're connected, remember?"

"Shall I get someone?"

"Yeah."

I hear Elijah's chair scrape, and the door clicks open and closed. I try to relax my mind and listen to the wind chimes.

Kade…

Emery?

Oh thank God, you can hear me. I tell him.

Emery. You're okay?

Yes. I just can't open my eyes, Kade. It's scaring me.

Hold on.

I feel some tugging and movement on my face, then suddenly, everything is brighter.

"Try now," he tells me aloud.

Slowly I open my eyes and try to focus on something, but the world is blurry.

"It's okay, princess. You had these pads covering your eyes," he explains. That still doesn't make any sense to me, but right now I only care that I'm awake and looking into the face of the man I thought I'd lost.

Opening my mouth, nothing comes out. "You had a tube in until this morning, it was helping you breathe. They said you might feel scratchy in your throat and have trouble talking when you finally wake. Just have some water, baby. Take it easy, and

Chrysalis

give it a couple of hours. Hopefully, then you'll have your voice back, okay?"

I nod my reply, before telling him with my mind. *Kade. I love you.* I watch as his eyes close, and his whole body relaxes.

"Whatever we do now, we do it together," he tells me, squeezing my hand, and I nod and smile.

Elijah bursts back into the room with a young doctor trailing him. She brushes her honey-blond hair over her shoulder in what seems like a nervous tick. Before I have time to think on it, Elijah takes my attention. "Em, you're awake!" he shouts.

"Shh… man. She can't talk, not yet," Kade snaps at him.

The doctor looks between Kade and Elijah, appraising them I think, although that could just be my overactive imagination. "Gentleman, please, let me speak to Ms. Laird."

I'm surprised. I mean, it hadn't occurred to me up to that moment that my surname was really Laird. I've been called Emma Breitsprecher for so many years, but I've never really been her.

"So you can't speak?" She asks and I shake my head no.

"Hmm, that's rare. A sore throat and a scratchy voice is very common. Maybe a little water will help." I nod again, and she turns to Elijah, looking him up and down. Now I definitely didn't misread that. Wow!

"Could you go and get Ms. Laird some water, please?" Taking no notice of the looks she gives him, he turns and is gone. She doesn't say anything else, just reaches forward, and something flashes in her eyes. It's enough to spark fear in me. Her hand descends toward my throat, and once again I find myself watching in slow motion as Kade's hand reaches out, striking like a snake, capturing its prey. He has her wrist in his grip before she even knows what's going on. Whatever was showing in her eyes before, she's now hidden it well. I watch her avert her gaze to Kade, putting on the pretense of being scared. "What are you doing?" she whispers. "You're hurting me."

"Do you think I'm *that* stupid? Do you think that I'm a level ten for no reason?" he spits, and she screws her eyes up at him.

"You're not that good, *Kade*. Otherwise, you'd have known the minute I stepped in the room," she hisses, and I watch as a pain passes over his face.

She's wrong. Stop it. You've been all about me. Plus, you haven't slept in days, I tell him in my mind.

Just then Elijah walks back into the room, unaware, and she turns to him, hitting him in the chest with a red light. He flies back through the air, smashing into the wood and glass that makes up the wall of the room we're in.

No! I internally scream.

Chrysalis

Kade jumps up, blasts her with a white light, then hits her again, this time with a gold flash - the same gold that shines in his eyes. He brings her up in the air and holds her there. She's trapped, immobile and unable to speak. "Call Katarina," he tells Elijah, and my body jolts. Elijah pulls himself up from the floor and walks out of the door.

Now what? I ask him.

"Now we wait. Katarina will be here soon."

You had to call for your sister. You couldn't have called Sicily or Tess… or I don't know, Zeit? Even he wants to hurt me less than your sister. Kade chuckles at me.

This isn't funny! I snap.

His lips twitch, but he says nothing.

A few minutes later, Katarina appears. "Good to see you awake," she tells me. Her voice holds no malice or sarcasm, and I frown as Kade's lip twitches again.

Douche.

"She can't speak," he tells Katarina as he moves his eyes from me to her.

"Oh, is she okay?" she asks, and it feels like genuine concern.

I wonder whether I've woken up in an alternate reality, nothing would surprise me these days.

"She'll be fine," he answers, glancing over to me. I see his eyes flash momentarily from hazel to gold, then back again. Then his head snaps toward the woman being held in the air. "If she had been alone, though…" He stops and I watch a muscle jump in his cheek. "Take her, deliver her. I'm off the grid for a while. I'm with Emery," he says.

"Of course. So glad you're okay, Emery. And when you're back home, I'd like to take some time to explain why I was a bitch before… and apologize," she whispers.

Shit, maybe I am still in a coma.

Kade doesn't respond to my thoughts, but Elijah snorts, and a smirk spreads across his face.

"Kat now isn't the time. Take this one…" Kade's voice is firm, and she nods, offers me a small smile, and then turns her gaze to the fake doctor. That's when I see the bitch return.

"Elijah," she says quietly. He walks over and holds his fingers to the doctor's head, and much like when he did it to me, she passes out. Kat catches her like she weighs nothing and walks away.

"Emery," Elijah says, walking to my bedside and grabbing my hand. "I was so scared," he whispers, leaning over me and pulling my head into his chest.

Can you hear me? I ask him.

Yeah, baby sister. He responds without speaking.

Only you? I query, my eyes quickly darting to Kade.

Yeah. Your mind automatically finds who you want to speak to, but if you're just thinking something

Chrysalis

out loud then any of us that are able to read minds will know what you've said.

I nod in answer and watch as Kade rolls his eyes, obviously aware that I'm talking to Elijah.

Don't worry, I'm not talking about you. I tell Kade with a wink, and he just shakes his head and sits down.

I might just start talking like this all the time, I say, smiling at Elijah.

You wouldn't be able to. It doesn't use much power, but I would imagine that if we only communicated like this for years, we would be in danger of doing ourselves some real damage. Although I don't actually know that. He grins.

Wow, really? I ask, shocked, and he nods. *I can't believe Katarina was actually nice to me. Then she carried that doctor out like she weighed nothing,* I say, looking back to the door.

She was being nice because she knows that, ultimately, Kade will always choose you. So, she has no choice but to fall in line. And she isn't that strong. She's a level six. You're about a five at the moment, although you have some gifts that I've only ever seen on level seven or higher. Your powers are still developing, you won't reach your full potential for a while—

How long? I cut him off.

He smirks at me. *Even when we're talking via our minds, you can't let me finish without asking another question.*

I bite my lip.

I don't know how long. And I don't know what level you'll end up being, but I would take a guess that you'll be a level eight like me, at the very least.

I can feel my eyes widen, the thought of being so strong both excites and scares me.

I have to tell you both what happened when I went with Iric and Isobel. I push my thoughts out to both of them.

Later. Right now, you just need to get better. You need your rest. Kade says.

The last sentence is obviously directed at Elijah, if the death glare Kade sends his way is anything to go by.

Elijah steps back, holding his hands up in a surrender pose. His face is totally at odds with his body as his lips move into a smirk. "I know when I'm not wanted. I'll leave you two alone. Love you, little sis," he says, leaning down and kissing the top of my head. He turns to Kade. "Look after her." This time his tone is serious, and Kade just growls back before Elijah chuckles and leaves.

Kade reclaims his place next to me, leans over, and kisses my mouth softly. My eyes flutter closed, and I can almost feel my lashes laying on my cheeks.

Chrysalis

You make me feel so calm, I tell him, keeping my eyes closed as he moves back out of my space.

"Rest," he orders. I open my eyes, narrowing them on him, but smile

What happened before? What if it happens again? My questions cause pain, I can see it in his eyes, and feel it bloom in my chest. I know it's because he didn't figure out the situation with the doctor sooner.

"It won't happen again," he snaps, a guttural harshness to his voice. "Now I know you're okay. My top priority is your safety."

But Kade, you need to go home. Rest. I heard Elijah. He said you hadn't slept for four days.

"Don't worry about me. You're my life, right by your side is where I belong. Making you safe is my only concern." I frown, and it seems to trigger a similar look on Kade's face before some sort of realization crosses his features and he continues, "Sorry princess. Loving you is my other priority. Although, that takes no effort. With or without you being my Pith, there was never any doubt I'd fall in love with you." I watch as his eyes roam over my face, the gold igniting. *Always for me.*

CHAPTER 16

Gentle snoring is the first thing I hear as my eyes flutter open. My vision is blurry again, so I squeeze my eyes shut and bring my hand up to rub across my face. This time when I open my eyes, everything is clear. Kade's head is lying against my thigh, his face completely restful as slumber consumes him. I've never seen him sleeping. The only thing close was when... *when he was pretty much dead.* The thought sends a shiver through me, and Kade stirs. I still, not wanting to wake him. He hasn't had much sleep over the last few days from what I can tell. Although we'd had a brief conversation, albeit with my mind, I had fallen back to sleep quickly, and now there are so many more questions I want to ask.

Your thoughts are projecting across this whole building, Em. Wrap it up.

Elijah? I think, looking around.

Yeah. I'm outside in the waiting room, we all are.

Chrysalis

All?

Me, Sicily, Tess, Tristan, and Kat.

No Miles? I ask him.

No. That's all the answer I get before Elijah moves on. *Kade still sleeping?*

I look down at his gentle face. I've seen him angry, dangerous, loving, and scared, but never like this. *You wouldn't think he was so lethal.* I murmur in my head.

He is. Just never to you. Elijah's thoughts flow back into my brain.

Shit, has something happened to me? I was able to keep my thoughts to myself, and now I can't?

You just haven't blocked off your thought process today. You're still weak, baby sister.

You know, Elijah, if Iric is right—

He isn't. Elijah snaps.

You don't even know what I was going to say! I retort.

That's true. But I can guess.

He told me that I would turn dark, that Kade would be the only one who could stop me. I don't want him to have to do that. It would kill him... if I didn't first. I rub the heel of my palm across my heart, feeling the sting of electricity sparking under the surface.

Calm down. It won't happen like that. You choose who you want to be. You decide, Emery.

But—

No. Stop. This is not the time to have this discussion. Elijah's voice is stern.

When, then?

Soon. He softens and the electric pulse calms.

Shit.

What? I question worriedly.

Your boyfriend has just told me to get the fuck out of your head and stop pissing you off. Apparently, he can feel your energy ramping up. Elijah's thoughts end with a chuckle, which I find slightly odd. I've just gotten used to hearing words in my head, without sounds being pushed into my brain, too. I move my head gently and look down at Kade. His eyes are open, and he's staring at me intensely.

"You okay, princess?" he asks softly, lifting his head from the bed.

I open my mouth, ready to test my voice again.

"Yeah, I think so." I smile as the words come out scratchy. I have a kind of *Janice Joplin* thing going on.

Kade smirks. "It's good to hear your voice again." He sits back slightly, and I watch as his jaw ticks. A sudden unease tickles my throat.

"What is it?" I ask him.

He stares at me for a few seconds, and the gold ignites in his eyes momentarily, before he blinks and it turns back to hazel. "Don't ever do that again."

I swallow. His words hold so much anger that my heart thumps against my ribs. "W-what?" I stutter.

Chrysalis

"Never put yourself in danger," he returns, no less angry.

I pull my eyebrows in, confused, as my head reels. This is the cold, hard Kade that I knew at the beginning.

"Kade?" My voice comes out wobbly, and I'm sure I see a flash of concern flit across his eyes before his resolve is back in place.

"It doesn't matter the reason, who you're trying to save. I need to know you'll never do anything like that again." His tone is strained now, and as I take a second to think, I realize he's talking about me saving *him*. Me nearly killing myself to save him. I feel a calm cover me. My heartbeat slows and I take a breath in, releasing it slowly. "Emery," he snaps.

I place my hand up in the air. "No. I will absolutely not promise that."

His beautiful full lips thin at my words, and a muscle in his cheek jumps. "Emery…"

"No, Kade. No," I return carefully, shaking my head for emphasis. "I will not stand by and watch someone I love die, not if I can prevent it."

"Dammit Emery!" he shouts, standing. Then he starts to pace.

Em? I hear Elijah question.

It's fine. Don't come in here. We're working something out, I quickly explain before looking back to Kade.

"If you die, that's it for me. *You're* it for me. Don't you understand that by now?" Kade snaps, pulling his hair with his hands.

"Kade," I whisper his name softly. He stops pacing and looks at me. The devastation I see on his face makes my lungs constrict, and I find air hard to capture. He's opening himself up, allowing me to see him at his most vulnerable. And right then, I can see it all clearly—this man cannot live without me.

"I swear I will always look after myself, and I promise not to purposefully put myself into dangerous situations. But I won't ever promise not to save you or someone I love if I need to. Listen, come here," I tell him, gesturing to the bed.

Sighing, he makes his way back to me and sits. I cup his face. "I love you. I no more could live without you, than you could without me. If I told you not to save me… knowing you could kill yourself in the process… would you listen to me?" At my words, his shoulders slump. He knows he'd save me. He already did, and I wouldn't ask him not to. It wouldn't be fair of me to ask that of him. I can feel that it's our instinct, and to let the one we love die would go against our grain, against who we are.

"Emery." His voice is much softer now, laced with his love and passion. "You're going to end up in a lot of dangerous situations. The dark wants you…we know that from the information gleaned so far from Isobel… but the light wants you too. We've

Chrysalis

also found out that there's a new mixed group. They consider themselves good, but we have yet to determine that. They're a new, evolved sect. A mixture of both dark and light beings. They deem that this is evolution, that this is the way of the future." Kade rubs the back of his neck and lets his head drop, so he's staring at the ceiling.

"Kade?" I question softly.

"Verum Novum. That's what they call themselves. New Truth - it's Latin. They think that you belong with them. They think you'll unite everyone," he says, bringing his eyes back to mine.

"Well, that's good, right? I mean, finally a group that doesn't want to kill me." I laugh sardonically.

"I don't know, princess. There's more to it, although none of us are sure what yet. We don't know nearly enough. But I have a bad feeling. For the first time in my life, I'm scared, Emery. They all want you. I will always protect you, but we might be fighting for the rest of our lives." His eyes search mine. Worry and anxiety is rolling off him, and I can feel it in my gut and taste it in my mouth, as though it's my own.

I reach my hand to his and thread our fingers together.

"We can't worry about the future, we can only take every day as it comes. We have each other. If I die tomorrow, I'll feel like I was able to live a thousand lifetimes, because I got to love you… knowing you loved me, too."

"Shit, princess," he says shaking his head. "No more talking about you dying, okay?" His eyes flash gold, and both of our emotions of love and desire mix together inside me, warming my body until my skin flushes.

"Rest some more. I have no doubt we'll be heading home soon. This is one of our special medical facilities, so they won't keep you long. They know how tough we are."

"They have special medical facilities just for people with gifts?" I question, surprised, although at this point I'm not sure why.

Kade nods. "Yeah, there are a few medical centers scattered across the country. We don't allow many of our kind to know about them, not nowadays, with things as they are. We started setting them up about six years ago, aware that the fighting would be developing, and that we'd need special care. They function as normal hospitals in every way, it's just the sections we control are run by people with powers, and the doctors and nurses all have powers too. So they're prepared should one of our kind need treatment." He closes his eyes and swallows, then opens them to stare at me. "I don't know where we would be if we hadn't had this place to bring you to, I can't think about it—"

Chrysalis

"Then don't." I soothe, leaning forward and beckoning him with my mouth. He smirks before angling himself toward me for a kiss. It's only a peck, and I pout as he pulls away.

Smirking, Kade rubs my cheek with his thumb. "Let's worry about getting you better before we worry about kissing." I stick my tongue out, and he chuckles.

"Oh, I wanted to ask you," I say, changing the subject.

"Why did I have eye pads on when I woke?" I touch my eyes, remembering the panic I felt at not being able to see.

"They have to do that to us. Remember your training? You can direct your power to come from anywhere, your fingers, arms, head—"

"Eyes…" I finish, and he smirks.

"Yeah, even your eyes. It's your choice, and your brain helps you decide. But when we're unconscious, we can't make those choices. The strongest of us—"

"Like you," I interrupt smiling.

He smiles back. "Yes, like me. We can control it, even our subconscious can be trained. You're too new for us to expect that you could control things when you're unconscious. They couldn't take that chance."

I nod at his explanation as my eyelids feel heavy again.

"Sleep baby, we'll be home soon." Kade doesn't tell me twice before I close my eyes and drift away.

Ten hours later, I'm on my way home. I grin at myself in the dark glass of the car as I watch the world whiz by. *I can't believe I actually consider that place my home now.*

I'm glad you do. Kade whispers in my head.

My home is wherever you are, Kade.

Same here, princess.

I close my eyes and relax. Elijah and Tristan went home earlier and collected Kade's car. By the time they got back to the hospital, I was almost ready to be discharged. The others all left about thirty minutes before us. Then Kade—being Kade—lifted me into the air and carried me to the car. I rolled my eyes, and he ignored me as people stared while we walked through the hospital. Now, in a matter of minutes, we'll be home.

As we turn into the familiar lane, my heart starts thumping. A buzzing zings across my skin, and I can feel pain, fear, anger and rage. I look at Kade. His eyes are alert, and I know he senses something too.

"I can feel fear… and anger. There are people in pain, too, Kade. What's going on?"

He looks over to me and back at the road. I can almost see his brain working through the movements

Chrysalis

and color changes of his eyes. His anxiety is spiked and adrenaline starts pumping through my system as words and thoughts start filtering in.

"They were ambushed," I whisper into the dark air.

"What else?" Kade snaps.

"The fight is over," I reply as we arrive at the house. Smoke billows into the night sky. Bright yellow flames shimmer through the windows that are still intact, showing me that our bedrooms are gone. I reach for my handle.

"Stay in the car," Kade demands.

"No," I reply, wrenching my arm out of his hold and swinging the door open. I said I wouldn't go into situations where there was danger on purpose unless I had to save or protect someone I love. My brother is in there somewhere, and I'm not about to let him burn. "Elijah!" I scream when my feet hit the ground running. There are trees lying on their sides, pulled out by the roots. Elijah's car sits in its usual place, dents all over, with smudges of what looks like blood, and the window screen is shattered. The downstairs windows in view are all smashed too. Then I spot Tess, her body is slumped at the front door, which has been demolished.

I run to her. "Tess," I call, shaking her slightly. She groans as her eyes flutter, and I release a breath knowing she's alive.

"I'm okay. Tristan?" Her voice is strangled.

"Where is he? Where are they?" I demand, feeling Kade sidling up next to me.

"Some are inside, some out the back. You need to get them… don't let them die." Her voice is barely a murmur, but her mind is screaming. It's so loud that I need to switch her off in my head.

"I'll go inside, you check the back," Kade tells me, disappearing before I have the chance to argue.

I grab Tess and move her to Kade's car, placing her on the back seat. "Stay here. I'll go look for the others." Her head rolls back as her eyes close. I monitor her for a second before making my way around to the back of the house. Kade is coming out the front door with Tristan as I pass him. He nods, letting me know that Tristan is fine.

The sight out back takes my breath away. Multiple fires are scattered across the yard. Rubble, wood, and scorch marks on the ground all litter the large space. I close my eyes and try to sense something, anything. The first feeling I get is of worry. I latch onto it and let it drag me to the far corner. Behind an upturned bench is Elijah.

I reach him and bend down, cupping his cheek.

I'm okay. Find the others. I think they were all inside. He tells me with his mind.

"I need to know you're okay," I reply, voicing my words.

I'll be fine. They hit me with something, not sure what. I haven't seen a power like it before, but it

Chrysalis

knocked me out. I've just come around. I could feel you and that woke me. Now help the others. Please.

"Okay," I tell him. Rising, I close my eyes again and feel pain. Moving toward it, I could choke on the agony. When I reach the blistering fire I can smell singed flesh, and I struggle to keep my stomach from lurching.

"You…" I hear hissed from behind me as an arm swings around my neck forcefully, pulling me to the ground. "His body burns because of you. Everyone wants you. The great *Emery Laird*. Well, now nobody will have you." I recognize the voice, it's Michael. I'm slightly surprised, and fear rushes through me as I try to pull his arm away but can't. Being ill has weakened me. There's a momentary tingle that spreads across me before Michael is ripped from my body, and my head falls backward, but Elijah captures me.

"Let's go," he says, pulling me up, and I look past him to see Kade with Michael.

"I told you, if you ever touched her again, I'd kill you," Kade growls.

"Do your worst. Without Danny I'm dead anyway," Michael replies, looking at the fire. Elijah pulls me away quickly, and I feel a split second of unbearable pain before I close it off. When we get back to the car I see everyone but Sicily and Miles.

Kade rejoins us quickly. "They took Sicily," he says, and I squeeze Elijah's hand as I feel the pain shoot through him before he locks it up. "Miles has gone, too, I don't know if he ran, or joined them." He looks around us all. "We need to regroup and settle. Tomorrow we'll have to analyze this. See what happened." He stops and looks around at everyone slowly, then states, "She's dead."

She? I question Elijah.

You remember the tingling when you went upstairs? Elijah asks me, and I look his way so he knows I'm listening. *She was an elder, helping us. She was very old, the oldest we knew about, at least from the light side. You got the tingles because you could feel her power, her knowledge. She was leaking it into you.* I raise an eyebrow at him as the others continue talking. *I Know more explanation is needed Em, for now just know that she's dead. They killed her. They will pay. They'll also pay for taking Sicily.*

I grimace at his words. I'm worried for Sicily, and my heart feels heavy. I now realize what Kade was talking about earlier today. We may never have peace. We might be fighting forever. As I look around the group that has quickly become my family, I'm pretty sure that if this is the way we will live, then we're not all going to survive.

Chrysalis

CHAPTER 17

We've been walking for thirty minutes. I don't know why we're walking rather than using the car, or at the very least doing the usual fly-running thing that they all tend to do. I'm also not sure where we're going, as nobody has uttered a word since Kade said, *'Let's move.'* As soon as the instructions were issued, everyone fell into line, like they'd done it a thousand times before.

Maybe they had. I'm the newbie, not them. I tacked myself onto the end of the line and wondered why they followed one behind another. Sometimes I forget that my time here has been short. With the love of Elijah and now Kade, there's nowhere else I'd rather be, and for the first time in my life, I know down to my bones, that I belong.

As soon as we'd started to walk away from the burning house, I could feel the pull inside me. Now, we're a few miles into our journey and the pull has turned into a burn. It blisters against me like there are actual flames licking my chest. *It's you. Accept yourself.*

"What the hell?" My whispered words reach the group and all heads turn to me. "Right, super hearing," I groan, rolling my eyes.

Kade stops, and everyone halts quickly behind him so as not to cause a human pile-up. "Emery?" he questions.

My brain flitters from one thought to the next. I'm somehow aware that I need to keep the voice to myself, for now. "A m-moth flew into me," I stutter. Kade just raises his eyebrow and waits, "I-I'm scared of moths," I continue with my stutter. This time I do it on purpose, trying to act out the fear, hoping I'll be believable. Kade tilts his head and stares at me. I bite the inside of my mouth, hoping he'll buy it, knowing that he didn't feel fear from me, so he's probably not convinced. I see a flash of something in his eyes, but then thankfully he lets it go. I huff out a silent sigh as we continue on in our formation.

We'll talk later, princess, Kade orders in my head.

I don't say anything because I don't know what to say. I'm starting to think that I imagined the other voice.

Emery, you need to accept yourself, the voice tells me again. This time I manage to keep quiet and continue walking in line with everyone else. My heart picks up speed at the unknown voice, and

Chrysalis

Kade—without missing a step—turns to look at me, his eyes narrowed and I know we'll be having a discussion sooner rather than later. As soon as he turns back around, I know what I need to do.

Who is this? I demand.

You already know. The voice is eerie. It takes everything inside me to keep shivers from running down my spine. There's also a melodic element to it, like there are musical notes attached to every word. It's a strange kind of hypnotic tone.

The woman in the house. You died, I say, answering my own question, confused as to how I know the answer.

You're quick. I can see why you were hidden, she sings in my head.

Stop, now. Tell me what's going on. I can't control my heart rate from getting faster, but it's anger that's causing it. Kade and Elijah both turn their heads to me as I stop walking. I ignore their stares, instead closing my eyes to concentrate. *Please tell me.* I beg this time.

I am the Convergence. Named as such because I am a normal human who lived with gifted beings, a human who should never have had powers. I do not come from a House, or even a bloodline that has power. I am merely a mortal. I will show you. As her last word leaves me, my eyes snap open, and I can see Elijah and Kade shouting while the others look on with wide eyes, fear displayed across their faces.

Although I can see them all, I can't hear, it's like watching a mime. I try to speak or to reach out, but I can't do anything. The feeling is similar to when I was *Earthed*, but I don't feel scared. It's almost as if I know this has to happen. This has to be the way it is, and that thought gives me peace as I fall backward, closing my eyes.

When I open them, I'm lying in a field. The sun is beating down so hard that beads of perspiration have already formed along my brow. I sit up and take in my surroundings. The first thing that strikes me is how beautiful this place is. The view spans for miles. A wide expanse of different colored fields are between where I sit and the breathtaking snow-topped mountains in the distance. The skyline is only broken up by a line of tall trees where a selection of different looking houses sit, complementing the scenery. They were obviously built to blend with rather than compete with the vista.

An explosion of noise captures my attention, and I stand, turning in the opposite direction. What can only be described as a brawl greets my gaze, and after taking a second to compose myself, I run in the direction of the rabble. While I'm running I realize that I have no power, and halfway to the fight I have to stop to catch my breath. By the time I finally reach my destination, there are only a few people left. Many have disappeared, much like I've seen before, where they seem to shatter into shards before

Chrysalis

vanishing. There are others lying on the ground, people helping one another up. The strongest seem to be talking amongst themselves. In the middle of them all is a vehicle, upside down. It looks like a cart, but without the horses to pull it. I take a few steps and move my focus from one person to another. Everyone is wearing old-fashioned clothes. It's then that my brain catches up, and I take another look around me. *I'm in the past.*

"Hello," I say tentatively. Nobody even looks my way. "Hello…" I say a little louder, but they still ignore me. I walk over to the tallest, broadest, scariest looking one there, and I feel strangely calm and safe as I tap him on the shoulder. He looks back and straight through me. His deep brown eyes study the immediate area, then he shakes his head causing his shoulder-length black hair to sway in the wind. I feel mesmerized by his familiarity as he pulls in his eyebrows, turning back with another small shake of his head.

"We'll have to take her with us," he tells the others. "People will not believe her parents' disappearance while she is seen alive and well. And anyway, the others will kill her if they find out she exists."

"Just a normal human family in the wrong place at the wrong time. They then fall prey to the ways of the dark. We need to stop them, Kalciffer. Otherwise, there will be more destruction of human lives for those who do not hold gifts. The time for keeping ourselves sectioned off is gone. This is a new age," another man with blond hair says to him.

They all turn toward me, forming a line and looking straight past where I stand. "It starts with her," the man called Kalciffer says.

I turn and see a young girl, maybe six or seven years old. She has brown hair in ringlets and is wearing an old dress with some kind of pinafore over it. The whole outfit is dirty and torn, and I look back and forth between the vehicle and her.

My parents died this day. Leaving me. If the dark had gotten me, I would not be of any world for longer than my mere seven years. However, Kalciffer and Edmond decided to save me. They didn't know then, but having a powerless human around those that are gifted for an extended period turns that person into the Convergence, the little girl tells my mind while staring directly into my eyes.

A jolt, followed by shouting, causes me to blink a few times as the little girl fades, and Elijah's fear covered face with the backing of a dark sky replaces her.

"Em, are you okay?" Elijah asks as my eyes move past him, catching onto Kade's, who is standing behind my big brother. The mixture of fury and fear causes me to stop breathing, and when it catches up with me, I end up having a coughing fit. Elijah stands me up and holds me, rubbing my back and soothing me.

It's taking everything inside me right now not to rip you from your brother's arms. You should be in mine. I know he needs to hold you. But damn it, Emery, so do I. I allow my body to relax and even let out a giggle as I peer over Elijah's shoulder and watch Kade pacing back and forth muttering to himself.

I feel my shoulders jostled as I'm pulled away from Elijah. He looks annoyed but then relaxes as another set of arms wind around me.

"Glad you're okay, little one," Tristan whispers his hot breath in my ear. "Watch what happens now." He chuckles quietly as he kisses my cheek.

A growl pierces the now tranquil night, and then I'm ripped from Tristan's arms and pulled against a solid chest. I ignore Tristan's laughter and people chattering as I gaze into Kade, right into his soul. "Why did I fall in love with someone who everyone wants?" he asks, shaking his head.

He remains silent for a few minutes, seeming to take in the warmth of my body, holding me and knowing that I'm real, that I'm here. "I'm so scared, princess. If I lose you, I'll lose me." He moves his thumb gently across my bottom lip. "You've always been my reason to fight. Do you understand that? You were the reason I became who I am even before you knew me... because, deep down, I knew the day would come, the one where I admitted my feelings for you. I knew that Pith or no Pith, I would have fallen in love with you and I would spend my life making sure you were okay. My world exists only because you're in it, and I fall in love with you a little more each day. The idea that you could be taken from me at any moment nearly brings me to my knees. I can't lose you, Emery. If something ever happened to you…" He breaks off and swallows, and a lump forms in my throat.

I open up and feel his pain and worry. It's unnerving coming from Kade, he's always so strong, so fierce. To know his very real fear of losing me is causing him this much anxiety is unsettling, to say the least, but I also know there's nothing I can do about it. I can't stop people coming for me. I just have to be strong, and as much as he wants to protect me, I have that same need to protect him too.

I grab his hand, and he focuses back on me. "I could walk away right now. Let you have peace."

He snatches his hand away. "You think I'd want that? Or that I would have considered it for even a second?" Kade snarls.

I smirk at him and bring my hand back up. This time I run my fingertips through his hair, and he lets a little sigh slip from his lips. "Then we have no choice but to make sure we both remain safe. Kade, you know I feel the same as you, we've been through this already. Do you not think that if I lost you it wouldn't tear my world apart?"

He grabs my hand and kisses my palm. "I know, princess." Leaning down he places his lips on mine. Unmoving for a split second, I suddenly feel his other hand wrap around my waist, hauling my body even closer into his while he kisses me. It's hard, needy and desperate, almost like he didn't think he would have the opportunity to kiss me again. His hand runs up my back and into my hair holding me close and tight. He slows down the kiss until his lips rest against mine once more.

I open my eyes and see his are still closed.

He breathes in and out slowly, then opens his eyes, pulling back an inch. "There's everyone else, Emery. Then there's you," he tells me, spinning around and morphing before my eyes into Mr. Alpha-Leader-Man, telling everyone that we need to continue and that we're going to split up and meet somewhere.

The others all talk at once. It's a mixture of jeering about our kiss and complaining. I block them out as I touch my fingertips to my lips and look at Kade's back. I'm drowning in this man, and it's everything I want. I'll happily close my eyes and let my hands and feet float unmoving and allow myself to sink into him, completely.

He moves back to me, collects me in his arms, and the next thing I know, the breeze is washing over us both. Looking down at my face momentarily he says, *don't think I've forgotten about earlier. We WILL be having a chat.* I just smile, letting the warmth and love flow over me.

Chapter 18

"I'll meet you in a few hours." I hear Kade's voice as I rouse from sleep. My head turns, and my eyes immediately seek him out, even though the room is almost pitch black. His back is to me, and he's on the phone.

Blinking, I do a quick scan of our surroundings. It's another hotel. That's clear within the first five seconds. Bathrobes hung up ready for use, a room service menu sits on the cabinet next to the bed I'm in, and I can see a couple of doors leading off to the bathroom and balcony no doubt. As I twist my head I spot the exit. It's a basic room, not as opulent as the one Elijah and I stayed in, but clean and warm and, most importantly, this room contains Kade, and that's all I need to consider any place home.

I glance down at my body and see that I'm still in my jeans and hoodie. My eyes wander back to the bathrobes, and I almost groan out loud with the thought of having a warm bubble bath. Pulling my hoodie over my head, I raise my butt and pull the jeans down my thighs, slipping them over my feet before leaning away from the bed and chucking them on the floor next to me. As I twist back into a sitting position, Kade is facing me. He's like a statue. The only reason that I know something awful hasn't happened to him is because his eyes are blazing golden. I look down at myself—a navy blue lacy bra and matching boy shorts are the only things covering me right now. I gulp as I open my inner-self to him. His feelings flood me, desire being the most potent, followed closely by a hunger and then love. The hairs on my body stand with anticipation, waiting for him to follow through with what his eyes so clearly display. "Kade," I whisper. My word breaks his fixed position, and he bites his bottom lip.

"Gotta go," he talks into the phone before throwing it to one side like it's acid in his hand.

"Princess, it's taking everything in me to stay over on this side of the room right now. I'm strong, I'm good at restraining myself… but right now, with you looking like that, I'm on the edge, and this isn't somewhere we're ready to go yet." He closes his eyes and shakes his head slightly.

I realize that this is hard for him. All his focus is on keeping me safe. I've just come out of the hospital and we've immediately escaped a fight which saw his home burnt to the ground. On top of that, Miles and Sicily are still missing.

"I'm sorry," I tell him.

"You have nothing to be sorry for. You wanted a bath, right? That's all this was." His reply is warm, comforting.

"You knew that?"

"You were thinking about having a bath," he tells me.

"Oh. I didn't realize I was thinking out loud."

Kade ignores my comment and walks toward me, his eyes changing back to hazel. He grabs a robe on the way, slipping it over my shoulders upon reaching me, and I thread my arms through the holes, wrapping it around my body so I'm covered.

"We need to discuss what happened earlier," he says, and I can still hear the need in his voice.

I hold my hand up to him. "Nuh-uh, we need to discuss the fight, the fire, the fact that Miles and Sicily are missing, and the secret old lady that died in the fire," I reply counting each thing off on my fingers.

Kade takes my hand in his, then raises his other one, swiping it down my face and capturing my chin in his fingertips. "Princess, please trust me. Everything you're asking I will explain. But for right now, I'm leading my family. I *know* all that information. What I don't know…what I *need* to know before I make my next move and possibly endanger everyone, is what happened with you."

My shoulders slump on a sigh as I realize he's right. And I hate that. I'm sick of always waiting to be told. Being kept in the dark is starting to grate on me, but I'm also acutely aware that we haven't got time to talk about it now.

"Someone was communicating to me in my head."

His body stills, his eyes more alert than before, which I didn't think was possible. "More," he growls through his teeth.

"Stop growling at me. I know it's your signature thing, but it's not my fault," I snap.

He grumbles but shakes his head, sitting on the bed. "Emery." His one word holds the demand in his tone.

"It was the woman who died in the fire."

"You knew about her?" he questions, tilting his head.

"No. I mean, not before. I knew something was strange upstairs in that house because I always felt a tingle when I passed her door, but nobody explained what that was." I search his face for a tell, anything to show what he's thinking, but he keeps everything locked up tight as usual. "When she started talking in my head, it was like she placed the information in there, too. I can't explain it, except to say that

Chrysalis

suddenly I knew she was the woman who gave me the tingles, and she died tonight in that fire."

"Mary-Ann... that was her name," he says, and I sit a little straighter, waiting for him to continue. "What happened next?" His words jolt me as I realize he's not going to continue with any sort of explanation.

I roll my eyes before continuing, "She told me she was the Convergence."

"Dammit," Kade hisses out.

"What?"

"Nothing. Carry on," he tells me.

Shaking my head, and more confused than ever, I explain what I saw. Once I'm finished, Kade says nothing for a minute, instead staring down at the bed as though transfixed. Then his head flicks up suddenly, and he studies me. "The Convergence is someone who evolves superficially into having similar characteristics as those with gifts but only when they're in the same environment. Basically, she was a non-gifted human who evolved into having powers," he tells me.

"But, I mean, isn't that what we've all done? We're human after all. We must have all come from non gifted humans at some point, right?" I ask.

"I don't know. As I've explained before, we don't know enough of our history to be sure how we came to be. What I do know is that the Convergence is one person, dark or light, good or bad. There can only ever be one. From what you've explained in your vision, Mary-Ann was a child whose family was killed by the dark. Our ancestors took her in, and she became the Convergence. It could be as simple as she was in the right place and time, or it could be that it was in a host waiting to jump, and she was just lucky or unlucky, depending on how you look at it."

"So, what's so special about the Convergence? I mean, firstly, you make it sound like this only happens if someone non-gifted lives with gifted people for an extended period. Then in the next breath the way you describe it… you make it sound like its own entity," I ask, biting my lip, trying to hide my concern.

Kade shakes his head at me. "The Convergence is what the person becomes, but as I said, there is only one. Otherwise, the dark would be kidnapping humans left and right to live with them. To become like them. The person evolves into the Convergence, but that person has to be chosen. I don't understand it fully. What I do know is, when a person becomes the Convergence, they're very strong, and can use power at will from anyone within their vicinity." He stands and walks over to the window, closing it before joining me back on the bed.

"Mary-Ann was very old, over one hundred years. As the Convergence, she could have lived for even longer. You know if we're not killed then our lifespan is often at least one hundred and twenty years, if not more. A Convergence can live *three* of our lifetimes."

My eyes widen at his words, and he nods, reading my expression.

"That's a lot of destruction if there were a dark Convergence," he tells me, rubbing the back of his neck. "Mary-Ann chose to keep herself hidden so she wouldn't use our powers. But she wasn't stupid. She lived with me, knowing I was the strongest. She was safer with me than anyone else. Still, she kept hidden even within the house."

I feel his overwhelming sorrow at her loss, and I reach over, grabbing his hand in mine. We both know, without any words, what the other is feeling. Pulling my hand to his mouth, he kisses my knuckles, and as he does his eyes alight, just for a second. Not letting go of my hand, his thumb explores mine.

"When there's no Convergence, the seed—or whatever it is that turns someone into a Convergence in the first place—finds a host. This can be anyone, gifted or not." He stops and clenches his jaw. "When this seed chooses someone, it's based on purity. Pure good *or* pure evil. It's not biased. I would assume that it chose MaryAnn because she was a child and therefore pure. Until that point, it had to sit with someone. You mentioned Kalciffer. He was my great-great-grandfather, and from what I know of my family tree, he was a leader and a good man. It is entirely possible that he was carrying the seed while it waited for a permanent host. However, he should have known. If that's the case, then he would've taken in Mary-Ann knowing what she would become—"

I interrupt him. "No, she told me that they didn't know what would happen."

"That doesn't mean that they didn't. She would *not* have been aware of their knowledge, and Kalciffer was very strong, able to withstand mind invasion amongst other things," he returns.

"Hmm, so I see where you get your abilities from," I complain, arching my eyebrow and thinking about how he locks me out from seeing inside of him sometimes.

He smiles but then mumbles, "If it were me, I would probably have done the same, based on the fact that I could raise and protect the child and guide them in the ways of the light." Kade is talking more to himself than me now. It's like he's thinking aloud, but his words make me pull my hand away. He looks between our hands at the broken connection and back to my eyes with a frown. "What's wrong?"

"Why would anyone burden an innocent young girl with that? How can that be something that someone of the light would do?" I snap, flustered and frustrated with everything, I'm aware that I'm taking it out on Kade but unable to stop myself.

"It would be the best thing for everyone, Emery," he replies, and I say nothing while I sit glaring at him.

Chrysalis

"Emery, the Convergence will *kill* a gifted person if it stays within them for too long." My head jerks at his omission, and I'm lost for words. "Not only that, but had Mary-Ann been left, the dark beings would have found and killed her. She was safer becoming the Convergence because, much like you're learning with your own powers, the Convergence would protect her without her realizing it." I find myself nodding to his revelation this time, my brain catching up and ready to chastise my overactive imagination.

"Emery, I need to know what it said to you." His words are quieter this time, and before I can ask why, he lowers his voice further. "We cannot trust that someone isn't listening. After your recent hospital visit, I can't trust that your mind is at full strength, your thoughts may be overheard. This is important, so we'll speak as quietly as possible, okay?"

I nod. "She said, 'It's you. Accept yourself.'"

Kade closes his eyes, running his palm down his face. Then getting up, he grabs the lamp next to the bed and throws it across the room. I startle, and my heart accelerates as I fling my arms out. Suddenly, a blue light blasts from my fingertips and catches the lamp in a bubble just millimeters from the wall. Kade stares at me for a second. "Emery, you're tapping into my ability to slow things down without even trying."

I look between him and the lamp and slowly lower it to the floor. "Why did you throw it?" I ask him quietly.

His jaw works as he says nothing, then stiffly he moves forward before dropping to his knees on the floor beside me. I twist on the bed to face him, and he lays his head in my lap. "It's chosen you to be its host." His words are sorrowful, and I swallow my emotion, locking it up inside as I reach my hand out and run it through his hair. "It's because you're both pure and strong, Emery. It chose you."

"But you're strong and pure, too, Kade. Why didn't it choose you?"

"I can't say for sure, but I think there was already a connection. You said you had tingles when you passed her room, right?" he asks.

"Yeah, but Elijah had them, too," I state with a shrug.

Kade looks up from my lap. "It picks the strongest. You're stronger than Elijah, princess," he tells me with what sounds like a hint of pride. "I don't think it's inside you yet. I believe you'll know when it is, but it's only a matter of time. Days… it could be less." His voice is pained again, and I feel inside him. Closing my eyes, I reach in and imagine myself coating his pain with a balm. A sharpness pierces my heart, and I instantly stop. "Don't try and take my pain from me. You can't rid me of it without taking it into yourself. I will not allow your powers to diminish because you lend them to me, even if we are in a fight. You must promise me, Emery. I can't take your powers yet, but you can freely give them to me. I don't want them. You're everything to me, keeping you safe is my priority. Treat your life with respect. Please. For me."

I say nothing and Kade buries his head back into my lap with a frustrated groan. I sit, watching my hand travel through his hair over and over again. I know the question I want to ask, but I'm not sure if I should ask it and risk upsetting him more.

"I don't know how long you'll have once it's inside you. Could be months, could be years, I'm not sure there's anyone alive today that knows the answer." Without moving his head from my lap, Kade has answered the question I couldn't ask.

"I'll be okay," I tell him what he needs to hear, even if I have no clue whether it's true.

Kade looks up at me and smiles. He wraps his hand around the back of my neck and pulls my head down to his, then kisses me. The kiss quickly builds up speed and desire as he moves to standing all the while still kissing me. He pushes me back onto the bed, not letting his lips disconnect from mine as he climbs over me. Only then does he pull away, his chest heaving, and I bite my bottom lip, feeling the swell of it.

"You're going to have more powers, both natural and from the Convergence. But because you're late developing, we won't know which is which. That means you'll need to learn any new powers that emerge. Emery, you need to learn to control your heart. The amount of powers that will be coming alive inside you can cause a sort of overload if you're not careful. You've not had your gifts for years. You struggle maintaining your heart rate now… if we're not careful you could either go into cardiac arrest like a normal human, or—"

"Or what?" I ask, gripping his muscular upper arms.

"You could die, like those you've seen break into shards before vanishing completely." His voice is guttural, and my stomach dips.

"I have to work out our next steps. It's only just after five a.m., but I'm leaving now and meeting with Tess and Tristan. He may seem like a joker, but Tristan is one of the smartest people I know. We also have to formulate a plan regarding Sicily and Miles. Elijah will be here soon, he'll stay with you. I'll brief him before I leave, and you can ask him about everything I haven't had time to share with you tonight. Go have your bath, princess."

"Kade," I whisper, and my voice breaks.

He places his hands on both sides of my face and kisses me once more. "I won't let anything happen to you, okay?" I nod in response. "Nothing. You're my forever, Emery. I'm not losing that. Not ever," he says, leaning forward and resting his forehead against mine.

I breathe in his scent and know that whatever happens in my tomorrow, having him in my today has made everything we face worth it.

CHAPTER 19

"Em." Elijah's voice makes me jump as I stare out the hotel window. The fact that he startled me is a surprise, not many people can creep up on me anymore, and it just shows how much I have on my mind.

Turning around to look at him, the worry is immediately clear on Elijah's face, as is the concern rolling around inside him.

"Elijah, what's wrong?" I ask, my voice slightly raspy. I make my way to the mini fridge and pull out two bottles of water, offering him one.

"Kade has caught me up with what's going on with you. The Convergence, Em… that's not good," he says, accepting the bottle from me, worry lacing his words.

I sigh and lean against the wall, dropping my head. "I know."

Chrysalis

"He's informed you of the possible consequences?" he asks.

"What? You mean that I could have a heart attack or break into a thousand shards and cease to exist? Yeah, he's told me," I say flatly. The moment the words are said, I feel bad. Elijah's pain slices through him and me. "Sorry, Eli," I say. It's the first time I've used a nickname, and his eyes widen before he smiles.

The smile goes as quickly as it came when he grabs my hand. "I can't lose you, Em. I know this isn't your choice, but I just can't lose you. When it enters your body, from that moment you have to focus one hundred percent on finding an ungifted human with a pure soul to take it from you."

I nod in reply. I know he's right, but there's little I can do about the whole situation. I'll have to let the chips fall where they may, as Jenny would say.

Jenny. I haven't thought about her since that night I dreamed about Elijah saving me.

"Could she help you?" Elijah asks, picking up my thoughts.

I frown and cross my arms over my chest. "I need to learn how to stop you from overhearing my thought process," I state grumpily.

Elijah smiles at me, as though I'm cute and clueless. "You know how to do it, Em. You just make the decision internally, like you've always done. You think it, and it happens." He ruffles my hair, and I'm an eye twitch away from kneeing him in the crotch. "You can't have forgotten the most basic stuff, so I guess it's probably just the fact that you were in the hospital and aren't fully recuperated yet." His voice has become more serious as he stares at me like I'm a problem to be solved.

I huff and move to sit on the single chair by the desk.

"Eli, Kade told me that I could ask you anything, seeing as he didn't have time to answer my questions."

Elijah chuckles. "Emery, there isn't enough time in the world to answer all the questions you probably have inside you." When I say nothing, he rolls his eyes and leans back against the wall, throwing one ankle over the other and slipping his hands into his pockets. "Shoot, little sister," he says, and it's all I need to start firing questions.

"When I was in the hospital, I could hear wind chimes, they were up in my room. Why?" I'm not sure where that question came from. It certainly isn't the most important one I need to ask, but it's a good place to start, I guess.

Elijah must think the same as me, because his eyes widen, and he shrugs his shoulders to himself. "Well, that's easy for you, Em," he says with a wink. "They're put in the rooms of gifted beings when they're unconscious, so they know that they're at the hospital and safe." He briefly stops speaking as my

Chrysalis

eyebrows pull in at my confusion. "Because we have to have our eyes covered for safety reasons, and often our hands and bodies have to be strapped down, too. The rest of us aren't blessed to have Kade as a constant protector, vouching for us. He wouldn't allow the medical staff to immobilize you."

My mouth hangs open, and I don't know what to say. The thought of being strapped down, unable to move, makes me feel uncomfortable, and I'm grateful that Kade was there to stop that happening.

"Why didn't you tell me about Mary-Ann?" I jump straight into my next question.

"What could I have told you?" he returns, and I automatically reach inside of him with my powers. He has no wall up, so I can sense everything he's feeling inside as he clams up. It's unlike him to feel uncomfortable. It makes me uneasy. "Whatever you knew about her."

"Nothing. I knew nothing," he snaps, pushing off the wall, walking back to the balcony and slipping outside. I let my head drop back and close my eyes.

Sorry. I hear Elijah's soft word in my head.

What is going on with you? I ask him, making sure to focus my mind so I'm only speaking to him.

I knew there was something different about MaryAnn, but I never knew what exactly. I thought she was the Convergence, but she wouldn't speak to anyone but Kade. She lived like a recluse for the seven years she spent with us, rarely moving outside of her room. Kade was the only one allowed inside. I was able to tap into some thoughts here and there, managing to work out that she was the Convergence. I never told anyone I knew. Then, about six months ago I started getting a tingling every time I passed her door. At first it confused me, then, somehow information was pushed into my brain. Not much, but just enough that it made me believe there was a chance that she was going to feed me her powers. The night I brought you to the house I could feel that you had the tingles too. I think I've known from that moment.

What did you know from that moment? I ask, greedy for information.

I knew she'd picked you instead. The tingles started for you. It was her way of passing tiny pieces of the Convergence to you until you were ready for the whole power. I knew because the tingling stopped for me the night you arrived.

I don't say anything. I'm unsure what to say. I sit at the desk and stare at the mirror in front of me. I'm different. I have been since the night my powers sparked to life inside me. That's a lie, I've *always* been different. But now, I can feel powers constantly building within me. I feel strong. I have family. I have Kade. I feel whole, like all my pieces are where they should be, and I'm finally realizing my place in this crazy world. I was a wallflower before, hiding in

Chrysalis

the shadows, trying to go unnoticed. I never really had a place.

Now I know who I am. I am part of the light.

I am Elijah's sister.

I am the Convergence.

I am Kade's Pith.

I'm not Emma Breitsprecher anymore. I'm not sure I ever was.

I'm Emery Laird, exactly who I was always meant to be.

Chapter 20

"Elijah, come sit in here with me," I demand.

Surprisingly, with only a roll of his eyes, he concedes and sits across from me on the end of my bed. "There are explanations I still need." He just nods in response, so I take that as my cue to question him. "Where are Sicily and Miles?"

I can feel the pain burn through him from my question. It's stabbing me inside like a thousand needles, and I wince before trying to cut off his feelings.

"They took Sicily. I watched, but I couldn't do anything." His voice is strained and I can see from the look on his face that he feels like he let her down.

"You didn't do this," I murmur.

"I allowed the dark to take her," he shoots back and heat prickles my skin.

"What happened?" I ask.

Chrysalis

"We arrived back at the house and Mary-Ann was fighting at least ten men, they were all dark beings. There were fires all over and already a few bodies on the floor," he says, dropping his head forward and rubbing the back of his neck. I fight my own urge to interrupt him and ask ten new questions that have just popped into my head.

"She was dying, and there was too many of them against… just her. She was powerful, really powerful, but she was old and her gifts had been unused for so many years…she was rusty." His head comes up and he looks pointedly at me. "This is why I've had you training. You need to pick that back up today. There's no time to rest and recuperate like Kade has led you to believe. We live in a world where they *will* come for you at your weakest." His words are rushed and panicky, and my stomach feels like a thousand moths are attacking me from the inside. It's all from him.

I reach across the small space and capture his hand.

"Elijah, I'm not going anywhere. Nobody is going to take me from you," I reassure him. He smiles, but it's weak, he doesn't mean it. He doesn't believe my words.

"You say I'm strong… Kade says I'm strong and when I have the Convergence in me I'll be stronger. It's unlikely that anyone will be able to kill me, Eli," I say, moving so that I'm sitting next to him now.

His shoulders drop, and he gives a slight shake of his head. "I know what you're saying, and while most of that is true, there's still the fact that the Convergence being inside you could—" he stops talking and grinds his teeth.

"Eli," I whisper, and after a few torturous seconds when I think he might lose it, he looks over to me.

"Nothing will happen to me. Even if you take away the fact that you and Kade wouldn't let anyone hurt me, there's still one fact that you're forgetting."

He frowns but says nothing.

"I'm Emery Laird, the head female of Laird House. I'm light, dark, *and* a pure soul. I will win. I will survive." My little pep talk for Elijah seems to work because I see the corners of his mouth twitch.

"I forgot, Kade calls you Princess. I guess that's what you are. I mean you're the strongest of our house now," he tells me. I can feel his pride swell, it warms me from the inside, spreading through my limbs.

"So, what happened next?" I encourage him to continue.

"Well, we fought the ones who were still alive. There were more than we realized. Mary-Ann was fighting ten, but as soon as we joined in, another twenty or so appeared from behind the house. Tristan and Tess fought side by side at the front of the house with Mary-Ann. I ran through to the back when they grabbed Sicily and hauled her to the garden. I

Chrysalis

managed to get her back, and for a few moments we were winning." He sighs. "Then all at once a bunch of them ran around from the front of the house. I knew right then that they had beaten the others, and I hoped that nobody was dead. We couldn't win, there were too many. They took Sicily, and I was knocked out for a few seconds by a power I've never felt before." He stops talking again, running his hand back and forth over his hair. An ache spreads through my chest, and I realize that I'm not cutting off Elijah's emotions like I had hoped I could. Maybe I want to take some of his pain, share it, so he doesn't have the full impact.

"Where was Miles?" I ask, suddenly remembering him.

Elijah's jaw works back and forth. "I don't know."

"But you suspect," I reply immediately.

He nods his head, and I give him a moment. "I thought I saw him leaving us and running with them. I heard a whisper in my head, but I'm not sure if I imagined it."

"What did it say?"

"Someone was saying, 'He's re-joined us now.'" I feel his anger a split second before he stands, kicking the chair I just vacated. Instinctively, I reach out and stop it from flying through the balcony doors. "Damn, Em," Elijah says, staring at me with wide eyes.

"What is it with you and Kade? Inanimate objects don't deserve to be punished." I grumble, standing and crossing my arms.

He laughs, but it's not real, he's trying everything he can to mask his pain.

"You can't hide from me," I tell him.

"I know," he whispers, letting his worry show.

I move over to the mini fridge. "You want another water?" I ask, but he just shakes his head. Rubbing my temples, I decide to keep questioning him. If I can at least keep his mind occupied then maybe he won't feel so desolate. "I know what I want to ask," I say, and he raises his head to look at me. "Why did some of the dark bodies remain? I thought we all shatter and disappear when we die?"

Elijah blinks a couple of times before answering,

"Oh, yeah, well... we only shatter if we're above a level six. It's to do with us being too strong, the whole stopping both sides from building an army thing."

"I don't get it." I shrug and sit back on the bed, this time positioning myself at the top, propping up the pillows so I can lean against the wall.

Elijah turns around and faces me, crossing his legs.

"Do you remember when I first found you and I thought you'd killed those guys?" he asks, and I nod, gritting my teeth as the memory washes over me. "Well, Michael didn't die, right?" I repeat my nod.

Chrysalis

"He would've been close to death, but he told you that he survived because
Zeit saved him. Well Zeit, like you, probably has the *Revive* gift. If someone with abilities dies or is close to death, and they're less than a level six, you can use the *Revive* gift on them and bring them back. However, if they were light and someone from the dark saves them, then they would turn dark, and I would assume it works the same way if a person from the light saves a dark being. Although, I can't be sure since I've never heard of this happening."

I can feel myself frowning, Elijah doesn't miss it. "Because we've been outmaneuvered and at a disadvantage for so long when it comes to facing the dark, most people of the light are wary. Most of us remain hidden and will not engage in fighting. The sections like us that fight are few, and we're trying to come together, to make ourselves bigger, stronger… it's hard. If we do engage in fighting, we wouldn't try to save a dark being. Therefore, I have no real idea if they would switch sides."

"So why do only level six and above shatter?" I ask.

"Because there's no coming back from that. Again, we don't know as historical documents aren't freely available, but we assume that we're this way so neither side has an advantage. Neither light nor dark can afford for the higher levels to be saved. If someone from the dark killed me and brought me back, I would be dark, it would be another addition to their ranks…and if it does work both ways." His words die off and he shrugs. "The majority of gifted people are level five, a few are lower. The amount of people, both dark and light at every level from when you hit six gets less and less. The stronger ones of us are rare. We would be an asset on either side."

"Why could I bring back Kade?" I ask, biting my lip.

"Why can you do any of the things you seem capable of, Em? You're special, born of both light and dark. You have more power than you can fathom. Obviously, your gifts go beyond the norm. Also, Kade hadn't shattered… did you notice that?" he replies.

"Well, I didn't think about it at the time, but I guess… yeah. I mean, he was dead, right?" "Yes. He was," Elijah answers.

I clutch my stomach to ward off the ache.

"How?" I rasp out.

"Kade is special, too. Nobody else has golden powers, Em," he tells me, but says no more, and I can feel that he's not willing to elaborate.

I blink a few times, trying to digest the information. Letting it seep in, I move onto my next question, pushing back the burning, knowing I need to ask this one.

"Why can't Kade use my powers?"

Chrysalis

Elijah swallows and blanches slightly. "I don't think I'm the one to answer that. Speak to your Pith when you see him." I bite my bottom lip for a moment then nod.

"Okay, another question, Elijah." This time I run through how to ask what I want to know.

"Em?"

"Before you rescued me, when Kade… when we nearly lost him," I whisper the last part, not wanting to relive that. "Eli, I want to know all of it. From who it was that took us to… well, everything."

He grinds his teeth. "I believe it was our Uncle Zed that came for you. I don't know how he found you or what exactly happened when you were out there. I'm sorry, Em, I don't even know what they had planned for you."

"What do you know?" I snap, agitated.

"I know that they took you to a safe house, one of theirs. We've been doing covert missions for the last three years, watching them, following them, and gathering intel. It was lucky we had our facts straight because it meant that we could find Kade, and then he was able to *connect* with you. As soon as he did, I ran to get you." Elijah hangs his head. "I wasn't too far away when I felt Kade. That was the only thing that saved you both." He clears his throat, his emotions. "It was only because of that we knew so quickly." He thumps his fist against the bed. "If I wasn't on my way back to you... if I wasn't near enough—"

"Stop, Eli. What's the point of dissecting things that don't require it? We can't change anything, and the only information worth analyzing is stuff that's going to help us. You *did* find him, and because of you, both Kade and I are alive today. So just stop, okay? You're making me feel hollow inside," I tell him, clutching my stomach, a mixture of annoyance and sadness echoing in my tone.

"Sorry," he breathes out with a huff. He knows I'm right, but he's still consumed by worry. It has seeped into every pore of his skin.

"I looked like my mother," I murmur, and he nods. "You knew our father was there?" I whisper this time.

"Yeah, we found him a while ago and have been watching him ever since. I'm sorry I told you he was dead, but honestly, the man you saw isn't our father, not anymore." I nod at his words. "He lost mom... Zarina... You already know what can become of us when we lose our Piths. He couldn't deal with it and has been with the dark, I assume, ever since. He left us when things turned bad when houses started being infiltrated. I didn't know back then. I mean I was a kid, they said he'd been killed, both of them had been. I wasn't to know any different. When we started following them, I saw him. I knew... could feel his anger and fear. I tried to speak to him once,

Chrysalis

and he didn't have even an ounce of remorse about leaving us. That's when I knew his light had been extinguished. His heart belongs to the dark now."

"And Zarina?"

"I don't know. I've never seen her, so I can only assume she's dead, but I have no proof." He rolls his eyes upwards. "Although nothing surprises me these days," he tells the ceiling.

"I have so many more questions, but I'm so tired, Eli. I don't think I can carry on."

"Awesome," Elijah tells me with a smile.

"One more, though." He groans but waits for me to ask. "Where is Kade? What exactly is he doing right now?"

"I thought he told you? He's going to meet with a new alliance. Erm... Verum Novum I think they're called."

"What?" I shriek, standing up.

"What's the problem, Em?"

I jump off the bed and scrabble around the floor looking for my sneakers. "The problem is, *Elijah*, that he told me this new group is a mixture of light and dark, that they think I'm their salvation. What the hell he thinks he's doing going to meet with them I don't know, but I intend to find out."

"I think you need to let him do what he needs to keep you safe, Em," Elijah chokes out, looking at the ground.

I pull on my jacket but stop with one arm in and one out, turning to stare at him. "You know where he is *exactly,* don't you? You've been told to answer all my questions and to keep me busy."

He rubs the back of his head, looking sheepish.

"Dammit, Eli!" I shout, then scramble to get out the door.

"Rethink this, Em," Elijah says, trying to grab my arm.

I shake him off. "You're either with me, or you're not. Make up your mind now, 'cause with or without you I'm going to him."

He groans, closing his eyes, and I slip out the door. Not a second later, I hear the door click as his footsteps fall in line with mine. "I'll take you to him," he grinds out.

"Thank you, brother," I answer.

We move out of the hotel, and Elijah leads me across the town until we're walking down an empty street. Buildings line both sides, but they all appear derelict. I stop, looking back down the road. It seems really eerie, something feels off.

"This place is strange," I whisper, turning back around to Elijah. When I do, I see that he's disappeared. I'm alone.

"Elijah!" I shout.

Laughter bounces around the deserted street.

"Elijah!"

CHAPTER 21

The laughter stops, silence replacing it. Fear throbs through me, but there's also something else. Power. It tingles like little spikes of electricity across my body. I take a deep breath in and steady my heart, and I know in that half second that I'm ready to face what's coming.

"Well, well..." a cold female voice pierces the quiet, and I turn toward her. The moment I do, my feet automatically take me a step away. Her face is the mirror image of mine. Her hair is the same. Her clothes are a little out there compared to my taste, but she looks like me— attending a slutty Goth convention. She stands at my height. It's unnerving, it's like looking in a mirror— one that just so happens to talk back.

"So... you're her?" she asks, staring at me with her eyebrow arched and her lip curled. Her mouth moves like mine, but her voice is her own. And that small thing allows me to corral my control, bringing me back into the here and now.

"Who are you?" I ignore her question, instead asking my own. She smirks, and as the corner of her mouth moves, turning her face from impassive to calculating, I open my heart, reaching out to feel her. I move another step backward, hitting a warm, firm and unwelcoming wall I didn't expect. Even while my brain splits two ways for a second, and I momentarily wonder about the person behind me, I'm quickly tugged back to her as I start feeling everything. She's consumed with hate. It's overwhelming and suffocating.

"I'm Elodie, your twin sister, and your worst nightmare," she says, stepping toward me. I'm immediately on alert as the fear flows, and I know Kade will be on his way as strong cold arms grip my shoulders and drain me completely. I have no time to prepare as Elodie punches me square in my jaw, and then pulls back before thrusting her fist forward once again. This time she hits my nose, and the cracking sound echoes through the air as pain ripples throughout my whole face, throbbing and temporarily blinding me.

My head springs backward from the force as everything turns foggy. None of my powers are within reach. They've been doused again. I have no fight as the big, strong, cold wall hoists me over his back. He walks a few feet until I'm next to a truck, then he chucks me in the back like a piece of trash, before jumping in next to me, making sure we're hidden.

I hear Elodie shout, "Stay over there. He'll be here soon. I don't want him to see you."

Seconds later I hear a whoosh, and then I feel him. The pull is as strong as ever. Warmth and power surround me, but I have no strength to move, to alert him to my whereabouts, and I know he can't see me.

"Kade, hey baby," Elodie coos to him. My stomach twists as I fight the urge to be sick as well as the need to shove my hand so far into her face that she'll never look like me again.

He doesn't say anything, and I can feel his hesitation.

"What's wrong, baby? Don't you want to go somewhere, just you and me? We've been so busy lately. It would be good to take some time for ourselves." I can see her through a crack in the truck bed, she's running her fingers up his chest, and the power that was absent is starting to sizzle in my fingers.

"Night, night." A deep rumble sounds from beside me, and then pain grips my scalp before my head is slammed down. I keep my eyes closed for a second as I roll away from the great lump crouching in front of me, standing sentry. He has a mixture of boredom and lust for Elodie flowing through him. I listen to his thoughts for a few seconds. Suddenly, pictures, words, and understanding starts filtering into my brain. He *is* level eight, but only because he has the power to drain people's gifts. But it feels wrong, like he isn't supposed to have that power. More information rushes through, and knowledge I can't imagine I'll ever even need settles itself somewhere inside me. It fills me so fast that it's like my inner being is on fire. I want to scream and cry and jump into a lake to take away the burn.

It's coming… clear your mind, Emery. The time is now.

Everything is suddenly silent, like I've lost my hearing. I know, without a shadow of a doubt that the Convergence is here, and it's ready to become a part of me. I breathe in and out, slowly, calmly, knowing this will change things. My brain switches, and I realize that since I could hear the thoughts of the meat-bag next to me, then I must be able to talk to Kade. But as soon as I think it, I know that there's no time to take in what's happening with him, as right then a green aura surrounds my whole body. It lifts me an inch off the truck bed. I glance toward Meat-bag, but he's entirely focused on Elodie and Kade. Abruptly, he jumps over the edge of the truck, running away, and that's when my back arches. Pain and power flow through every vein within me as the green aura turns electric, sparkling like glitter in the air surrounding me. My eyes shut of their own accord, and I see maybe a thousand women.

Chrysalis

We were many. We move to one. We came before. Now is your turn. You are worthy, we will give you our light, our love and our protection.

My eyes pop open and calm settles over me. The green mist has gone, and I'm once again lying on the truck bed. I sit up and see Kade fighting both Meat-bag and Elodie, as well as five other dark beings, his eyes are blazing golden, and I can feel his rage. I jump over the edge of the truck and jog over to him. The minute I arrive, three of the dark beings turn to focus their attention on me. They all rush me at once.

"No!" Kade bellows, jumping in front of me and fighting them while moving backward, trying to herd me away.

Kade. I have this. I whisper into his head.

No. I need you safe, Emery.

Trust me. I'm still whispering to him, and this time I place my hand against his back. His shoulders drop, and although I can feel it pains him to do it, he steps to the side, allowing me to face off against them. I glance over to Elodie. The smirk that she wears drops quickly from her face when she looks at my nose. I reach up and touch the tip. It's not broken anymore. It's completely healed. I smirk at her. She's the one I want. I can still see her purring at Kade while touching his chest, and it sets my teeth on edge. Meat-bag stands next to Elodie, seemingly guarding her, and two dark beings run at me as Kade fights the other three. I raise my hand, clench my fist, and punch the first one in his stomach. He's thrown backward into the other guy and they both fly across the street, smashing against the truck then dropping to the ground. I'm momentarily stunned at my strength.

Kade finishes off the three guys he was dealing with, and they shatter before my eyes. Meat-bag runs at Kade just as six more seem to come from nowhere. Two of them come toward me, and I notice Elodie trying to slip away. Something inside snaps, and I raise one hand allowing a crackle of white power to flow from my fingers. I capture and hold her in the air while I use my other hand to blast the men coming at me. They try to shoot me with their powers, but mine are stronger, and they all panic as one by one they shatter. The two I knocked over earlier get up, making their way over to join back in the fight.

"Oof..." Kade grunts beside me. I glance at him and see his eyes have dimmed as he fights Meat-bag and the other four men. My mind works quickly, picking up everything and assessing it like I'm a machine.

I'm draining your power! I shout in his head.

He doesn't reply, and it's then that I drop Elodie. She scrambles away. I pull everything back into me and watch as Kade's eyes ignite. Before I have a chance to help him, Kade has dispatched everyone except Meatbag, who Elodie calls, and he quickly

Chrysalis

runs to her. They disappear as the last remaining dark beings shatter.

"Kade!" I cry out, running to him, but his strength is all there now. He doesn't need me to worry. I can feel anger, I can almost taste it on my tongue. His arms pulse, as does a vein in his neck as his jaw ticks.

"You should never have put yourself in harm's way, Emery. Something could have happened to you," he says, shaking me gently.

Emery.

"Elijah!" I shout, and Kade steps away, looking around. "He's in my head, Kade. He's here somewhere." *Elijah, where are you?*

Feel me, Em. Even though he's talking in my head, I can hear the struggle in his voice. It's like he's gasping for breath.

I close my eyes and feel him. Pictures run through my head, and I open my eyes moving forward.

"Princess, where are you going?" Kade asks, all anger now forgotten.

"I can feel him. I can't explain it, except to say it's like a beacon in my stomach, and the closer I get to him, the hotter it burns."

"Okay, I have your back," he tells me.

"You always do, Kade. You're my savior."

He follows me as I move toward the heat. Upon reaching a pile of dirt, everything that was dragging me to Elijah vanishes, and I feel nothing. *Elijah!* I scream internally.

"There's nothing, Kade!" This time, my scream is external.

"I feel it," he replies.

"What?"

"This space, it's some kind of hold. There's something here that's tramping down our powers. Now don't freak out," he says, cupping both sides of my face. "I think Elijah is buried beneath this dirt, and there's something that's been placed with him to stop his powers."

"What the what?" I shout.

"Calm down, princess, I'm going to get him out."

"How? You have no power either," I cry out, panic rattling around, trying to push up my throat.

"I have my strength. Step away until you feel your powers and watch my back, okay?" I nod, immediately taking a few steps away until I feel revitalized. I know Kade doesn't really need me to watch his back, he just wants me in a place where I can restore my powers, enough to protect myself.

Elijah. I try again, but he doesn't answer me.

Kade digs into the clay-like substance until I can't see him. It takes three whole minutes—

I count every second—until he pulls a mud-covered, unmoving Elijah from the hole.

"Elijah!" he shouts, shaking him, but he just lays limp in his arms. I rush over and grab Elijah, tugging him, trying to pull him from the pit.

Chrysalis

"Wait," Kade says, and before I have a chance to complain, he feels up Elijah's arms then moves to his neck. "Here," he says, pulling something from his skin. It looks a little like a pellet. "I don't know exactly what this is. I'll have to get Tristan to look at it." He drags Elijah away. "There's still something here dousing our powers. Otherwise yours wouldn't have evaporated when we were in the vicinity." He turns from me to Elijah and shakes him gently. "Elijah. Elijah." He shakes him again, more vigorously this time. Panic builds in my chest as I realize that Elijah is dying. I spread my hands out and close my eyes.

Revive. I whisper in my head and open my eyes to see white and blue light flowing from my fingers into my brother's chest.

Elijah splutters and moves to sit up. Unable to get his breath, he falls back to the ground. I slump next to him.

"Elijah, slow breaths."

Kade leans down and passes him a bottle of water. I have no idea where it came from, but I don't care as I watch Elijah sip gently until his breathing is easy and his eyes are alert.

"I'm fine. I'm good," he tells us both, and I know he's right. I can feel him.

"Come on," Kade says. He picks me up, and we rush through the streets.

"You know I can run myself, I'm fast enough," I tell him as we fly.

"I like you here. I know I have you. That you're safe. I can breathe when you're in my arms." We say nothing else until he stops.

"Where are we?" I ask, looking around at the lone house and hundreds of trees surrounding us.

"This is one of our safe houses. The others are here," Kade tells me as I feel a gust of wind blow past me, and I know that Elijah has arrived too.

"If you've been here with the others, why did you leave me at the hotel?" I ask him, feeling something scratching across my heart.

"I had to know you were safe. I didn't know if this place had been found by the dark, and I wasn't going to risk your safety," he tells me, and just like that, a balm covers the surface wounds.

Once we're inside, the hellos pass quickly until we're all sitting around a table in the kitchen.

We go through what happened with Elodie, and everyone is as shocked as me that I have a twin. Elijah is probably the most freaked out. He tells us that when the dart hit him from behind, he was paralyzed and then lost his powers. He was buried but never saw Elodie. I decide to move the conversation away from long-lost siblings, mainly because I can't deal with that situation right now. "Why were you visiting that group of people, Kade?" I ask him, narrowing my eyes. "Shouldn't you be

Chrysalis

figuring out a way to get Sicily back?" I demand, my words causing a sharp pain to slice through Elijah and then, in turn, me.

"We were figuring out a plan," Tess tells me quietly. I look between Tess and Kade.

He sighs, shaking his head. "I wanted to find out if they really were friendly," he tells me. "I wanted to see if they truly believe that you are the Chosen One." He smirks at me, and I roll my eyes.

"And? What was your conclusion… oh Wise One?" I mock.

"I'm not sure, I was only there for an hour before I felt your fear and rushed away. Their leader, Genna, she explained how they want to shape a new future. She was very accommodating before I left."

"I bet she was." The words slip out of my mouth, and I slap my hand across it as everyone except Kade bursts out laughing. He stares at me, his eyebrows showing his surprise.

Are you jealous? He whispers into my head. I don't answer him, but an image of a woman, a year or two older than me, long gray hair with cat-like silver eyes passes through my brain. A smirk adorns her face and she wields a knife.

"Come on, it's been a long few days. Let's get some rest and talk over our plans on getting Sicily back tomorrow," Kade says, and everyone gets up, moving in different directions to go to their rooms.

When everyone has gone, Kade walks over to me and pulls me out of my chair. "Emery, were you jealous?" he asks me again.

"Honestly, I don't know," I answer, staring into his eyes. I'm not sure what my brain is trying to tell me, but I do know that there's something I need to decipher when it comes to my instant feelings about Genna. I just need to be sure what they are before I share.

"You don't ever need to be jealous," he tells me moving closer. "When I met Elodie today, she threw me for about a second. Then I knew she wasn't you," he says, cupping my cheek. "There's only one woman I love. There is only one of you, Emery, and I'll accept no poor substitutions," he tells me, leaning down and placing his lips on mine. He kisses me slowly, lovingly, before pulling back and looking into my eyes.

"Remember, it's always been you," he tells me, and just like always, those words wrap around me and make me feel safe and loved. "Today you used my powers, I could feel it draining me. I told you before that we were different than all other Piths. I think when we get a chance, we need to look into that further. Even so, my mind hasn't changed… if you're in danger, you tap into my powers, Emery, even if it drains me."

"Kade, the Convergence entered me today. It flows through me now."

Chrysalis

Kade stills and closes his eyes, taking a breath through his nose and blowing it out of his mouth.

"If that's the case, then why didn't you use the power of the Convergence when we were fighting?" he asks softly.

"I don't know. There was a green light, and I knew it had entered me. I saw a bunch of women, all the ones who have come before. There was a reason it didn't choose Elijah or you. It only takes women," I tell him.

He tilts his head from one side to the other, clicking his neck.

"I know it's in me, but so far the only thing I seem to have been given is a bunch of information. I can see things, and I know things I never did before. I have no idea where the knowledge has come from, and to be honest, I wonder why I even need to know it, but that's all it's passed on to me so far."

Kade runs his hand over my head and down my hair, threading his fingers around the back of my neck.

"Everything that has come before and everything they foresee is all being passed to you. You'll have the rest of the Convergence power once you've been filled with knowledge," he tells me. "I've read about it, but I thought it was lore. It seems, however, that it's the way of the Convergence. Now we need to find someone to pass it on to."

He pulls me toward a bedroom and ushers me inside. "Go take a shower and get ready for bed. I'll be back," he says, dropping a kiss on my forehead.

Ten minutes later and I'm finally alone. I find the quicker I move my brain from one thing to another, the quicker my thought process picks up until I'm not trying to think about anything at all. My brain just naturally carries me through a multitude of thoughts. It started when I climbed into the shower. Needing to get some space and not having had time to soak in the bath earlier like I wanted—Elijah having arrived sooner than I thought he would—the moment the hot water hit my skin, my quiet introspection ran riot. I needed to push out the feelings rolling off everyone in the house, especially Elijah, he seemed unable to lock himself up today, and I was suffocating in his emotions. Closing my eyes and trying to clear my head hadn't worked. Instead my brain bounced from one thought to the other until ten new things passed through me every second. Now I can't stop it, and I can't control it.

Suddenly, and without warning, everything stops, and I see a picture behind my closed eyes. Molly. It's like the Convergence is trying to pull me to her. It wants to slip into her. I haven't seen Jenny or Molly for years. Not since they were rescued by their aunt. Sadness tingles down my spine as I wonder what they've been doing, if they're okay, and whether they're still close. I know I'll be seeing them again.

Chrysalis

The Convergence wants Molly, and I don't think I have a choice in the matter.

I sigh and lean forward, resting my forehead against the tile, letting my arms hang by my sides. I can only hope that if this is the choice of the Convergence, it's because pure goodness still flows through them both and that they don't hate me when all is said and done.

Chapter 22

After my shower, I decide to stay in the bedroom. I find some clean PJs in the closet and light the log fire in the corner of the room. The space isn't big, but it's old, and therefore has lots to take in. The large window has twelve panes of glass all separated by thin pieces of wood in a rectangular pattern. The window ledge has names etched into it, and on the inside of the frame going up the wall are blue handprints that start small and get bigger. At first glance, I think it's a family, but on closer inspection I notice that the index finger has the same print on it, so it must be handprints the same person as they were growing through the years.

I hear the door open behind me, but I had already known Kade was coming. I could feel him before he entered.

"You okay?" he questions, clicking it shut.

"I can see the fingerprints," I blurt.

Chrysalis

"What?" he replies, confused.

"Here," I say, pointing to the hands splayed up the inner window wall.

He walks over and wraps his arms around me, resting his chin on my shoulder.

"These hands, they get bigger. At first, I thought they were a family, you know… baby, child, teenager, mother, and father. But then I looked closer and could see that the fingerprints match. I realized it's the same person as they grew."

He nods against my shoulder but says nothing as his warmth coats my back.

"I can see the fingerprints, that's crazy!" I exclaim. "How can I see that? I mean, they're tiny and probably years old." I shake my head in wonder.

"Princess, you have gifts. You must know by now that anything is possible? Even so, *Excelled Vision* is one of the most basic of our powers. You used it when you saw Zed from the balcony of the hotel before… remember? You were seven floors up but could still see him." I still in his arms as my heart flutters.

"What is it?" Kade asks, moving away, then turning me to face him.

"I've just remembered something. Elijah told me he suspected that the person who attacked and captured us was Zed, but it wasn't him. I saw that man's face. That day in the hotel, when I looked down seven flights, I saw Zed. Clearly. They weren't the same person."

Kade's eyebrows cave, and his eyes narrow, then he glances to the door. "Then we need to find out who he was." He turns back to me. "But not tonight." He steps forward and claims my hand, pulling me toward the bed. "Tonight, we rest." He gets in and pulls me with him until I'm lying on his chest with his arms wrapped securely around me. He kisses the top of my head, and I close my eyes, feeling a peace envelop me.

"Kade, we should talk about our powers, and our connection," I say softly as I lay tucked in his arms.

"I have a feeling we'll be working this stuff out for the rest of our lives. Without someone to ask, we have no way of knowing anything for sure. What I do know is that you can use my powers at will. As I've explained before, that's because you're classed as the Princess of your House, and as such, you can summon my powers whenever you need them." He sighs and breathes against my hair. "The others can use the powers of their Piths, but to drain their other half completely, they would need to have a *Consume* power, and typically that power only seems to naturally occur on the dark side."

"Naturally occur?" I pick out the words that cause confusion.

"This power is one that can be developed."

Chrysalis

"You can do that?" I screech slightly, amazed that I'm only now learning this.

"I don't know," Kade murmurs into my hair.

"What do you mean?" I ask, pushing myself back until I'm sitting upright. I twist myself so that I'm looking back at him.

He rubs his forehead. "There's so much I don't know, Emery. Like I've said before, a lot of it is lore. I don't know what's true and what isn't. They say that some powers can be developed, taught or learned. It supposedly takes a lot of time, and it can kill those who are too weak. I don't know if it's true," he tells me, shrugging slightly.

"So why are we different?"

He leans forward and cups me around the back of the head, pulling me until my face is an inch from his.

"Because you're special," he whispers, then kisses me on the lips. It's chaste, and I'm lying back in his arms before I really know what's happened. "With the others, tapping into each other's powers doesn't harm them, they can only use about twenty percent at any one time. You, Emery...you can take *all* my power, without even realizing it."

"Why? How?" I fire the questions out, still confused.

"I told you before, baby, you need to be protected. It's natural, the way things have always been. If someone was attacking you, and you needed to drain me to save yourself, that's what I would expect you to do." The words reverberate around my head and slowly piece together to cause a crack in my heart.

"But—" I try to argue.

"No. This isn't a negotiation," he says, and I can feel him tense against my cheek. "Anyway, if that time came, you wouldn't have a choice… like you didn't earlier."

"That scared me," I admit. "I can't live without you," I whisper.

"I know," he tells me, softer now as his warm breath blows across my face. "Sleep now, princess, there will always be more to discuss."

I don't really have a choice, and I feel my eyelids drooping as sleep takes me.

The sun blinds me, and I blink, trying to bring myself into the present.

"Em, you need to get up." Elijah's voice filters through the mush that is my brain.

"Where's Kade?" I croak out.

"He's gone to do some scoping."

"Scoping?"

"Just get up, shower, throw some clothes on, and come down to the kitchen, you can have breakfast, and we'll fill you in," he tells me. Then he leans over, kissing my forehead before moving to the door and

Chrysalis

leaving me alone. I stretch my arms out behind my head, and they slip under the pillows. Something catches my hand, and I pull at it. It's a note from Kade.

> Morning Princess,
> You looked so serene sleeping, and you still need to rest, so I left you be. I'll be out for a few hours, but I'll see you later. Don't leave the house, and make sure to keep Elijah up to date if anything new passes to you from the Convergence.
> Remember, it's always been you, Emery.

I clutch the piece of paper to my chest like a silly schoolgirl.

Rushing through my shower, I find more clothes in the closet and dresser. Then slipping the note into the back pocket of my jeans, I make my way downstairs. "We're going to break their shit. His too." The voice belongs to Tristan, and I stop, shocked at the vehemence in his tone. Tristan is the joker. He's always making me laugh and seems light-hearted most of the time. I move again, purposely bouncing around the corner, trying to inject something lighter into the atmosphere.

"There she is!" Tristan stands up and walks over, pulling me in for a hug. All the anger has disappeared, and he's back to being the guy I've grown close to. I hold him.

"We're going to get Sicily back, right?" I ask.

He pulls away and looks me straight in the eye. "Oh, hell yeah!" His reply is firm and confident.

I make my way over to the table where Tess is sitting. She's studying her hands and biting her lip, nervousness spills out of every inch of her body. I sit down next to her and know I have to finally do this. "Tess, I'm sorry I used the *Entrance* power on you. In my defense, I didn't realize I was using it, and what's worse is that I've left it so long to apologize to you. I know you were away on different missions, and we haven't had a lot of time together, but I should have made the time to say sorry."

She looks up at me. "Don't beat yourself up about it. I know you didn't realize what you were doing. I'm not mad. And anyway, we have been on different schedules for the last while, so don't sweat it."

I nod at her answer. "What's up then?" I question, feeling that something else is bothering her.

"I was getting close to Miles," she tells me, dropping her gaze back down to the table.

I jerk my head back at her reply. I'm unsure what that has to do with anything, and my silence makes her glance across at me. She obviously reads my confusion well.

"Miles is dark." Her words make my chest compress. "I should have known, I could have

Chrysalis

stopped him." She's very clearly beating herself up about this.

"Why is this on you? Hasn't Miles been here for a while?" I ask.

Tristan comes and sits next to me, placing his hand on my shoulder. "Yeah, he's been with us for a couple of years. It isn't Tess's fault," he says, his voice flat like it isn't the first time he's said the words or tried to convince Tess of her innocence, something she's obviously struggling with.

"He dated Sicily before he became part of our group. Only for a short while… maybe three months before she split with him. She's always had a thing for Elijah," he says glancing across the room to my brother. "Even though he was blind to it until recently. At that point Tess wasn't living with us. She was still staying with our Aunt and Uncle over on the south side. I guess she met Miles and they dated." Tristan's jaw ticks as he tells the story. "About a year after Tess moved in with us, Miles followed. It was awkward at first, but Miles convinced us all that he was into Tess. Kade was the last to take the bait. He never trusted him, though. Never."

"I brought him here, and now he's betrayed us," Tess whimpers.

"Hey, stop it, he had us all fooled." Tristan's voice is warm as he comforts his twin, slipping his arm around her shoulder and hugging her to him.

Without warning, a crippling pain flows up my spine, and I can't help the scream that rips from my throat as my body automatically arches.

"Someone has her in a *Command Grip*. I'm going outside. Watch them," Elijah orders Tristan.

I can't think clearly as a throbbing engulfs my head, and I can feel the internal battle my body is waging, trying to keep control while someone else is attempting to climb into me, endeavoring to take over. The pain running down my spine spreads across the backs of my legs and up my arms. It feels like my skin is being ripped from my flesh. I have to close my eyes.

No! Stop! I scream, and instantly everything stops.

There's no movement, no sound, no life. I slowly open my eyes back up and realize that I've frozen *everything.*

Princess. I hear Kade whisper to me. I jerk and know in my bones that this is his power, the one that slows time. That's what I'm using, and that means I could be draining him. I close my eyes once more, and without a second thought I scream, S*tart!* Into the darkness behind my eyelids. The pain comes back all at once and in full force, bringing me to my knees, but I know that I'd do anything to keep from hurting Kade.

"Emery, I have you." I hear Tristan whisper as he lifts me into his arms, cradling my body to his. "Just breathe, sweetheart. Elijah will stop them. Kade will

Chrysalis

be here soon. Nothing's going to hurt you." I feel his breath caressing my face and try to focus on his warmth, knowing that Kade won't be far away. It takes everything I have to try and ignore the agony inside. It's like it's alive and trying to spread from the inside out.

The pain stops. It's so sudden that I can't control my body as all my limbs fall limp in Tristan's arms. He leans down and rests his head against mine, stroking my hair.

"You're okay," he tells me gently. "You're okay."

"You wanna pass my girl to me." Kade's voice is tight as he growls the demand through his teeth. Even so, it fills my chest with peace, knowing he's okay. I'm passed into the arms of the man I belong to. Without saying a word, he carries me up the stairs and into bed, and I fall to sleep with his hand holding my face. When I wake, Kade is still sitting on the edge of the bed beside me.

"They tried to control you," he tells me, staring at the wall with his back still to me. "I went out to do some recon. I thought you'd be okay here, I thought this place was secure." He rubs the back of his head. "But it's not. I was careless, Miles knows about this safe house. We have to move from here soon."

I say nothing, just reach up, placing my hand on his back. His muscles bunch, then they relax under my palm.

"You needed to sleep. That gift is rare and strong. I've never seen anyone resist it, not until you. You were in so much pain because your body wouldn't allow you to be controlled. I felt you and knew that you needed to sleep. You were exhausted, but now we must move. We still need to go and get Sicily, and today something occurred to me that hasn't before." He twists on the bed and stares at me. His eyes move languidly across my face, taking in all my features before he brings his thumb to my bottom lip and runs over it with his pad. "We're stronger together." His eyes close for a second, and a look of pain passes over his face. "I was away, doing something that someone else could have done when I felt your pain. It sliced through me. It was like my heart was being ripped out. It wasn't pain enough to stop me coming for you, but I knew that I was close to losing you. What I didn't know was that they were trying to take you over, and I would have lost you to the dark… not to death… and honestly? I'm not sure which is worse. I do know that neither option is acceptable." Leaning down to me, he kisses my lips softly. "If you're with me, then no matter what happens, I know I can protect you. There may be times when we're split up, but leaving on purpose to go on a mission is a no-go, not anymore. My place is beside you."

"I love you," I say the first words I've spoken to him today, and I know that's all I need to say when

Chrysalis

his eyes glow golden and he kisses me again, harder, faster, and more passionately.

"Come on, grab some things. There should be a backpack in the closet. We need to leave in ten minutes."

I nod as he moves out of the room, then I touch my lips for a second, knowing that with all the threats on my life right now, there's still nothing I regret. I've been with them for just under three weeks, but it feels like three years.

I'm still learning, still gaining power, but this is where I belong.

This is my family.

And I know, dead or alive, Kade is my future.

Chapter 23

Where are we going? I ask Elijah.

We're once again walking in a line, except for Katarina, who has been sent on a recon mission, apparently scouring for new dark locations. Much like us, they have many safe houses, at least that's what Elijah tells me. Katarina is searching for the ones we don't already know about. Kade leads us, and Elijah pulls up the rear. I've been placed in the middle with Tristan to my front and Tess at my back. Kade told me this was because I'm the one everyone's after. An attack could come from anywhere, and he wanted me protected. There was no point arguing. When we first started walking, I was talking to him internally, then he began ignoring me, so I started talking out loud. That's when he decided to send his thoughts to me. Those thoughts didn't make me happy. Basically, he told me I was to be quiet so that he could concentrate. Something

Chrysalis

about how he wasn't going to let anyone get in the way of my safety—not even me. I rolled my eyes but also shut up.

I hear Elijah's chuckle in my head. *Baby sister, I never know what your boy has up his sleeve.*

Well, I asked Kade, but he told me to stop talking and pay attention to our surroundings, I whine.

Maybe you should listen to him, Elijah says. *Watch out, Emery!*

The moment Elijah's scream rips through my brain, I jerk backward, smacking straight into Tess and am just missed by a flying body aiming straight for me. Looking to my left, I see that the culprit is already on the ground with Kade on top raining punches down onto his face. No sooner have I taken in that situation when more people run in from different directions, crashing into us all.

I feel a fist connect with my cheek, and I fall back until I'm horizontal and looking up at a fuzzy sky. Blinking a couple of times and trying to decide whether my eye is about to pop out of its socket, I manage to catch a momentary glimpse of Kade. What I see has all the power in me buzzing to life. He's underneath a mound of bodies. I can't see a way out for him, there must be at least thirty people on top of him, while another twenty swarm around the outside, waiting for their shot.

He's gonna die. The words rush through my head, and the next time the guy on top of me lands a punch, he shatters into pieces without me doing anything. I jump up and realize there are at least ten more surrounding me. Their smirks match the arrogance rolling off them.

"Little Emery Laird, I'm going to enjoy this," a guy on my right sneers.

"Do it, Marr," someone says behind me.

But I don't take my eyes off him… *Marr*. His stance is confident. He thinks he's got this in the bag. The dirty blond hair, slightly unkempt, and a scar running from his cheekbone to his eye and up through his eyebrow gives him a menacing air. However, as I take a breath and reach inside of me I know, with one hundred percent confidence, that I have no fear of him, of any of them.

The only thing that I'm scared of now is that someone from my family is going to die.

My eyes move around the field. Just like the small group that I'm surrounded by, the others are in similar situations. I risk a glance in Kade's direction and see at least three people shatter one after the other, which means he's fighting them off.

Before I know what's happening, two men move toward me from behind, but the moment they touch my arms, they both shatter. I can feel a spiraling power starting in my core. It's pushing throughout me, spreading quickly, and my body can only yield to it. My breath hitches, and I know Marr thinks it's because I'm scared when I see him smile. My limbs

Chrysalis

pull taut, and the sensation clawing underneath my skin is unlike any other I've experienced in my life. My blood is buzzing. It must be moving through my body so fast, because it feels like it's going to burst through my skin. Suddenly, everything calms, and I'm finally able to take a deep breath. At that moment, I know I'll be okay. My main focus now has to be the others.

"Well, well, it seems the little princess here does have her charms," Marr speaks again. "Forgive me for being so rude. I'm Marr, and I'm going to kill you today," he tells me with a matter-of-fact tone. All the other people surrounding me laugh.

I tilt my head slightly. "I don't think she'll let you," I tell him with a smile.

I watch as his eyes flash with anger.

"And who might *she* be?" he snarls at me.

"The Convergence." My smile spreads, and I watch for the briefest of seconds as his eyes widen, then I feel the heat and power that has collected in my chest pulse, before shooting out of me from every side, bathing the bodies surrounding me in a green light. They all shatter. I look around at the fighting and don't know where to go first. *Tess*. The voice inside me says, and I know that's not my family speaking to me, I know this is *her* talking to me. My eyes zoom in on Tess, who's fighting one on one with a guy, but she's still surrounded by a group, and it doesn't look like she's going to make it much longer.

Without even taking a second to think about what I'm doing, I shoot my arm out and blast the guy she's fighting with. This time it's a blue light that hits him, and I know it's all me. *Her* powers are always green. The guy drops to the floor, and his eyes roll back in his head. My brain catches up with my actions, and I know that he could have only been a level five. He didn't shatter, and she was struggling to hold him off, which means Tess is weaker than I thought.

Making my way into the circle of the enemy, I push my back against hers and whisper in her head. *I'm here. We'll be fine. Trust me.* She doesn't say anything, and I don't know whether she's heard me or not. I don't have time to dwell on it though, because a woman comes at me, anger in her eyes and teeth bared.

"That was my brother you just killed," she hisses.

I raise my eyebrows and hit her with the same blue light that I used on her brother only moments before. Her eyes widen before she shatters.

"Sorry," I whisper, before turning to the next in line.

Tess jerks behind me as I simultaneously fight with my fists and my powers, until one by one all the assailants are either shattered or on the ground. It doesn't take long.

Chrysalis

"Tristan!" Tess screams, and my eyes take in the scene not twenty feet away.

Tristan is being held by three big men, while two others are throwing blast after blast at him, and it looks like he's minutes away from death. Before I get a chance to help, Elijah is there. In the blink of an eye, he's killed the two men who were taking potshots, and he's ripped another from Tristan's arm.

I run over and get in-between the other two. Tristan groans as they pull him in different directions, the strain in his voice betraying how close we are to losing him. I reach forward and grab one of the men by his head. I pull, and it's clear that he's no match for me as we both fall backward with him on top. I push the top half of my body up – taking his with me - and cock my elbow, giving myself enough room to slam my fist into his nose.

There wouldn't be much force in my thrust if it weren't for my super strength. The crack that follows tells all— his nose is now broken as he falls sideways off me. There's a quiet moment where everything slows down, and I take time to breathe. Closing my eyes, I assess everyone internally. Tess is scared, but even so she's fighting full on with the other man who held Tristan. Her heart beats fast, and she hasn't got a lot left in her.

Tristan is angry and trying to pull himself together to fight, to help his sister. He'll be okay now, and between them they will dispose of the guy.

Elijah is completely focused, so focused that he can't feel me digging inside. The man trying to kill him will die, Elijah is about to land the final blow.

I center myself and move to Kade. He's angry, frustrated, and scared. He doesn't know where I am. I look across the expanse of field that separates us. He's still surrounded. There are less of them, but he's buried and won't be able to see me. *I need to get to him.*

The thought brings me back to the now, and everything moves at normal speed again. I stand up, and quickly, the man I was fighting jumps up to face me, blood running through his fingers as he cups his nose. "Bitch," he seethes.

His eyes widen, and my hand flickers just once before I bring it to his chest, touching him until he splinters, then I turn on my heel and run. My legs burn as I pump them harder than I knew possible while I almost fly across the field. When I get to the mound of men and women, all dark beings, I listen to their feelings—they just want to kill us, *kill Kade*.

A few individuals that surround the scrum of fighting bodies move. The moment they do, I'm spotted. A group of six dark beings, all wearing the same sinister smile, break from the thrall and approach me. They form a circle around me and gesture to one another, smirking and laughing, like a woman is no match for them, despite who I am. Arrogance rolls off them menacingly.

Chrysalis

A tall man with a ginger tinge to his hair takes a step forward. "So this is the famous Laird? I thought she was supposed to be stronger than her brother... she doesn't look more than a level two, barely worth calling her gifted," he says to the others. They laugh again but stop the moment another man steps into the circle. "Marvin." The ginger one gasps and steps back. Marvin looks exactly like the first dark guy I shattered today, not ten minutes ago, except he doesn't have a scar.

"Be careful, do not underestimate this one. She has an insane amount of power, much like Kade over there," he tells his men—calmly, quietly, knowingly. The men grumble, but I look toward Kade, who only seems to be left with about thirty men to overcome. He looks fresh, like he's just had a full night's sleep followed by a hearty breakfast, not like he's just fought twenty plus people off. Elijah moves up beside him, and they're now back to back.

Princess, tell me you're okay? Kade demands.

I'm okay. I reply calmly, and I know, even though I have seven men to contend with, that I'll win. Just like I knew the outcomes of Tess, Tristan, and Elijah's fights only moments ago. I also know without a shadow of a doubt that these people cannot harm me. The Convergence is telling me so.

"She has more powers than we realize, probably than *she* realizes. We need to get her to Elodie," Marvin tells the herd.

The name of my twin causes a ripple effect in my stomach like my lunch is trying to crawl up my insides, ready to make a reappearance.

Marvin smiles. "We're tied to our twins in a way that you cannot yet begin to imagine. Normal humans always talk about having a connection, but when you have gifts, it's so much more than that. Elodie is strong, maybe not as strong as you… yet." He rubs his chin and glances toward Kade before bringing his attention back to me with a frown. "For some reason, you took the majority of the power, but we just need to get you back to her and then she can *Siphon* from you." He quickly glances back to Kade, and I know what he's looking for. He wants to check that both Kade and Elijah are occupied.

"Grab her," he commands, and the other men move quickly but not quick enough.

Move! I demand in my own head, and in less than a blink, I am out of the circle and standing in front of Marvin. His eyes widen momentarily before he schools his features. I can see a plume of green smoke where I just stood, and I can feel that Kade and Elijah are distracted from their fighting worried about me.

I'm fine. I reassure them both before my attention moves to Marvin.

"You know, you look like him," I speak quietly, loud enough so he can hear me, but not enough to make a statement. The words I'm choosing are for impact, not attention, and I know they're coming from *her*. I don't have a vengeful streak, but, without a shadow of a doubt, *she does*.

"Him?" he replies, full of arrogance that doesn't mask his concern.

I reach up and run my finger down his face while biting my lip. "Except he had a scar," I say with a smirk. Two things happen right then. Kade appears and wrenches my hand away from Marvin's face, then pulls me behind him. At the same time a roar bellows from Marvin's mouth.

"You killed him!" he screams. "You. Will. Pay."

He jumps back and Kade pulls me until my chest is pressed against his back.

We will talk about you touching him later. He confirms what I already knew, and I smile inwardly.

"Bring her!" Marvin commands with a shout, and the remaining dark beings move to his back, creating a space between us all, like a divide. Light on one side, dark on the other. The contrast is stark and permeates the air around us. Shuffling comes from behind the group of twenty or so dark beings that are left, and it looks like someone is transported in at the back of the group. A gap forms as two figures move through the tunnel. "Sicily..." I gasp as I spot her, but my body stills when I see Elodie next to her.

"This is what I can do to you, little girl. I will take everyone you love and I will kill them..." Marvin shouts, then smirks as he continues, speaking low, "…or I will turn them."

"No!" Elijah yells, and my body jolts, coming out of the freeze I was suspended in.

Sicily laughs and spreads her arms wide. Red power runs down her arms, zapping above the skin, waiting to pounce on something. I can see more dark beings arriving behind the group already here. Quickly their army builds.

Emery, you need to use my powers and get out of here. Now. Kade tells me.

No. No way am I leaving without you, I reply, knowing that no matter what he says, I'm not going anywhere.

Dammit, Emery. We can't win this. There are too many of them. Tess is out. Tristan doesn't have much left. You, me, and Elijah cannot overcome them all.

Yes, we can. I tell him with certainty.

Before we have an option to talk, decide, or make a plan, Elijah screams and runs toward the group. I take in the kiss between Sicily and Marvin and rush after my brother. Kade is a few steps in front of me in the two seconds it takes to reach Elijah. Suddenly the war erupts.

There's screaming and shouting, fists thrown, bodies flying, and a mass of powers used. I take down at least six when they rush at me and hit a wall of my *Revive* power. It prickles across me and they break into shards before disappearing forever.

Chrysalis

As I continue fighting, throwing power out of my fingers and battling hand to hand, I notice that we're winning. I glance over my right shoulder and quickly scan the field. There are a lot more people now. I catch Kade's eyes, and he must see my confusion. *Verum Novum. They came to help us*, he tells me, and my eyes zone in on a woman fighting close to his side. I let out an involuntary growl.

Only you, princess. It's always been you, Kade soothes, sending a quick smile my way before turning back to the fight.

For one delightful moment, I know we're going to win. We're going to survive, and it's bliss.

Then my world is rocked. I didn't see it coming.

"Elijah," I scream suddenly, surprising myself. I drop to my knees as I feel his pain and anguish but mainly his hate. I've never felt that from him. It's almost—*dark*.

I look up to Kade. The fighters are backing away... receding. We've won. Yet somehow, I know we haven't. My eyes find Elijah. His arm is around Sicily. His eyes are low, and an evil grin dances on his face.

"I guess it's time to be with my other sister now," he tells me, laughing.

Elijah. I plead for him to hear me. *Elijah.*

Em... I... His voice fades away and he says no more.

Elijah! I scream as I feel Kade lift me into his arms.

We turn and so do they, all retreating to fight another day. I feel my body slump in Kade's arms, and I allow my head to fall back. As I do my eyes catch Elijah's. He's the last to turn, and for a split second I see something beautiful in his eyes, something loving, something regretful. Then Sicily grabs his hand and pulls him away.

Elijah.

I get no reply.

Chrysalis

CHAPTER 24

"Emery, it's been three days," I hear Kade say, but I ignore him. My focus is on Sid as I punch him once, then kick twice.

Punch. Kick, kick. Punch. Kick, kick. Sid is the man-shaped punch bag that lives in the gym, which is actually the basement of the new house we're holed up in. For the last three days, the body opponent bag—who I lovingly call Sid—has been my only friend. I know Kade's worried, but I need to do this, to expel the pain so I can breathe.

A month ago I was alone, I could only rely on myself, and then I got given a family. Now they're slowly being taken away—one by one. It's cruel and heartbreaking, and if I stop for even a second, I'm afraid I'll break. I keep going because I have to focus, and right now Sid is what I need. I couldn't sleep last night, so I came back down to the gym. The last straw for Kade, it seems, was finding me asleep on the mats this morning.

Now he won't leave me alone.

"I'm fine, Kade," I grind out between punches.

"Emery, stop! I know you're not fine."

I spin around and advance on him. "You know *nothing*," I shout, slamming my closed fists against his chest. He doesn't move, not even an inch. "All my life I've had nobody. *No one,*" I continue on my rampage, yelling in Kade's face, but he still doesn't move, taking what I throw his way, all my anger, all my fear… all my pain. "Then I find out that this whole time I had a brother. And that he *loved* me." I waiver, sadness coupled with worry is unfurling in my stomach, and I'm not sure that I can hold it in anymore. "He watched over me. He *wanted* to be my big brother." The fight seeps out of me, replaced entirely by grief, as I hang my head. "I had no one," I whisper, as my voice hitches. The emotion finally bubbles up my throat, and I try desperately to swallow it back down.

Suddenly, I'm in Kade's arms, and I'm not sure if I fell forward, or if he pulled me into his protective embrace. I close my eyes and smell him, taking in the soft fabric detergent. The tears that were forming now freely travel down my cheeks, dripping off my chin and onto his chest. I feel like I'm never going to stop crying, but I couldn't hold it in any longer. Kade just stands with me the whole time, holding me, supporting me, and loving me. When I open my eyes fully and see that my skin has a blue glow, I try to jump back, away from Kade, but he holds me still.

"Shhh... princess, it seems your powers mean me no harm." He breathes the words across my cheek, and I let my eyes flutter closed once again, laying my face against his chest. For that one moment, I allow him to be my strength.

I stand still for a few long minutes until Kade lifts me up in his arms. "I'm taking you to bed. You need to rest." He looks down at me with such love in his eyes that it feels like my heart is smiling when it misses a beat.

I breathe in and slowly blow the breath back out.

"He's my brother, and now he's gone. What am I supposed to do with that?" I ask him, my voice gravelly.

"Know that he's *not* gone. Know that when all is said and done, we will do everything we can to get him back. And *know* Emery, that he loves you. Dark or light, Elijah has never loved anyone as much as he loves you. I don't care that Elodie is your twin. She is not, and never will be you. Elijah will be disappointed with what he finds, and he'll come back to you. For now, though, we have to let him go. He needs to do what he feels he must, and we have other things to attend to." He carries me into the bedroom that we now share and lays me down. "For now, my princess, sleep." He strokes the hair away from my face and lays on the bed next to me.

"Don't you have important leader-type things to be doing?" I ask him, my voice strained.

"Nothing's more important to me than you, Emery. Nothing. Now, sleep."

I turn toward him and lay in his outstretched arms, relishing the warmth of his chest, and I finally allow myself to sleep, without thought.

Elijah! I scream in my head as I bolt up from the bed. For a moment upon waking, everything was good, everything was as it should be, and all was right with the world. Then I remembered.

"Shhh… it's okay." Kade sits up next to me and pulls my body into his.

I rub my eyes, holding my hands over them for a second longer than necessary, using my palms as a shield so I don't have to face reality. Kade gently pries them away. He leans forward and kisses me.

"Ewww, don't kiss me. I have morning breath," I tell him.

He smiles and claims my lips again. "I don't care." Kade threads his fingers into my hair at the back of my neck. "I love your taste, no matter the time of day." I sink into him and let his power alight mine. Kade pulls back and smiles. "It seems your

Chrysalis

powers can't stay dormant around me anymore." I glance down and see that my skin is once again lit up like a Christmas tree.

"How…" The words die in my throat as I look back to Kade, and his eyes are golden. They look like they're on fire, and I know it's because of the make-out session we just had.

"I'm not sure, but I know it's all you, because you're glowing blue," he answers my unspoken question.

"Red is when you tap into the dark side. I've never seen you do that, but I've been told you did when you revived me from death."

His words elicit an involuntary shiver as I remember Kade's lifeless body that day. Everything inside me clenches as I strain not to vomit.

Kade ignores my reaction. "White is the light side. Blue comes from you. They're your own gifts, from your House. Whether you were light or dark, that would be your power, and that means you don't need to draw power from either side. Then you have green, which is the Convergence. I've also seen gold used by you. That color appears when you use my powers."

My eyes widen, and I tuck that little piece of information away. I need to make sure that if the power that comes out of me is ever gold, I switch it off immediately.

"So… my power… it doesn't hurt you because I love you?" I murmur.

He nods and his eyes let me in, all his love flows through me, filling the gaps and the crevices of pain.

He grips my chin in his fingers and pulls my face to his. "I love you… as my Pith, my muse, my friend, my love… my forever. And I promise I *will* do whatever it takes to make everything right in your life." I'm able to stare into his golden, determined eyes for a second before his lips crash into mine again.

You chase all the bad thoughts away, and no matter what the future holds, as long as I have you, I know I'll be living my life exactly how I always dreamed. You're the answer to all my questions, Kade. I open my feelings to him as our mouths dance and caress.

Kade lays me down without moving his lips from mine, and his hand slips onto untouched places of my body. As his fingers massage me, heat infuses my pores, and I can feel a buzzing in my core, right under my belly button. It's like having a thousand grains of sand swishing around causing tiny scrapes and cuts but in the most beautiful way. It's telling me I'm alive and that right now I don't want to be anywhere else but here with Kade. The only way to douse the sharp grains of sand is if he takes me, finally. Allowing him to break my seal would mean that I'm

Chrysalis

truly his. It's what I've wanted since he became mine.

I'm ready, Kade. Please, I need you. Love me.

All at once Kade pulls back so he's sitting up.

"W-what?" My brain is struggling to catch up with the speed at which he pulled away from me.

"I'm sorry, Emery, I shouldn't have let it get that far." His words are pushing through his teeth, and his chest rises and falls with such speed that I worry he's about to hyperventilate.

"Kade, w-what's wrong with me?" I sit up to face him, finally asking the question that always plays on my mind every time he pulls away.

His head jerks up, and he locks into place for a moment. I blink a couple of times trying to clear my thoughts and my eyes before he relaxes. His shoulders hunch forward slightly, and his black hair - which has grown a little over the last month - drops into his eye. I push it back, and he captures my hand, holding my palm to his cheek. "I want you," he whispers. "God… I want you so bad it's painful. But I can't. I won't risk you, not with the way things are right now. I can't."

"I don't know what you mean, Kade." The tremble in my voice is unmistakable, and his eyes soften on me.

"If we take it to that next step, Emery, I will then be able to claim all your powers, like you can claim mine. I would be able to take them at will. That's how it works for you, the female Head of the House." His eyes bore into mine, pleading with me to understand.

"But, I'd be happy for you to use my powers. Then I know you'd be even safer."

"No." He pulls away, shaking his head.

"Kade?" I whimper.

"If I were in a fight, I might take your power without realizing it. Then you would be helpless. Could you imagine if I fought and won, only to find out that you hadn't survived because you had no protection… that I took your powers from you?" He grabs my head, a hand on each side and once again lowers me down onto the bed, but this time he hovers above, staring at me like I'm *his* answer. "No, if I lost you, I'd give up. I'd let them take me, kill me, turn me… do whatever they want."

"Kade, don't say that." My reply is weak as I try to rein in the pain currently stomping on all the sand grains that were in my stomach.

"It's true, princess. There's no world for me if you aren't alive in it. I need you by my side, and if that means we need to wait a while to physically love each other, then that's no hardship for me, as long as I get to kiss your beautiful full lips," he says, his voice barely there before he kisses me again.

I keep my eyes open this time, and so does he for a few seconds, allowing his golden gaze to pin me before I watch his eyelids close, his long lashes stroking the top of his cheekbone. Then I follow suit

Chrysalis

and close mine, and I know that this right here will always be enough for me. If this was how I was going to live the rest of my life, whether it be minutes or centuries, not a second of being in Kade's arms would ever be a waste.

Chapter 25

This is probably the nicest place we've stopped at in the last three weeks. I never realized just how many safe houses Kade had secured for us.

Five days after Elijah went with Sicily and Elodie, we moved on from where we were staying. Tristan told me it was a risk, staying there as long as we did. It was too close to where the fight had happened, but I know Kade had allowed us to stay in case Elijah came back. He's my brother and Kade loves me, so he partly did it for me.

But Elijah is also Kade's best friend, a member of his family, and I know that Kade wants him back as much as I do. We all do.

Since then we've moved through five different houses. This one is my favorite. It's light and airy, modern and pretty big. All the rooms are on the ground floor, but it's not cramped in any way. The

Chrysalis

biggest bonus is that the house sits on a cliff and has a huge backyard that overlooks the sea.

I stand at the boundary edge. The only noise is that of the waves crashing against the shore. It's the closest to peace I've felt since Elijah left. But it's not quite peaceful enough.

My hairs stand on end as I feel Kade before he arrives. His raw magnetism is connected to me. It's times like these—when he's walking up behind me—that I can sense the Pith connection between us.

"I'm okay," I whisper softly. My voice floats forward on the breeze, and anyone else, anyone *normal,* wouldn't be able to hear me.

"You're not, but it's understandable, princess," Kade answers, proving that he *always* hears me, even when I'm trying to hide.

I wrap my arms around my chest and let the first few tears silently escape from my eyes. I've cried so much. I'm sick of myself, but I feel helpless. Kade steps up behind me. His body is pressed against mine, the warmth somehow managing to wrap me up, even though his arms remain at his side.

"He'll come back," he states, his voice firm above my head.

Biting my lip, I continue to stare at the sea. Waves crash against the cliff's edge, and although I can't see it, I can hear every movement. My senses are even sharper now that the Convergence has fully awakened inside of me. I thought there would be a struggle for supremacy, I thought there might be a chance I'd lose myself to *her*. I've since found out that that's never going to happen. She's quiet, in the background, but supportive. She'll only appear if I'm in danger, and at those points I'm not going to complain about her arrival.

However, I can feel her drain and her pull on my natural self. I haven't told anyone, not even Kade. He'd only worry more than he already does, and I sense that there's little I can do. She'll need to move into a pure host before I'll be safe, but for now at least, I'm not condemning anyone to this life. I know she'll look after them forever, that they'll be safe, but I'm not sure if my old friends are the way to go. I sense the Convergence should settle in someone without family to mourn, someone who'd be happy outliving their current life expectancy and would welcome this new, unknown and sometimes slightly strange world into their lives.

"Emery, he'll come back," Kade tells me again.

I nod, allowing a small sigh to blow through my lips. Turning, I bury my face into his strong, firm, and warm chest. Instantly, Kade wraps his arms around me, dropping his chin onto my head.

"I love you. Always you." Kade's voice vibrates through me, and I close my eyes, relaxing into him. Leaning down, he lifts me up easily, placing his arm up my spine for support. I wrap my legs around his waist and pull back slightly. We stare at each other.

Chrysalis

Cupping the side of his face, my eyes follow my thumb as it moves across his cheek and brushes over his mouth. I admire the contrast of his face, the strong edged jawline against his full, soft lips. Then I take in his straight manly nose and the deep hazel eyes, big and full of love.

I know that he's waiting for me to do something. The last few days, he's taken a step back, allowed me space without actually giving me any real distance or time away from him. Every touch has been instigated by me.

He's making me set the pace, and as I take in his face, I realize that I've missed his touch and his kisses. I don't want to push him away. Slowly I lean forward and tentatively place my lips against his, keeping our eyes locked the whole time. I move my mouth slowly, peppering kisses along his lips.

Suddenly his eyes ignite. Gold blazes fiercely, and it's enough for me to let my eyelids close as Kade takes over. With one hand still supporting my back, he pushes the other into the hair at my nape. Nipping my lower lip, his tongue trails along the top. Automatically I open, aware of what he wants and knowing I need it too. The second I do, he slips his tongue into my mouth and touches it to mine, causing them to dance together. Kade groans down my throat, and I feel my whole body tingle. It's the first time in days that I've felt something real. My skin is prickly with need, and my heart beats like it might punch out of my chest at any moment.

Kade pulls away, and it takes a second for my brain to catch up. When it does, I open my eyes and find I'm looking directly into his. The gold is still blazing, and there's a lopsided smile on his face. The fingers threaded in my hair move slowly, massaging my scalp.

"I've missed you," I murmur, touching our lips lightly again.

"I've missed you too, princess. It's been hell without you." Kade's voice is gentle, but I can hear his pain laced within the words.

"I'm sorry," I return. My heart squeezes as a sad smile appears on his face.

"Nothing to be sorry for, Emery. None of this was your doing. I have to say, if *you* were taken and converted to the dark…" he trails off, scrubbing a hand down his face. I keep my silence, waiting for him to finish whatever it is he needs to say, "I'd do the same as him."

I gasp at his words, my mouth hanging open. Kade's eyes drop, and then I feel him move until he places his fingertips under my chin, closing my mouth.

"It shouldn't surprise you, princess. You're my world, above all else, above everything I fight for and everything I am. More than the battle of light and

Chrysalis

dark, and above the destruction of this world as we know it, there's you. Above everything."

My heart speeds up as the meaning of his words penetrate, and the emotions completely overwhelm me. A mixture of amazement, concern, and mostly relief, takes over my body, and I close my eyes, dropping my forehead to his.

"It's not right," he mutters, and my body stills in his arms. "I don't mean what I feel for you isn't right." My breath releases, and I sink into him. "It's the fact that I'd let the whole world destroy itself before I'd let you go. That's never been the way I've worked, but…" he shakes his head as a chuckle bubbles up from his throat, "…although I'm pissed that Elijah has gone, I do understand. If it were you…" He shrugs, and I get what Kade's telling me. He pulls his head away until our eyes meet. "You're the most important person in the world to me. Nothing comes above you, Emery. Nothing." He stares at me for a few seconds before he moves, keeping me in his arms. He strides across the yard, into the house, and right to the back where our bedroom is. He doesn't use his super speed, instead going slowly, the whole time keeping his eyes trained on mine. Sitting on the edge of the bed, with my body still wrapped around him, Kade's eyes move over every inch of my face, leisurely, lovingly, almost like he's scared he'll forget.

"Kade?"

"I can't have sex with you."

My body jerks in his arms. Shock and concern course through my veins because I know we've already touched on this subject.

"W-What?"

"I'm sorry to throw it out there like this again. It's just been on my mind since we spoke. It's what I want, so much that my actions are almost uncontrollable. But it can't happen, and I'm now starting to realize that it's going to be a long time before there's even the smallest chance that it can."

"Kade." My voice wobbles with emotion.

"Shhh…" He strokes the side of my face.

"You've told me this. Why are you bringing it up again?" I whisper, frowning.

Kade shakes his head as his eyes dip down. "I just can't. If we did, I'd be worried the whole time. Then, at every fight I'd be scared that I'd take your powers. It's not an emotion I'm used to feeling. I wouldn't be able to fight properly. I'd put you, me, and others in danger. I need to always be at my best, and at the top of my list is keeping you safe." His eyes move back to meet mine, and once again the golden color is like a fire facing me.

"Kade, why are you repeating yourself?" I snap my question.

"Because I need your help." He admits, leaning his forehead against mine. "I need you to control the situation too. I'm not sure I'll always be able to stop."

His hand spasms on my back and a sigh slips from his mouth. "You're my weakness, Emery."

I pull myself back so I can look at him, but I can't speak. Kade slides his hand into my hair and drags me closer, so our lips nearly touch. "I plan on spending my life with you, Princess, however long that might be." His words elicit a pain that jabs at my heart. The thought of not having Kade with me makes me feel hollow, and I know that I would be barely a shell if he left me.

I blink away the tears gathered in the corner of my eyes, the ones I'd been ignoring.

"Hey…" Kade soothes, kissing my wet, salty lips. "We have the rest of our lives to do what we want. Let's just be happy we've found each other and try to stop the dark from winning." He kisses me again and moves back, placing his thumb on my lower lip. I quickly open my mouth and take his thumb between my teeth, letting my tongue swipe across the pad. His eyelids dip as the hunger swirls. "Doesn't mean we can't do other things… lots of other things," he rumbles slipping his hand up the back of my top and tracing circles against my spine.

My breath catches in the back of my throat, and I close my eyes, leaning my forehead back against his. "Kade, just tonight, do whatever you can to help me forget, to make sure I remember what we're fighting for. Show me that you love me," I plead.

Kade lifts us both back up, then lays me down in the center of our bed.

"That, I'm more than willing and able to do. Your wish is my command, princess," Kade tells me, then proceeds to show me just how much I'm loved, without breaking the protection I have on me. Protection that he deems so important, his love for me bigger than anything else I've ever known, felt or seen before.

Chrysalis

CHAPTER 26

"Elijah!" I shout. He's across the field, but I know he can hear me. I see his head twitch when I call his name, but just like all the other times, he ignores me. "Elijah!" I scream louder, pushing my voice. I try to move, but both my legs are still Earthed. I swing my head to the right, seeing the back of the dark being who took control of my feet. A strange sense of familiarity washes over me, and I tilt my head slightly, wishing he would turn around.

"There's no point trying. You should know when you're beat," Elodie sing-songs from next to me. I spin my head the other way, glaring at her, trying to shoot fire from my eyes, even though I know it's not one of my gifts.

Hopefully, it's not a gift anyone else possesses, either. "You shouldn't believe everything that comes out of your own mouth, Elodie. You may have Elijah right now, but he'll come back to the light. He'll *come back to me. It doesn't matter what you say because I know it's true. I'll never give up," I hiss out, anger bubbling inside me.*

Elodie throws her head back laughing. I feel the frown spread on my forehead and start paying attention to the situation I've found myself in. I slowly peruse the field. Dark beings are everywhere, and they seem to be creating some kind of machine—no, it's a building. They're building a base. I can see a tent, inside of which it looks like something is being worked on. Vials, both empty and containing liquids, are visible as are people with white coats… maybe scientists?

Elijah pulls my focus toward him when he walks up, standing shoulder to shoulder with my twin.

"Emery." My full name sounds wrong coming from him now. I'm so used to him calling me Em. It's cold and emotionless, and I want to scream at him. Instead, I feel the tears start gathering, and that only makes me angrier. I pull at my feet but cannot seem to gain my freedom.

"Elijah," I whisper, and there's a glimpse of him, a momentary flash of pain crosses his face. It's so quick that I find myself wondering if I imagined it.

"We're building a lab… making lots of interesting serums," he tells me, his voice flat.

"Serums?" I mimic.

Chrysalis

"We're creating things to help the dark be the leaders that they should've always been," he says as his eyes bore into mine.

"Elijah, enough," Elodie snaps out.

"You'll never win." I shout to them both. I can't hold the tears back anymore, and they erupt onto my cheeks. My heart hurts looking at Elijah and seeing someone completely different than the brother I love.

"I don't think there's much you can do anymore," Elodie snarls with a smirk on her face. I stare at her pinched face. "You see, we have something special now. Something that would have been your saving grace before, but now you have nothing."

Her words cause my insides to freeze. The tone in her voice makes me realize that she isn't bluffing. The dark being that was to my right, the one who has me grounded walks over, but I can't look at him. My eyes are pinned to Elodie's, and I somehow know that he's been doing it. I see an arm slip around her shoulder in my peripheral vision. At that moment my body becomes my own again, and my eyes immediately move to the being that's connected to the arm. Soft full lips, masculine jaw, straight nose, dark hair, and hazel eyes look back at me.

There's no emotion in his face.

"Kade?" I whisper.

He says nothing, just stares at me bored.

"See, I have everything you had, everything you ever wanted... ever needed. It's all mine now." She *throws her head back once again and laughs. I take a stumbling step backward, then I do the only thing my body will allow, I run, and run… and run. A sharp pain slams into my back, and my eyes close as my body hurtles toward the ground.*

I bolt upright, gasping for breath, my heart beating a mile a minute.

"Breathe, Emery. You're okay, I'm here," Kade murmurs in my ear before I shriek and edge away from him, falling off the bed.

"Hey, it's okay," he soothes as I crab crawl backward until my head hits the wall. Kade frowns, worry and sadness warring on his face. The door swings open, bouncing off the wall and an arm pushes out as it tries to slam closed again.

"What's going on?" Tristan questions, stepping into the room with Tess trailing behind, rubbing her eyes.

"There was a bang and some shouting. Is everything okay?" Katarina asks, rushing in after them.

Kade looks like he's about to lose his patience as my eyes flit between them all.

"Do you not think if something were wrong I would handle it?" he grumbles, pulling his hand down his face.

"Dude, you can never be sure," Tristan returns, and I smile slowly.

Chrysalis

Kade sees it and uses that moment to edge forward, carefully like I'm a feral animal.

"It's okay," I tell him, biting my lip. "I had a bad dream." I look down at the floor and quickly move myself into a sitting position, my back against the wall and my knees pulled up to my chest.

Kade crawls over and sits next to me. Our bodies touch each other, but he makes no move to hold me, obviously fearing I might freak out again. I make a decision and thread my fingers through his. The second I do, his body relaxes.

"You turned dark. You were against me with Elijah, and you were… you… you…" I squeeze my eyes shut and take a breath.

"What, princess?" Kade demands tentatively.

"You were with Elodie. You chose her, over me." The words are so quiet coming from my mouth that I wonder for a moment if he could hear me, even with his super hearing. I know my answer when his body stills and his hand squeezes mine so tightly that it begins to hurt.

"You're hurting me," I tell him, and instantly he loosens his grip.

"Sorry, baby. You just… even in a dream, you can't… never… just…" Kade starts to say, then abruptly he stops speaking and pulls away from me. He stands up, clenching his fist, and punches the wall, before stalking out the room, slamming the door behind him.

I stare at Katarina, Tristan, and Tess with my mouth hanging open. Their faces pretty much mirror my own.

"I'll go speak to him," Tristan spits before storming out the room too, Tess hot on his heels.

Katarina tentatively walks over to me. "Come on." She eases me up off the floor and brings me back to bed, tucking me in. I feel my heart rate pick up now that I'm back in the bed again. With the rapid beating of my heart lately, it's lucky that I now have full control of my own powers. Although, new ones can appear at any time, so I know that I have to be mindful.

"He'll come back and tell you what his issue is. You know he can be moody sometimes… Mr. Growly, remember?" she says, smiling down at me, trying to make me feel better. I give her a small smile back.

"Thanks, Katarina," I whisper, and I genuinely feel grateful that she's taking care of me right now. We haven't been close, but I can see lately how much she's been trying. "I'm fine now, you go back to sleep," I whisper, squeezing her hand.

She nods and walks out, giving one backward glance at the door.

I stay squashed in the middle of the bed, between Kade's pillows and my own and stare at the ceiling.

I miss you. My mind whispers to a lost Elijah.

Chrysalis

I miss you, too, Em. I almost believe I hear him whisper back.

"Emery." The word wakes me from the restless sleep I'd managed to find after hours of lying here alone and scared. "Emery."

I open my eyes and look straight into Kade's. They're hazel now, no gold shimmers back at me in the early morning light.

"Kade, what do you want?" My voice is flat, and it's because I've had enough.

Enough of everything.

I live in a world I never knew about after being left alone for so many years of my life. The brother who pulled me from my sad existence has now left me, instead, joining with a twin sister I never knew I had. A twin I hasten to add, who seems to want to kill me. Add that to a father who also tried to kill me. I've seen people die, and I, myself have killed. My life is not my own anymore since the Convergence now inhabits my body, and it *will* kill me if it stays inside too long. It seems that not only the life of my brother, but also the fate of the whole world lays solely with me, Kade, and our ever-shrinking group. To add insult to injury, Kade explains nothing, decides to storm out, after punching the wall, when I've had a nightmare—one that scared me to my bones, leaving me alone in the bed, afraid and thinking that it may have been better if I died that night. I stare at him, this handsome man, and I know he loves me, truly loves me, as I do him. I'm just not sure how much more I can take until I end up breaking. I can feel my resolve crumbling already.

"I'm sorry. Really I am. Stop thinking what you're thinking right now," he says quietly, sitting carefully on the edge of the bed. He doesn't touch me, yet again. It's something he does less and less lately.

"I know." I reply with the words he needs to hear. I'm not entirely sure I believe them right now, but I'm still willing to give him this.

"Don't lie to me, Emery. You may not be thinking out loud, but your feelings are as clear as day to me. I'm your other half. Even if I wasn't your Pith, I love you and I know you. I know I don't deserve it but… talk to me… please."

I sigh and sit up. "Why did you storm out?" My question is snapped at him. I don't mean it to come out so harshly, but I won't apologize when he hasn't explained anything to me yet.

"Your dream—"

"Nightmare," I correct.

"Nightmare." His voice has a tinge of anger. "I needed to check some books, needed to make some calls.

But it only confirmed what I already thought."

Chrysalis

"Which was what?" I reply.

"There were stories, years ago. There are some who can talk in dreams or nightmares," he tells me.

I gasp, pulling both my hands to my mouth.

"They say that some people can talk, make dreams go the way they want, influence people even." Kade drops his head, shaking it from side to side, before looking back at me. "There are those… although I've never met even one… who can supposedly make actions happen *in dreams*. For example, if they want you to cut your hair off when you wake up, you've already done it. If they want you to steal something, upon waking it's in your room. And if they want you to die—"

"Upon waking—"

"There is no waking!" he shouts. "If they want you to die then you *don't* wake up." His breathing is rapid and harsh. I watch his chest heaving up and down.

"So you think…" I get to my knees in the bed and shuffle forward, placing my hands on his shoulders and steadying myself while the reality sinks in, "…that somehow Elodie might be trying to kill me in my sleep?"

He looks up at me, his face blank. "Yeah." He clenches his jaw, a muscle jumps in his cheek. Suddenly he lifts me up and pins me to the wall. His hands hold my butt and he stares into my eyes. "I don't care what new tricks they have, they're not going to get you. I'll kill them all if I have to." Kade grits his teeth with rage.

"We'll figure it out," I reply gently, even though I have no clue how.

We stay in that position for a while, Kade working out whatever he needs to while holding me tight.

Hours later, as the sun is starting to set once again, he leads me to the back of the yard. There's a bench now, near the cliff edge, a blanket and cooler rest at the side on the grass.

"Sit," he tells me, once we're at the bench. He then proceeds to lay the blanket across my lap before grabbing the cooler and placing it down next to me.

I look over to him, raising my eyebrows.

Kade shrugs. "If we can't have normal once in a while, then what's the point?" he explains with a smile, while passing me a Diet Coke.

"Thanks," I say, grabbing the Coke, then leaning over to touch my lips to his. "For everything."

He smiles back at me, and my heart skips a beat.

We sit quietly listening to the sounds of the ocean beyond, both in our own heads. Kade fits my hand in his and strokes his thumb over mine. He then readjusts until I'm in the crook of his arm, my cheek resting on his chest. I wonder if this is what it would be like, if there were no threats, if our lives were crazy-free. My eyes feel heavy, and I start allowing myself to doze. Suddenly, something at the edge of

Chrysalis

my conscious is nudged by my falling asleep, and I sit bolt upright.

"Emery?" Kade sits up with me.

I turn toward him. The concerned look on his face registers in my mind, and I flap my hands slightly.

Kade grabs a hold of my flailing arms. "Emery, what is it?" He centers my focus, and I nod.

"You never asked me about my dream... nightmare," I tell him.

His eyebrows pull in. "Yes princess, I did. You told me about Elodie," he growls.

"No. I mean yes, I did. But there was more. I never thought about it at the time, I was too upset when you left," I explain and watch as he grinds his teeth. "It's possible for people to talk to you in dreams?" Kade nods at my question. "Tell me, has Elijah ever been able to do that?"

"I don't know. I mean, he's never told me of such a gift," he replies, and I feel my shoulders drop as my hope deflates. "Princess, that doesn't mean he hasn't got that ability. This gift usually comes from people who can speak with their mind, like you and Elijah. Maybe he has it but never told me. Maybe he never knew. There is one other possibility," he says, looking out to the sea and rubbing his chin.

"What?" I ask, grabbing his shoulder.

Kade turns back to me. "Well, if he has that ability, maybe it's something he can only use with you, since you're his sister and have family gifts. Or maybe he knows that Elodie has that power, and he's able as your brother to jump into her dreams himself." Kade shakes his head. "Either way, why is it you're asking? What happened in the dream that makes you think this might be possible?" he questions, sitting back on the bench and pulling me into his lap almost subconsciously. I snuggle into him and start explaining the nightmare, the whole of it. As soon as I stop talking, Kade asks, "Is that *all* of the dream?"

I nod in reply, and he shoots out of his seat, dropping my feet to the ground. I've barely stopped myself from falling over before he rushes off, his lightning speed means he's disappeared in less than a second.

I drop my head back and give the sky my angry glare, before stomping off after him at a much more sedate pace. I feel him before I even reach the house. Panic, concern, and excitement fill the air as I walk into the office.

"Get me Genna... *now*," Kade growls into the phone. My body goes on alert as I wonder who he's talking to.

"Genna, I need you to meet me in the morning. No, Emery will be there, too," he tells her, looking toward me. "There's new information that I'm not willing to discuss over the phone. We need to meet, and we need to talk strategy. This has been going on for too long. Planning is good. Doing is better," he

Chrysalis

snaps, holding out his hand to me. I take a few steps forward and reach out to him. The second our fingers entwine he pulls me down to sit on his lap once again. "Yeah, that works. Okay, ten it is. Bye."

"What was all that?" I ask, turning to face him.

"Verum Novum. That was their leader, Genna," he tells me.

"The woman you were fighting side by side with?" I grind out.

Kade smiles and strokes my face. "Firstly, princess, *always you*. You should know that by now. Secondly, she has no interest in me, so stop worrying. Most of her interest lies with you. I should be the one concerned. If it weren't for what I already know I would wonder whether she had a thing for you. She talks almost nonstop about you." He chuckles easily.

But I pull away from him, my body stiffening. "How much do you talk to her... exactly?" I ask, harsher than I mean.

Kade laughs, throwing his head back, and I watch him for a moment as his shoulders shake and his throat moves, enjoyment filling every inch of his face.

Dammit. I'm supposed to be annoyed with him.
"Kade!"

"Sorry, princess. It's just your jealousy is unnecessary, but at the same time... I kind of like it," he tells, me capturing my lips with his own, and as usual, I melt into him. He leads our kiss, but ends it before we get carried away. "You have to know, Genna will never look at me like that. She's only a friend, trust me on that. We can take a chance on her. I know that you've yet to get to know her, but you know *me*, you know I would never do anything to put you in harm's way. If you let the jealousy slide for a moment and think, you'll know. Please, trust me."

I nod at him and lay my cheek against his. "I trust you, completely. I'm meeting her tomorrow then?" I ask.

"Yeah, but this isn't a get-to-know-you chat. This is a strategy meeting. We've been talking regularly, but that's only because she has people that believe in what she does. They believe you're the savior for us all. Well, you *and* me. Apparently, it's the two of us together that will save the light from the dark. We'll be able to stop the darkness from taking over the world. We've been trying to put plans in place and scope things out. With the information you've just given us… if it turns out to be real… we could make a massive change," he tells me.

I nod and smile, glad that finally things might be starting to piece together. I know it's going to be a long road, but we have to start somewhere and now we have a bigger army at our backs.

"There's something else that I don't think has registered with you yet, Emery," Kade tells me softly. I look to him, tipping my head in question. "If Elijah did step into Elodie's dream… and remember,

Chrysalis

this is a big if… maybe, just maybe, he isn't lost to them. I mean, that would be a huge piece of information to pass along. If it's true, we could make a real dent if we pull that new venture apart. It would be a massive win for us."

My chest compresses as my brain thinks back, over and over again as his words loop. I miss Eli. It's like losing a limb, I could learn to live without him, but I'll never be whole.

"We'll know more once we've done some recon and can find out if this place does exist." He shrugs his shoulder. "If it does, that's a big way for him to tell us that he's still with us." Kade pulls me into him, and I bury my face into his shoulder.

"I love you," I tell him, my voice muffled.

"Always you, princess."

Chapter 27

That's her then.
She doesn't look like anything special.
I wonder if she's really supposed to save us all?
Wow, she's so pretty.
I would love to be her, I mean look at the guy she's got with her. Hot Damn!

People keep talking and I can't seem to clear my mind. Since I came into my gifts—really came into them—I haven't been around this many people at once.

This morning Kade woke me with sweet kisses and then whisked me down to breakfast, telling me that Tess, Tristan, and Katarina had all gone out. We ate croissants on our bench, listening to the waves, then I took a shower. After that, we took a walk along the cliff top. It was all so normal, holding hands and just *being*.

Chrysalis

I knew why Kade was doing it. He thinks I needs a slice of normal, and he's probably right. It was bliss, and I know I'll hold on to the moments he gives me, especially while we face the other—much less normal— side of our existence.

I take in the large room as we wait for Genna. It's a huge space, laid out like a dining hall. An old bar sits at one end, dark brown wood that's worn and cracked, but gleaming all the same, arches around a small floor space. A large mirror makes up the wall behind, and glass shelves hold both glasses and liquor. An old man stands behind the bar, propping himself up and chatting to people, who I assume are regulars, content on their barstools. To the left there's a type of food court. Three different serving stations are set up, all seeming to provide different food to choose from. Tables and chairs are strewn about haphazardly, and there are at least a hundred people sitting and talking, eating and watching.

This place seems to be some sort of compound. We rode here on Kade's bike. It took us over an hour, but the ride was nice, holding him as the wind blew around us. We turned off onto a path I never would have noticed and traveled at least five miles up a dirt track. This opened out into a wide field enclosed by tall trees. There were more dirt tracks, three to the right and two on the left, but Kade rode straight ahead. I pulled my head away from his and tried to see where he was going, but even with my super abilities I couldn't see a gap. My grip on his shoulders tightened and I'm pretty sure I heard him chuckle, although I couldn't be sure as everything was muffled due to the motorcycle helmet he insisted I wore. As we approached the trees, Kade didn't slow down, not even for a second. Just before impact, I closed my eyes. After another second, I realized my body was still in one piece. I opened them again, blinking as they adjusted to the dark tunnel we were flying down. It felt like we rode through that tunnel for hours, and after emerging into the light, I hissed at the sting my eyes felt.

We entered a town. People watched us as we passed until finally Kade stopped at a large building that looked like a typical City Hall. He got off the bike and pulled me off after him, taking my helmet from my head. That led to me snapping at him that I wasn't a child, which in turn caused his lip to twitch while he tried to hold off a smile. He threaded his fingers through mine and pulled me up some steps and into the building. Without any haste, we navigated through small corridors until we arrived at this very spot.

We've only been waiting for Genna for ten minutes, but I'm apprehensive. Worried thoughts have invaded my mind, and I can't seem to calm myself.

"Something feels off," I whisper to Kade.

Chrysalis

He looks at me with a sharp nod. "You feel it, too," he states but says nothing else, moving to look back toward the door.

I can't question him further as suddenly he pulls me up out of my seat and gently tucks me into his chest. His eyes are trained on four people who have just entered the room. The first person is a woman. She's a couple of inches taller than me, about five foot seven and has curves that make me want to cry out with jealousy. Her long gray hair falls dead straight down her back, and when she steps up to me I can see the violet tinge to her silver eyes.

This was the woman Kade was fighting next to—this is Genna.

Instantly she smiles, and it lights up her whole face. A dimple appears on each cheek, and I have visions of stabbing her with cocktail sticks, but she makes me swallow the green-eyed monster when her excitement shines through.

"Emery, finally!" she breathes out in wonder, then proceeds to fling her arms around me in a tight hug.

"H-Hi," I stutter, slipping out of her embrace. Immediately Kade pulls me back to him.

"Genna." He nods his head but makes no move toward her, which allows me to relax slightly.

"Kade, good to see you. Please, won't you both sit?" She gestures to the table and we all settle into chairs. "This is Lucian," she says, her hand aiming for a tall, well built, brown-haired man sitting to her right. He's clean cut and suited, his eyes are sharp, and no emotion passes over his face. "The one next to him is Leon, his brother." I move my gaze to the next tall, well built, brown-haired man. This one however, is rough. His beard is at least four days old, and his hair is slightly longer and unkempt. A scar curves from the side of his neck, across his lower cheek, and just touches the tip of his upper lip, where he wears the biggest grin as his green eyes sparkle.

"Been waiting to meet you," he says, leaning across the table toward me. Kade growls and I bite my lower lip to stop the smile trying to form as I feel his jealousy zinging in my stomach.

At least it's not just me who gets jealous, I say to him, the humor in my words unmistakable.

Kade just grunts in my head which makes me bite my lip harder.

"Thank you, I guess?" What starts in a statement ends in a question as I lean over and take his offered hand. He doesn't shake it. Instead, he stands up and bows over the table kissing the back of my knuckles.

Kade growls again, and Leon holds up his hands in surrender. "Okay, big guy, I'm just saying hello. I know she's your Pith," he tells Kade, winking at me. He sits back in his seat, leaning toward his brother, and his single whispered word, "Shame," isn't quite quiet enough.

Chrysalis

Kade jerks forward, and that's when the man to Genna's left speaks, "Enough, Leon. This is not how these talks need to start," he snaps.

Leon immediately sits back. "My apologies." His words are aimed at Kade, who just nods in acceptance.

"I'm Goran. Genna is my sister. Between us, we lead the Verum Novum. Welcome to our compound, our base, our strategic headquarters…" he looks around, a small smile playing on his lips, before turning back to us, "…our home."

"It's extremely well hidden," I state and then feel like an idiot for pointing out the obvious.

"It is. We cannot go by normal human measures when hiding. The dark are a forceful opponent, and are never to be underestimated. We've been setting this site up for many years, since before your birth, Emery," Goran tells me.

I feel my eyes widen as shock registers.

"There is much to tell you. You are still new, my dear. Some things will come with time. Some… we can guide you," he says, pinning me with his eyes.

Kade sits next to me and is looking around the room. I can feel something coming from him—a displeasure of sorts. Without warning, he suddenly leans across the table. His move is threatening, and his gaze is aimed at Goran. "You have humans here," he hisses. Nobody moves as I convulse in my seat. Kade squeezes my thigh.

"Kade, you do not know the full extent of our organization. It reaches far beyond the normal spans of light and dark. I can explain all the inner workings over time, but I fear this is not for the here and now," Goran explains calmly.

Kade still doesn't move, and I think maybe it's time for me to talk him down. But before I have the chance, Genna speaks, "Kade, please, you must understand, we have no time. You trust me... remember?" she says, and her hand snakes across the table. She's about to clasp onto Kade's arm when I put my own hand in the way, thwarting her attempt.

She smiles at me, but I can't see past the anger that's sparking to life on my fingertips. Kade grabs my hand in his, kissing the back of it in the same place Leon did not ten minutes ago. I feel my temper dissipate as I realize we're both battling the same emotions.

My eyes move back to Genna, and she offers me a genuine smile before she rocks my world.

"I'm not interested in Kade. I figure it's best to lay that out there. He's gorgeous," she says glancing at him then back to me. "Anyone with two eyes and a penchant for men can see that. But I also understand the meaning of our other halves, or *Piths*. I know Kade will never look at another woman. He would be no more interested in me than he would be in my brother," she tells me, glancing at Goran then back to

Chrysalis

me. "Your Pith is the one your whole world revolves around."

My eyes automatically move to Kade, and I see that he's already looking at me. I can't seem to pull my gaze away as I listen to her words.

"The day begins and ends with them… no being, item, power, or gift is more important. Every decision you make revolves around their happiness. This is the meaning of true Piths, this is what we're made to feel. Of course, the natural love that some of us are lucky enough to have is extra special… another layer that connects the two Piths. Love that isn't because you're meant to be, but exists instead because you have your own connection. Love that would have evolved between the two of you, even if you weren't each other's *other half*. Making that connection even more unbreakable. If you die, he will kill himself."

I frown as a pain like barbed wire tightening around my heart makes me clutch my chest.

"And it would be the same for you. If he dies, you would feel unable to continue, you would die too." Kade squeezes my hand harder, and if it weren't for my super strength, he would have broken it already. "You're lucky and unlucky that you have found each other. I, myself, have found my Pith. However, he has never laid eyes on me, so he doesn't know I'm here for him. Everything I have done over the last two years, since seeing him for the first time and realizing who he was, has been to keep him as safe as possible. However, by doing that, I have inadvertently allowed harm to befall him anyway." I feel Genna's pain in my tight chest. She's tormented, grief-stricken, and desperate to help her other half. I blink and look away from Kade, searching and finding Genna's eyes instead.

"The reason I could never think of Kade as anything more than a friend is because my Pith, the man I am bound to be with and the man I have watched from the shadows over the last two years and fallen in love with, is Elijah. My Pith is your brother."

Chrysalis

CHAPTER 28

"So you and Elijah, huh?" The question tips off my lips as I take a seat next to Genna, carefully placing my small tray containing a burger and fries down. I throw back some Diet Coke from the can in my other hand and wait for her response.

Her eyes dart around the room, and I wonder if I've made her feel uncomfortable.

"Well, not exactly," she finally mutters, and the burger that was moving toward my mouth now hovers in mid-air as I wait for her to clarify. Genna stares down at her hands, fiddling with a ring on her thumb. "He's meant for me, and I for him. He is my Pith. I wasn't lying, Emery, but "

"What?" I encourage, finally moving to take a bite.

Damn this burger is good. I can't remember the last time I ate.

"I saw him, two years ago. I was hiding from dark beings." She pulls her ring off and slips it onto the thumb on her other hand.

"Were you being hunted?" I ask, feeling a spasm of pain shoot through me from her.

Genna nods. "Yeah, they took my family, everyone but Goran and me. We were out training." She stops talking, and I watch her throat bobbing up and down. I can feel the emotional war inside her. So far, she's managing to keep a lid on it. I remain quiet, eating my food, letting her speak in her own time. If she's my brother's Pith, then I can only hope that one day things will work out positively, and that she and I will be close. More than that, hopefully, one day we'll be family.

"If you don't want to say any more that's okay, we can talk about something else," I offer, popping a handful of fries into my mouth like a ravenous pig. I feel a burn coming from my right, and I glance over, catching Kade looking at me. His lips twitch when his eyes drop to the new bunch of fries in between my fingers. I smirk before shoving them into my mouth and turning back to Genna.

"No, I want to talk about it. It's something I need to do. Goran hates it. He doesn't like to think of his losses, but I like to remember them. Always." She smiles sadly at me. I swallow my full mouth of food and wait for Genna to unload.

"Take your time," I tell her gently.

Chrysalis

"Goran and I were the strongest, except for our father who was the same, all of us at level eight. It was decided that Goran and I needed to train as much as possible. My father believed a war was coming, and he wanted his family to be able to defend themselves. I don't think he realized just how soon the war was going to arrive at his door." Genna shakes her head and touches the ring again with a sigh. "The dark went to my home. I have no idea what was said or what happened... but when I got back they were all dead."

I gasp at her words. I knew what was coming, and I could feel her pain, but still, her confirmation and the agony she felt while telling me hurts, a lot.

"My dad was barely alive. He lasted for a few minutes after Goran and I got back. Enough time to tell us the dark had attacked them. My dad was the only one left. The others..." She drops her head, and I see a tear drop onto the table in front of us. I don't think, I just reach across and grab her hand, knowing she needs this comfort. "My mom, dad, my two younger sisters, twins, they were ten..." I squeeze her hand, "...and my little brother..." her voice is thick and choked up as she wipes her nose with the back of her other hand, "...he was two years old."

Her words bring my body so much pain that I almost crumble with it, but I need to shoulder this for her, and I don't let her see my silent tears that fall on her behalf for her loss.

"Goran went crazy for about a month, trying to find any dark being he could and then killing them. I think he had a death wish. I truly believe he just wanted to be with them, and I totally understood, so I was there, by his side at every fight. One day we got drawn into a fight. Traveling from place to place meant we were always on the lookout, and this particular day there was a fight already waging along the path we were traveling. The ones fighting for the light were losing, and so we joined to help their cause. But even though we were both level eight, we weren't fully trained, and we were severely outnumbered anyway. The dark started picking the light off. I remember I was down and next to be killed. It's all as clear as if I'd just lived through it- the two men walking toward me, black eyes and nasty grins on their faces. They raised their hands, and red light sparked. I knew it was the end for me, and I welcomed it. Peace existed for a moment when I knew I'd be with my family once again. Then *he* arrived. Elijah."

She looks up at me, and her tear-stained face is now smiling. "He pulled them both away, decimated them and saved me. He didn't look at me, he didn't have time to. There was a lot of darkness still to fight, but I saw him, and at that moment right when I thought I might die, my hope blossomed again as I realized I had a reason to live… because I had a reason to love. My Pith, he existed, and it filled me

Chrysalis

with a hope I hadn't felt for a long time. I never had a chance to speak to Elijah, though. I never had the opportunity for him to see my face, to confirm we're meant for each other because Goran grabbed me and dragged me away. He told me that he had lost everyone, he wasn't willing to lose me, too. I managed to grab this ring," she tells me and holds up the thick silver band that she keeps twisting on her thumb. "Elijah was wearing this when he arrived. I watched it drop to the ground just a few feet in front of me when he was fighting. It was probably wrong to steal this, but it has brought me some comfort over the years."

She stops talking and offers me a small smile, I lean into her and wrap my arms around her shoulders, bringing her body into mine and closing my eyes, hoping to lend her some of my strength, although I'm not sure she needs any. She's a fighter, a survivor, all on her own. That much is clear to see.

"I'm sorry you lost them all," I whisper into her ear, and I feel her nod as she holds me tight.

I pull back and tip my head slightly, a question sitting on my lips. "If that happened two years ago, why haven't you found Elijah again?"

She pulls off the ring and holds it in her palm. "I have. I mean, when I saw him for the first time, I didn't know him. I didn't even know his name. Now, I know everything, including the fact that you're his sister. You could say that I'm his professional stalker," she tells me with a grimace. I don't say anything. I can feel a burn blossoming in my tummy, so I know the same is happening to Genna.

"My brother recognized Kade. Goran and I disappeared when Kade and Elijah arrived, but once we stopped running, he explained that a bunch of light beings turned up and dispatched the dark. When I asked why we didn't stay and help he told me I was near death. He needed to get me away because he couldn't lose anyone else. I explained that I'd found my Pith, told him what he looked like. Goran said his name was Elijah that he was there with the strongest… with Kade. Once he told me who they were, I kind of turned into a crazy person. He was my Pith, so the need inside to connect with him, to see him, to touch him… it was almost overwhelming. My every waking second was consumed with thoughts of him. Honestly, I don't know how people manage to stay away from their Piths once they know they exist," she says with a shake of her head.

I think of Kade and how he managed for years to not reveal himself to me, and I know he was horrible to me when I first arrived with Elijah because he was trying to protect us both. Even so, I'm glad he gave in. I'm not sure I could have lasted around him while never being allowed to touch him, and the thought of seeing him with someone else makes me want to sink to my knees and howl.

Chrysalis

"I found him, eventually." Genna bites her lip and stares out of the window, looking at the view that stretches as far as the eye can see with nothing but fields and mountains.

"What happened?" I question, wondering why Elijah never mentioned her.

"Nothing," she answers.

"Nothing?" I repeat the word, confused.

"I never showed myself to him, I never *have*. He was with a girl, he was laughing with her."

"Sicily?" I interrupt her with my question.

Genna nods. "Yeah, I found out that was her name. He seemed happy. Who am I to take away his happiness? Honestly, if he saw me, then immediately he would recognize me as his Pith, and whether he wanted to or not, his body and mind would tell him that he belonged to me. I couldn't do that to him, to them. They looked so happy. I didn't want to take his choice away from him."

I close my eyes and let my head drop back. I can feel her pain, and I understand her choice. There was a time when I thought that Kade's love was a fabrication, some kind of spell put on him and outside of his control. I've since realized that's not quite how it works.

"You know, the choice thing... Piths have it. How do you think so many decide *not* to stay together? If it were that hard, then they wouldn't be able to make that choice," I tell her.

Genna shakes her head. "I can't believe that. I mean, I know how I feel, and it kills me seeing him with her, but I love him enough to want him happy."

"Yeah, I get that, but you've made a choice not to show yourself to him. You're making a choice not to be with him, so the point is… you *can* make that choice. The other thing you have to consider is that if you can make that choice, then so can he, and right now you're taking *his* choice away."

Her eyes widen in surprise.

"Secondly, being someone's Pith isn't something that's thrust upon us. We still decide. It's just that our Pith is our exact match in every way. It's like saying, 'Don't worry about trying with different people anymore, this person is it for you. They'll be able to give you what you want and what you need to make you happy for the rest of your life. There's nobody out there who you'll love more than this person.' When you think of it like that, it's kind of a no-brainer that you'd want to be with your Pith. The fact is, by thinking the way you have, you've kept both him and you from having that happiness. And if Sicily were free, maybe she would find her Pith, too."

Genna drops her forehead on the table. "I never thought about it like that. All this time I could have been with him. I might have been able to keep him from going over to the dark," she whispers to herself.

"We're going to get him back," I tell her with a fierce determination. "He'll be coming home… and soon. After tonight's strategy meeting, we'll have a plan. Then it will be *all systems go*." My voice doesn't falter, even though I'm battling with my own feelings now. Rage and a thick sadness wash over me in waves, and I clench both my teeth and my fists.

Warmth runs up my spine, and unexpectedly I feel two big hands on my shoulders. *Kade*. Immediately, as if knowing everything will be okay, my body relaxes into his. Goran, Lucian, and Leon all seat themselves opposite Genna and me.

"Tristan, Tess, and Katarina will be arriving within the hour. We can all sit and have a meal, then we'll strategize. Soon the first battle will begin, kick-starting the war," Kade tells us all.

After he makes that statement, no one speaks. All normal thoughts have now disappeared, leaving only the world that faces us.

Chapter 29

"That isn't how we do things around here!" Lucian's fist slams onto the table, and my body automatically jolts.

The thumb that Kade was leisurely stroking along the back of my hand stills. "I'm only going to tell you once. Calm down," he grinds out through clenched teeth.

We all hold our breath until Lucian nods and returns to his seat. The room fills up with air all at once when everyone exhales simultaneously.

"My apologies," Lucian tells Kade. I try to probe his outer shell, but I only manage to scratch the surface.

Lately, I've been trying to control my emotions, caging myself off from feelings, or specifically other people's emotions, trying to stop them from affecting me. Now I'm scared of opening that channel again. I do it with people I know, but I avoid it with people I

Chrysalis

don't. The problem is that I *need* to do it with people I don't know, so that I can gauge their honesty and know that they aren't leading us into a trap. But a while ago I put up a barrier, and ever since, I seem to be blocked. The worse thing is that I've done it to myself. Now I can only sense emotions that are simmering under the surface, clear and easy for even normal people to read. It's frustrating, to say the least.

"This is what I do," Tristan chimes in, anger displayed on his face. "I scope things out, collect intel from different sources, and then decipher what stuff is worthy information and what stuff needs to be disregarded. You don't know me, but if you want to work together then you'll have to trust me." I watch as he finishes his words and then twists his neck from right to left, clicks from both movements echoes around the now silent room.

"I don't remember saying *you* were needed." This voice comes from our left, and I look up as a new man approaches.

"Saracen, please, join us, but we don't need negative input," Goran snaps at the newcomer.

I look between the two, trying to gauge their reactions. I lamely attempt to sense anything from Saracen, but he's locked up tight. His blue eyes find mine, and he runs his hand through his wavy brown hair, which stops just above his shoulders, and smirks at me.

"Don't try and pretend Goran. You don't want *him*," he says, obviously meaning Tristan, but he doesn't move his eyes from mine. I feel Kade tensing next to me. "It's *her* everyone wants. *Everyone,*" he states, sneering, but he's trying to make sure I know it's me he means.

I feel Kade's heart rate pick up, and I know he's about to explode, so I do what I can. I go first. I launch myself upward into a stiff standing position. I know I've even shocked Kade when he questions me.

Emery, are you okay?

I ignore Kade as my eyes stay fixed on Saracen's.

"Listen, you may be something special with these people…" I state, gesturing around, "…but to me, you're unimportant, no more than a blip on my radar." I watch as his eyes harden, the smirk slipping, and it gives me a small thrill. "These people…" I tell him, pointing to Tess, Tristan, and Katarina, "…they are more than friends. These people are my *family*. You may or may not know my history, but I'll make it easy. I've never had family, so to have that now means *everything*. Every damn thing. I'll walk out of here in the blink of an eye if they do… Where they go, I'll follow. If the world falls apart around me, then so be it. As long as I have my family, then I have everything I need. Are we clear?" I huff out a breath as my chest heaves with anger.

Chrysalis

Kade grabs my arm and eases me onto his lap. "Shh... princess," he whispers in my ear while rubbing my back.

Still, my eyes don't leave Saracen's as I glare at him, making sure he understands that I'm as serious as a heart attack. His eyes narrow, and I see a twitch in his jaw before he spins around and storms away. "My apologies," Goran tells me.

"Did you ask him to behave that way?" My voice is harsh, and I know it's not his fault, but I also feel the need to be clear. These people are all I have left. Everyone accepts Kade easily, not only can he be scary and he's the strongest light being that we know of, but he's also my Pith. And apparently to win this war, they need the two of us as a team. So if they want me, they know he comes as part of that package. What they now need to understand is that I have a family, and I will stand by them all. Always.

"No. In fact, he was told to behave," Goran replies, glancing over at Lucian, who in turn nods and rises from the table.

"Sorry, I have things to attend too. I'll be as swift as possible," Lucian calmly tells us, moving his eyes around the table.

"Tristan," Kade rumbles, looking toward him while rubbing his hand along my spine.

Tristan nods, then looks back at the plans. "I have intelligence that tells us that the dark do have a lab and it's for testing. They have vials, which we believe possibly contain a serum—" "Possibly?" Leon questions.

Tristan's eyes find Leon's, and he nods. "Yes, we have information, but we have yet to check it out.

There's a chance that we do have someone on the inside." Tristan cautiously glances at Kade before moving back to Leon, and it's enough to spark my interest. "But we're not sure yet. There's a lead Kade's working on, but until the lead is one hundred percent fact, then we can't use it since it would be too dangerous. Until that's clear, all we have to go on are rumors. Still, it's better than knowing absolutely nothing."

"What is the serum?" I ask, and everyone looks at me.

Tristan does too, but his eyes smile at me while he replies, "We believe they're trying to create something to turn normal humans into dark beings."

My whole body spasms, and I throw my hand over my mouth as my eyes widen. "What?" I whisper through my fingers as my heart picks up speed.

Calm, Princess, Kade orders gently in my head. I take a deep breath as Tristan continues, "We're not sure, but so far all the information coming in indicates that they're trying to create a serum that will turn humans into gifted beings. I'm not sure whether they've managed to perfect the concoction. I'm going to go out on a limb and say no, because if they had, then I'm pretty sure we'd be fighting hundreds by now. I don't know much more than that. The questions I've been asking myself are things like... Can they create a serum in the first place? If they can, would it just give humans gifts, or can they manipulate them so that they turn either dark or light? Those are only the first things that spring to mind. If we can get information back from our possible insider, then we might know more." Tristan gets up and starts pacing back and forth. "The main thing we have to decide is, do we have time to wait for our potential insider, or do we start the war without knowing all the details?"

"The sensible thing would be to wait," Katarina adds from the corner she's been quietly sitting in for the last two hours.

Leon swings his head to her and looks her up and down appreciatively. "Every second we wait, they have the potential to grow, to get stronger," he tells her with a smirk.

"I'm very aware of that. However, playing the smart game is what will win the war. Running into something we know hardly anything about, like a bunch of school children, is the sure-fire way to get everyone killed," Katarina deadpans.

They continue to bicker, and Kade and Goran discuss the way forward in a more sensible manner. I pull myself from Kade's lap and walk to the big window overlooking what can only be described as a makeshift town. Wrapping my arms around myself,

I watch the people go about their business, smiling at each other and chatting when passing. There are a few stalls selling goods, like a marketplace. They barter for cloth and basic cooking ingredients. Someone sells wool and another trader sells slabs of meat. It makes me think back to my history lessons. It's like looking at a painting of the Middle Ages. I huff out a laugh. With the battles that await us, it *will* be like I'm living in the Middle Ages.

Suddenly, a scorching pain shoots up my neck and causes me to throw my head back. The burn that accompanies the pain continues behind my eyes and I have to shut them. My throat is closing as I drag my hand up and around it, holding on like I can somehow stop the pain that is assaulting me.

Em... I'm here, can you hear me? The words are almost screamed at me, and my eyes spring open again when I realize it's Elijah.

Elijah? I choke out his name, even though I'm saying it in my head.

You can hear me. Fantastic. There are some things I need to tell you, he replies.

Elijah, you're hurting me.

I know. I'm sorry, I can't help it. I want you to know that I haven't really left you, baby sister. I just saw an opportunity, and I took it. Don't hate me, please.

Elijah...

Chrysalis

Em, sorry to interrupt, but you need to listen. I haven't got much time. I managed to project myself, but it's hard to do. Tell Kade, yes. A million times. Tell him I'm glad to know my brother knew me well enough. Emery, I love you, baby sister. Elodie is nothing like you – you're irreplaceable.

Elijah… I can't—

Em, I'll be back. As soon as I can, I'll be back—

"Ahh!" I scream as the pain explodes in my whole body. Every inch of me feels like I'm being burned alive. "Emery!" Kade roars, and I can hear movement, but all the noise drifts away as the blackout takes me, saving me from the pain.

Peace.

Chapter 30

Elijah? You're still here? I'm confused, I thought that you didn't have much time?

I can't break the connection.

What? My question goes unanswered.

Em, I need you to know that I'm sorry I hurt you by leaving and that I'll be back. I promise. He rushes out.

It's okay, Elijah, I understand. I'll be here waiting. I realize my thoughts are pure. I truly mean it when I say I'm waiting for him.

Don't let them trick you. These new people you're with… Trust is earned, remember that, little sister. You might have to make a decision one day, a decision about who to trust. There are things going on over here that I can't talk to you about now, but not everything is as black and white as it might at first seem. You may have to make a choice between dark and light someday.

Chrysalis

I take a moment to really think about what he's saying, but I already know that I don't trust easily. The things he's just told me are both confusing and scary, but I can't dwell on them. My brain will turn to mush if I try to work it all out. Anyway, right now I'm more worried about him.

What are they doing to you over there, Eli? Are you safe?

Don't worry about me.

I'll always worry about you.

Emery, the spell I've used on you... on us, it's strong. It's pulled us both under. Nobody from my end should suspect, for now, but I'm not strong enough to pull us free. You need to be the one who breaks the connection.

Elijah, I-I'm so confused. Everything that's happened... I don't know what's real anymore or who to trust.

Trust Kade.

I always do.

Good. You only need to trust him, Em. He will keep you safe. He will protect you. He would die for you, and he will love you. He always has

I miss you, brother.

I miss you too. Now listen, you need to think about something... something that you can focus on and let it free you... us. Remember to tell Kade, I said yes. Love you, little sister.

Page | **329**

See you soon, Eli. I whisper the thoughts in my head before trying to focus on something.

The only thing I know that can consume me completely is Kade. I think about his smile. I think about the way he looks at me like I'm his every answer. Then I think about his golden eyes, blazing, setting me on fire from the inside out. I listen to my heartbeat and let the love I feel for him take over.

Thump.

Thump, thump.

Thump, thump, thump.

My body jolts internally, and I know I'm awake. I also know that on the outside, my body didn't move an inch. Now I just need my physical body to wake up too.

Kade

"She's still asleep?" Katarina asks from behind me. My eyes are fixed on Emery, so I don't even turn to acknowledge her. Kat can see that Emery is still out, and I could do without stupid questions. I'm holding onto my control just barely right now. I feel a hand touch my shoulder, and I flinch. "Kade?" The word sounds like an accusation.

"What is it, Katarina? Is there some new intelligence?" It comes out harsher than intended,

Chrysalis

and I catch her slight intake of breath. My shoulders slump, and I feel like crap. "Sorry Kat, I'm not in the right headspace to be chatting with anyone at the moment," I tell her.

"I'm not just anyone." Her words are whispered, and I can hear the hurt in her voice.

"You're not her."

Saying nothing else, she gets up and quietly walks out. I should feel bad, but I don't. I just feel numb. Emery brought all my feelings up from the dark recesses that I'd buried them in for so many years. Now she's sleeping, and I'm desperately waiting for her to wake. Goran spoke to a doctor on the phone, someone whom they employ, he told us that she's obviously under some kind of spell. There's little he can do. Everything now is a waiting game. I know she isn't dying. My brain tells me that she'll be fine. She's strong, so much more than she realizes. But knowing that doesn't help when all I can see is the person I love lying there vulnerable, and I'm helpless to stop it. I can't control the growl that claws its way up my throat on that thought.

I let my eyes glide over her face. Her hair is such a light blond that it shimmers, but her long eyelashes are brown, the same as her arched eyebrows. The normal pink tinge on her cheeks is missing. Instead, her skin is pale, and if it weren't for her plump lips, slightly parted and allowing little puffs of air to blow out, I would be in a totally different frame of mind. I look at the door where Kat just exited, then I turn back to Emery. I'll stay here until she wakes. No matter if the walls fall down around me.

Closing my eyes, I rest my forehead on the edge of her bed.

I'm scared. I've heard things—things I believe are going on inside her head, conversations that she seems to be having. I have no idea if these conversations are real, or if it's a construct, something she's dreaming. I can only hear one side. It's like I'm blocked from the other. But the message is clear, she's talking to Elijah, and I hope to God that whatever he's doing he realizes that it's hurting her and lets her go soon. I need her back, I need her with me. I miss my family, but I miss her more. She's the only person I can't survive without.

Emery

After hours of lying here unmoving, the world on mute around me, suddenly everything changes. I feel a spark inside of me. *She's* waking up, the Convergence. I can see green smoke behind my own eyes, and I know she's helping me to take back the control. To break the spell fully.

With a huge intake of air, my lungs fill up, and before I realize what's happening, I'm sitting up and

Chrysalis

coughing the breath back out. My eyes open and immediately meet with Kade's. He tries to hide the emotion behind his eyes, tries to convince me that everything is fine. I don't mention it. I'm aware he doesn't want me to notice, and instinctively I know he's desperately fighting against it.

Fear.

It's an unknown and unwelcome emotion for Kade. And just like every other time in his life Kade has felt fear, it's always for me. Only me.

"Princess..." His voice is raspy as he leans over, placing a tender kiss on my lips. My insides scream for more, so I push my fingers into his hair and kiss him back softly, lovingly, telling him with that one kiss that I adore him.

"I'm okay. I saw Elijah."

"I know."

His reply stops me in my tracks, my mouth hangs open while my brain catches up.

Kade doesn't wait for my unasked question. "I could hear some of your thoughts. You seemed to be talking to someone, and I figured it was Elijah when you said his name. What I couldn't work out was whether you were dreaming it, or if you really were connected to him."

"Oh, I was definitely connected. He told me to tell you, 'yes.' Actually, he said to tell you 'a million times yes.'" I smile thinking about Elijah and Kade's eyes soften on me.

"That's good news," he replies and kisses my forehead, his mind suddenly elsewhere.

"You can go, if you need to," I tell him, and his eyes snap back to mine.

"Absolutely not. I will not leave you. Emery, remember, there is no one more important to me, dead or alive, than you. That means I'm right where I need to be. My thoughts may wander away sometimes, but that's only because I'm thinking about another way to make you safer."

I nod my response and he sits on the bed, lifting me and placing me in his lap. Kade rains kisses down my cheek before things become more heated, and his lips move to my throat and then my collarbone.

"Okay, lovebirds, we don't all need to see that you're hot for each other all the time," Tristan says with a smirk as he breezes through the door.

Kade, as usual, announces how he feels with his trademark growl, and I can't help the giggle that bubbles up inside me.

"The doc is on his way, but as you're supposed to be resting, I'm here to chaperone the two of you," he says, pointing back and forth between us, a glint shimmering in his eyes.

Kade gently places me back on the bed and stalks to Tristan, telling him to shut up and get out, but there's no heat behind his words, just brotherly love.

I sigh happily as Kade and Tristan banter back and forth. I close my eyes thinking about today's events.

Chrysalis

My stomach dips and swirls as my mind fights internally. I think about Elijah and about what he said.

One day I will have to make a decision about whose side I'm fighting on. Right now, it's easy, but I know that if it happens, it will take everything within me to stay on this side—the side I want to be on.

I look over at Kade. He catches my gaze and stares back with his hazel eyes, brooding, menacing, suddenly his whole face softens as he blinks and his golden eyes alight. He smiles. The love I see, the playfulness he shows me, is just for me.

Yes. One day I will have to decide. But today isn't that day.

TO BE
CONTINUED

Maria Macdonald

PLAYLIST

Christina Perri – The Lonely
Little Mix – Salute
One Direction – Drag Me Down
Flyleaf – All Around Me
Flyleaf – Fully Alive
Christina Perri – Human
Firelight – Unbreakable
Sleeping At Last – I'll Keep You Safe
Jessie J – Flashlight
Killswitch Engage – Always
Starset – My Demons

Acknowledgments

My first thanks, as always, goes to my family: my constant source of love, support, understanding and unwavering encouragement.

To my betas – Beth, Laura & Morgan: Thank you for always being excited about my work and dropping whatever you're doing to ride this wave with me.

A special thank you to my beta Klaire: You didn't really have time to read this book, yet you made time, even though Paranormal hasn't really been your favorite genre in recent times. You have become the voice in my head when I'm writing, for that I'll be eternally grateful.

To my Misfits: Your never ending support keeps me going, literally. Love you lot!

Lastly, thank you to all the readers who have taken, and will take a chance on me. I hope you loved this book.

Feel free to message me via Facebook, IG, Twitter, or even via my website to let me know if you love it. I can't ever thank you all enough. You're the ones who truly make my dreams come true. I do this for you and me. I love you guys. <3

Chrysalis

CONNECT
WITH ME ONLINE

Thank you for reading Chrysalis.

If you enjoyed it, please consider leaving a review at your point of purchase and on Goodreads. It means a lot to me to hear what you think.

Also, feel free to join my street/reader group:
https://www.facebook.com/groups/mariasmisfits/

More books from Maria Macdonald
Love Reflection - An Entwined Hearts Novel Book 1
Love Resisted - An Entwined Hearts Novel Book 2
Love Renewed – An Entwined Hearts Novel Book 3
Finally Unbroken – Finally Unbroken Series Book 1
What's Left of Me   Finally Unbroken Series Book 2
Chrysalis – The Emergence of Emery Book 1
Dazed – Deliverance Series Book 1
Conflicted – Deliverance Series Book 2
Formative – Deliverance Series Book 3
Twisted Truth

Maria Macdonald

Website
http://www.mariamacdonaldauthor.com/

Email
mariamacdonaldauthor@gmail.com

Facebook
https://www.facebook.com/maria.macdonald.71?fref=ts

Goodreads
https://www.goodreads.com/MariaMacdonaldAuthor

About the Author

Maria Macdonald is a full-time working mum, she has two beautiful daughters, both of whom love books as much as she.

She has loved writing since she was a little girl.

Reading and loving books, as well as blogging, has inspired her to write and publish.

Maria, her husband, and children now reside in Wiltshire, England.

Printed in Poland
by Amazon Fulfillment
Poland Sp. z o.o., Wrocław